MARVEL

AVENGERS
ULTRON REVOLUTION

MARVEL UNIVERSE AVENGERS: ULTRON REVOLUTION VOL. 3. Contains material originally published in magazine form as MARVEL UNIVERSE AVENGERS: ULTRON REVOLUTION #9-12. First printing 2017. ISBN# 978-1-302-90257-5. Published by MARVEL WORLDWIDE, INC., a subsidiary of MARVEL ENTERTAINMENT, LLC. OFFICE OF PUBLICATION: 135 West 50th Street, New York, NY 10020. Copyright © 2017 MARVEL No similarity between any of the names, characters, persons, and/or institutions in this magazine with those of any living or dead person or institution is intended, and any such similarity which may exist is purely coincidental. **Printed in the U.S.A.** DAN BUCKLEY, President, Marvel Entertainment; JOE QUESADA, Chief Creative Officer; TOM BREVOORT, SVP of Publishing; DAVID BOGART, SVP of Business Affairs & Operations, Publishing & Partnership; C.B. CEBULSKI, VP of Brand Management & Development, Asia; DAVID GABRIEL, SVP of Sales & Marketing, Publishing; JEFF YOUNGQUIST, VP of Production & Special Projects; DAN CARR, Executive Director of Publishing Technology; ALEX MORALES, Director of Publishing Operations; SUSAN CRESPI, Production Manager; STAN LEE, Chairman Emeritus. For information regarding advertising in Marvel Comics or on Marvel.com, please contact Vit DeBellis, Integrated Sales Manager, at vdebellis@marvel.com. For Marvel subscription inquiries, please call 888-511-5480. **Manufactured between 10/13/2017 and 11/14/2017 by SHERIDAN, CHELSEA, MI, USA.**

10 9 8 7 6 5 4 3 2 1

MARVEL

AVENGERS
ULTRON REVOLUTION

Based on the TV series written by
PAUL DINI, TOM PUGSLEY, EUGENE SON, RICK WILLIAMS & JENNA McGRATH

Directed by
PHIL PIGNOTTI & TIM ELDRED

Art by
MARVEL ANIMATION STUDIOS

Adapted by
JOE CARAMAGNA

Special Thanks to
HANNAH MACDONALD & PRODUCT FACTORY

Editor
CHRISTINA HARRINGTON

Senior Editor
MARK PANICCIA

Avengers created by STAN LEE & JACK KIRBY

NIFER GRUNWALD
ITLIN O'CONNELL
itor: KATERI WOODY
: MARK D. BEAZLEY

VP Production & Special Projects: JEFF YOUNGQUIST
SVP Print, Sales & Marketing: DAVID GABRIEL
Head of Marvel Television: JEPH LOEB
Book Designer: ADAM DEL RE

Editor in Chief: AXEL ALONSO
Chief Creative Officer: JOE QUESADA
President: DAN BUCKLEY
Executive Producer: ALAN FINE

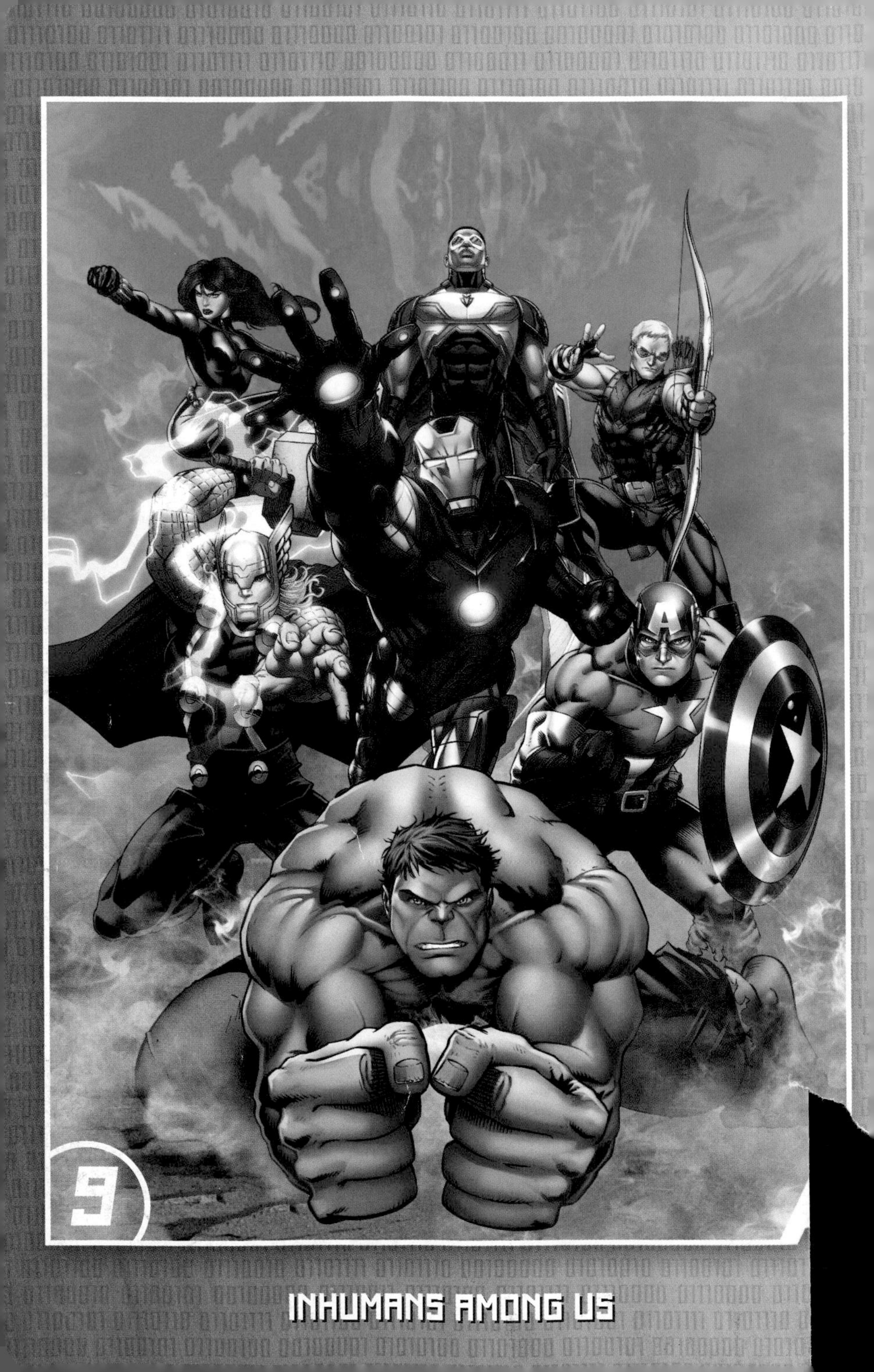
9

INHUMANS AMONG US

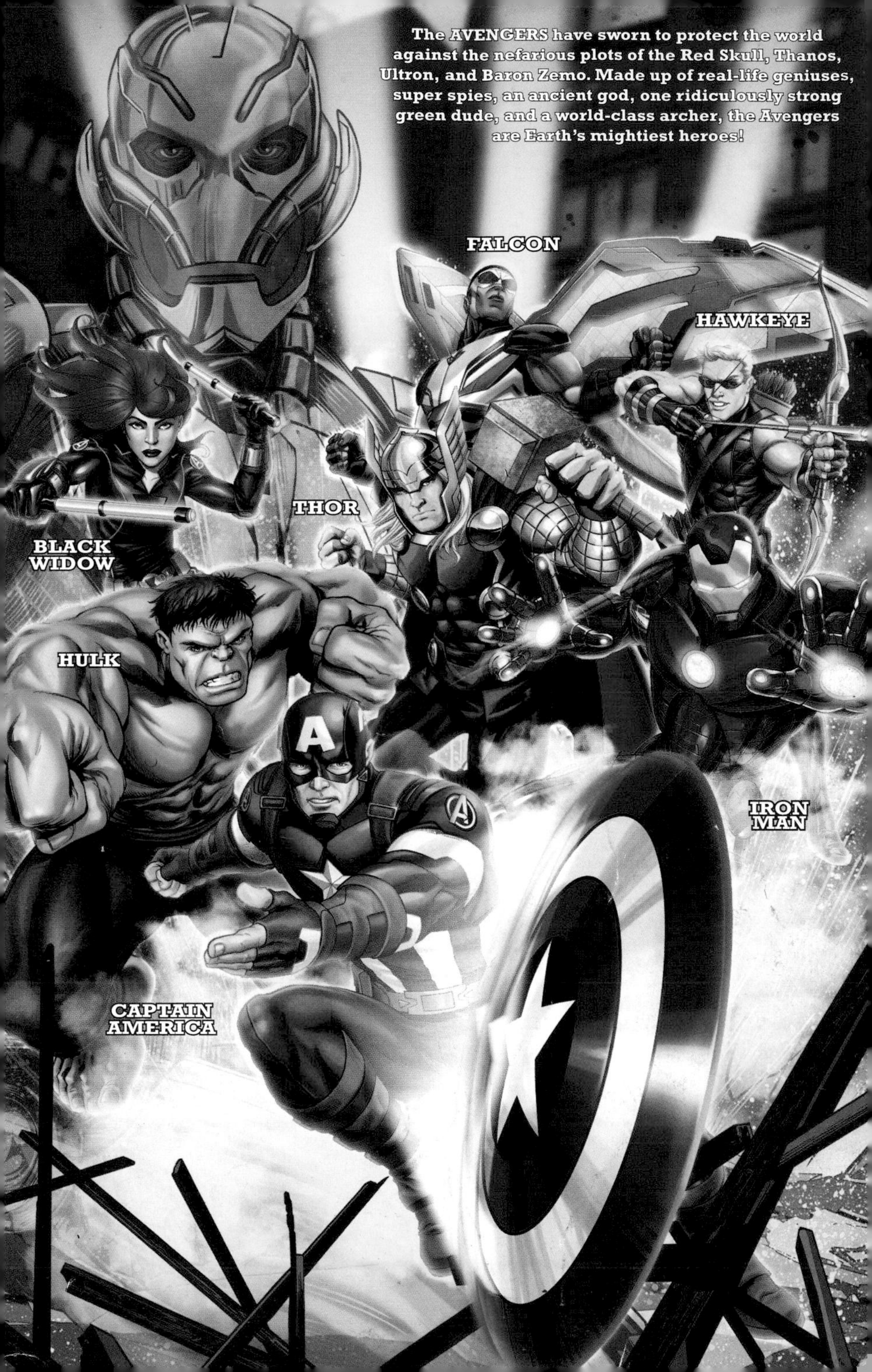
The AVENGERS have sworn to protect the world against the nefarious plots of the Red Skull, Thanos, Ultron, and Baron Zemo. Made up of real-life geniuses, super spies, an ancient god, one ridiculously strong green dude, and a world-class archer, the Avengers are Earth's mightiest heroes!
FALCON
HAWKEYE
THOR
BLACK WIDOW
HULK
IRON MAN
CAPTAIN AMERICA

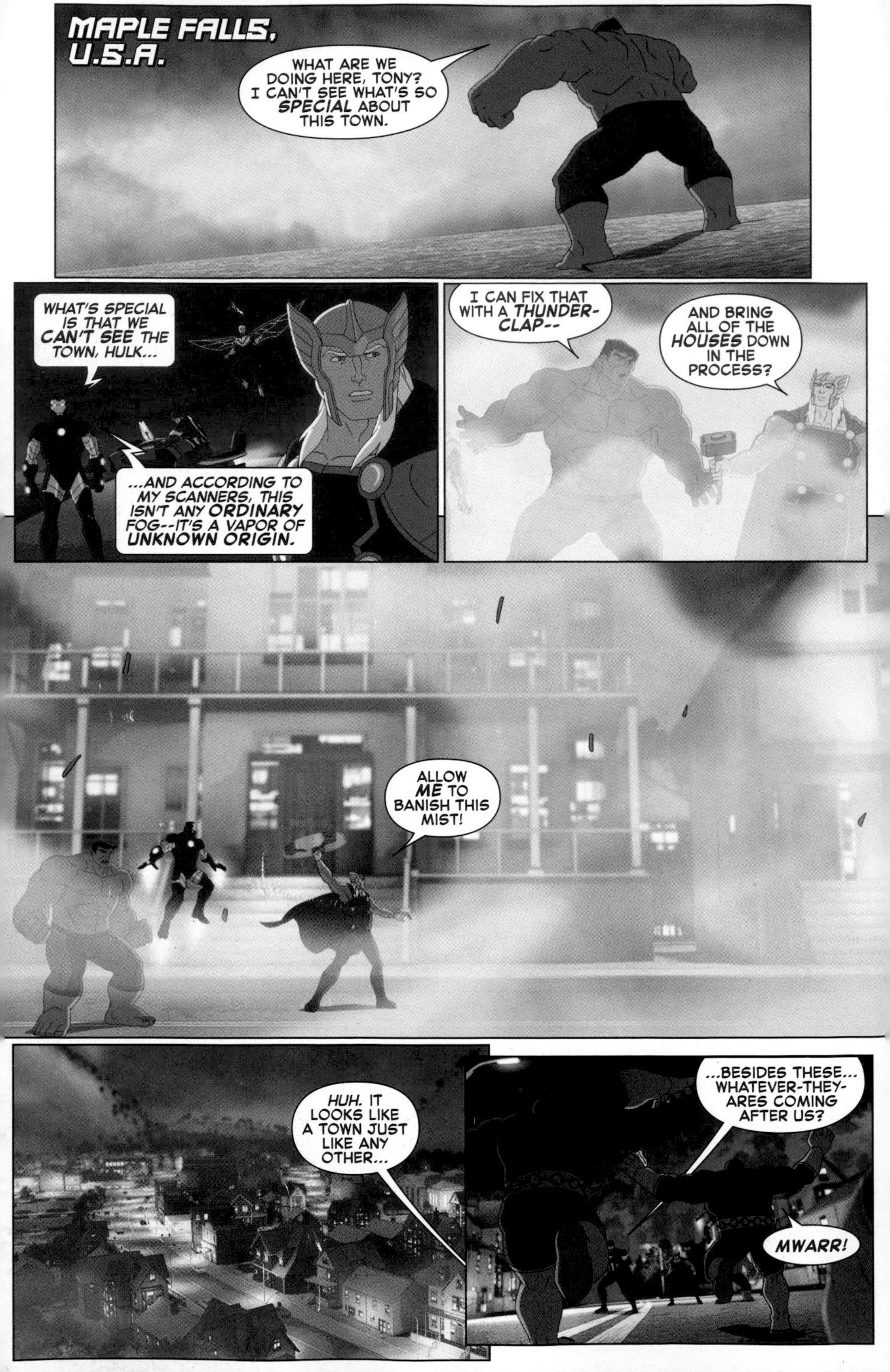
MAPLE FALLS, U.S.A.
WHAT ARE WE DOING HERE, TONY? I CAN'T SEE WHAT'S SO SPECIAL ABOUT THIS TOWN.
WHAT'S SPECIAL IS THAT WE CAN'T SEE THE TOWN, HULK...
...AND ACCORDING TO MY SCANNERS, THIS ISN'T ANY ORDINARY FOG--IT'S A VAPOR OF UNKNOWN ORIGIN.
I CAN FIX THAT WITH A THUNDER-CLAP--
AND BRING ALL OF THE HOUSES DOWN IN THE PROCESS?
ALLOW ME TO BANISH THIS MIST!
HUH. IT LOOKS LIKE A TOWN JUST LIKE ANY OTHER...
...BESIDES THESE... WHATEVER-THEY-ARES COMING AFTER US?
MWARR!

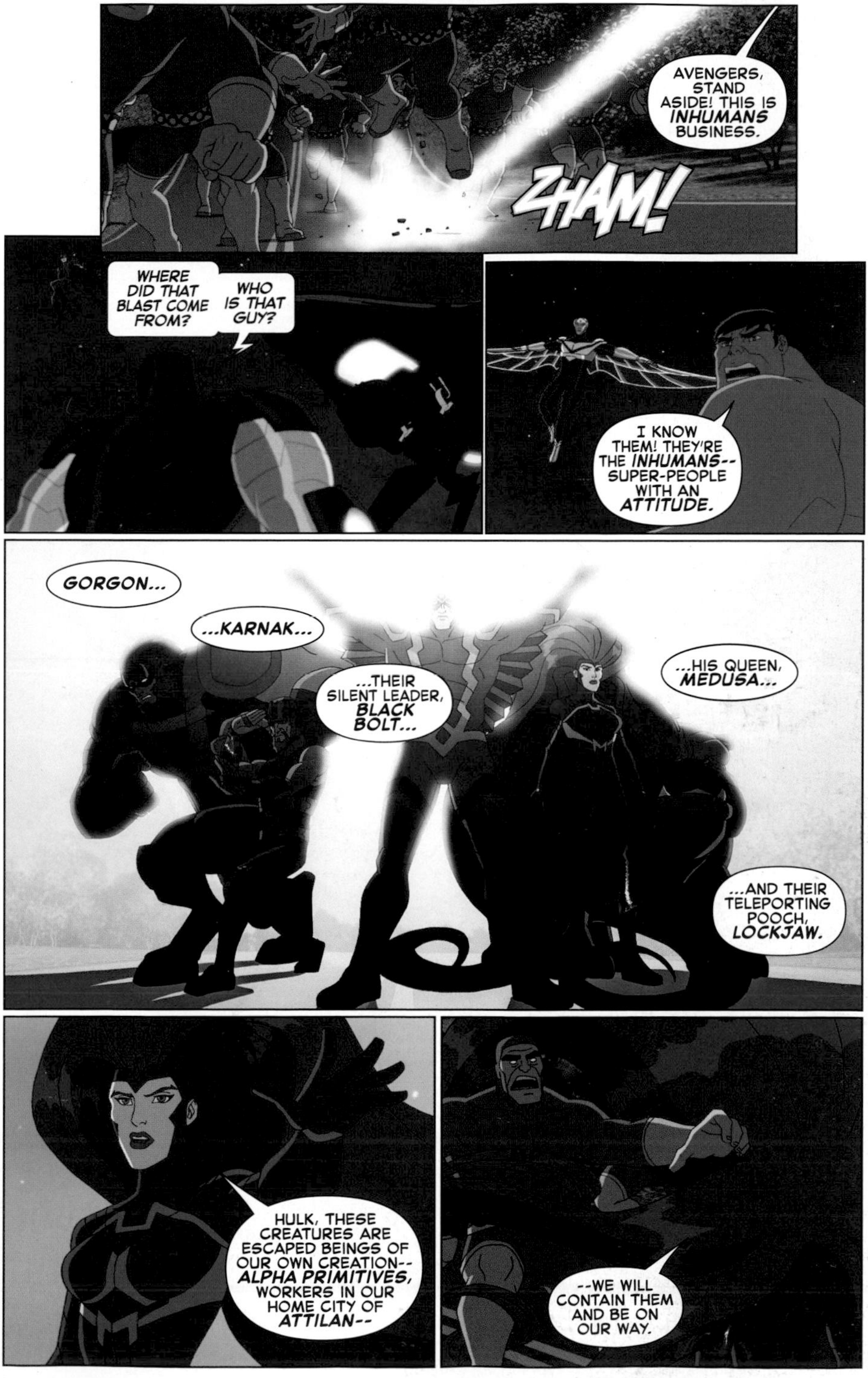

AVENGERS, STAND ASIDE! THIS IS INHUMANS BUSINESS.
ZHAM!
WHERE DID THAT BLAST COME FROM?
WHO IS THAT GUY?
I KNOW THEM! THEY'RE THE INHUMANS-- SUPER-PEOPLE WITH AN ATTITUDE.
GORGON...
...KARNAK...
...THEIR SILENT LEADER, BLACK BOLT...
...HIS QUEEN, MEDUSA...
...AND THEIR TELEPORTING POOCH, LOCKJAW.
HULK, THESE CREATURES ARE ESCAPED BEINGS OF OUR OWN CREATION-- ALPHA PRIMITIVES, WORKERS IN OUR HOME CITY OF ATTILAN--
--WE WILL CONTAIN THEM AND BE ON OUR WAY.

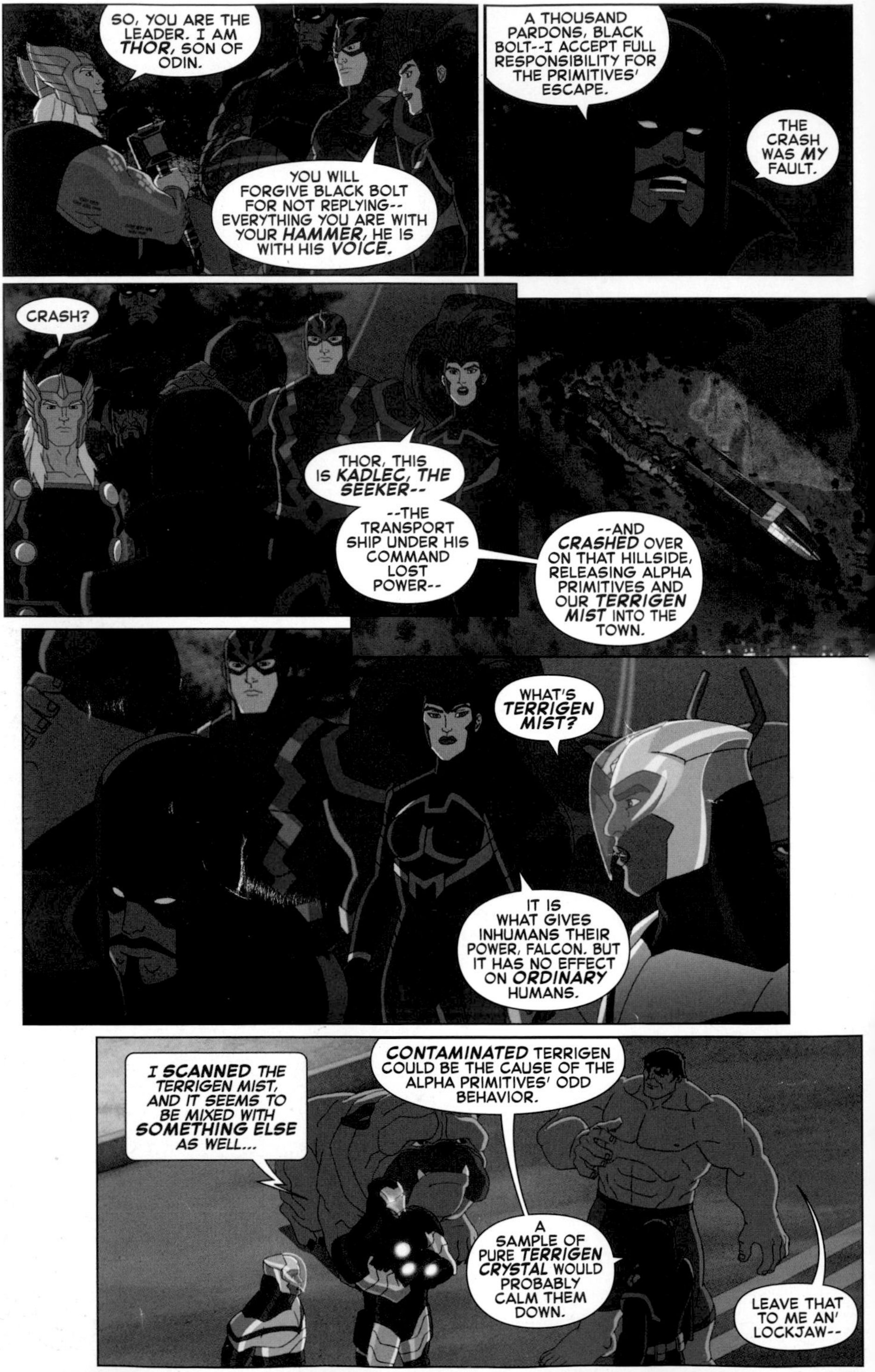
SO, YOU ARE THE LEADER. I AM THOR, SON OF ODIN.
YOU WILL FORGIVE BLACK BOLT FOR NOT REPLYING-- EVERYTHING YOU ARE WITH YOUR HAMMER, HE IS WITH HIS VOICE.
A THOUSAND PARDONS, BLACK BOLT--I ACCEPT FULL RESPONSIBILITY FOR THE PRIMITIVES' ESCAPE.
THE CRASH WAS MY FAULT.
CRASH?
THOR, THIS IS KADLEC, THE SEEKER--
--THE TRANSPORT SHIP UNDER HIS COMMAND LOST POWER--
--AND CRASHED OVER ON THAT HILLSIDE, RELEASING ALPHA PRIMITIVES AND OUR TERRIGEN MIST INTO THE TOWN.
WHAT'S TERRIGEN MIST?
IT IS WHAT GIVES INHUMANS THEIR POWER, FALCON. BUT IT HAS NO EFFECT ON ORDINARY HUMANS.
I SCANNED THE TERRIGEN MIST, AND IT SEEMS TO BE MIXED WITH SOMETHING ELSE AS WELL...
CONTAMINATED TERRIGEN COULD BE THE CAUSE OF THE ALPHA PRIMITIVES' ODD BEHAVIOR.
A SAMPLE OF PURE TERRIGEN CRYSTAL WOULD PROBABLY CALM THEM DOWN.
LEAVE THAT TO ME AN' LOCKJAW--

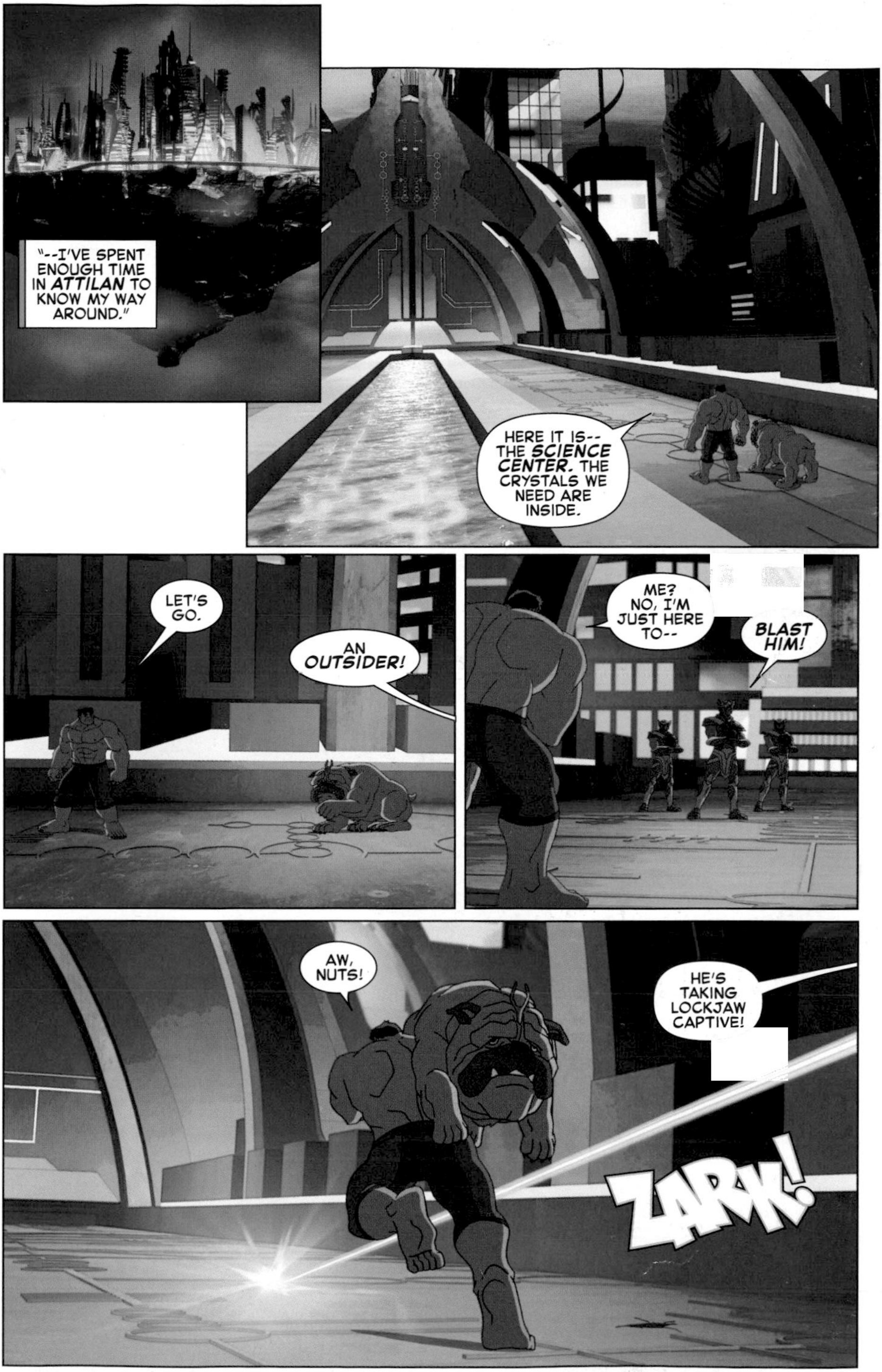
"--I'VE SPENT ENOUGH TIME IN ATTILAN TO KNOW MY WAY AROUND."
HERE IT IS--THE SCIENCE CENTER. THE CRYSTALS WE NEED ARE INSIDE.
LET'S GO.
AN OUTSIDER!
ME? NO, I'M JUST HERE TO--
BLAST HIM!
AW, NUTS!
HE'S TAKING LOCKJAW CAPTIVE!
ZARK!

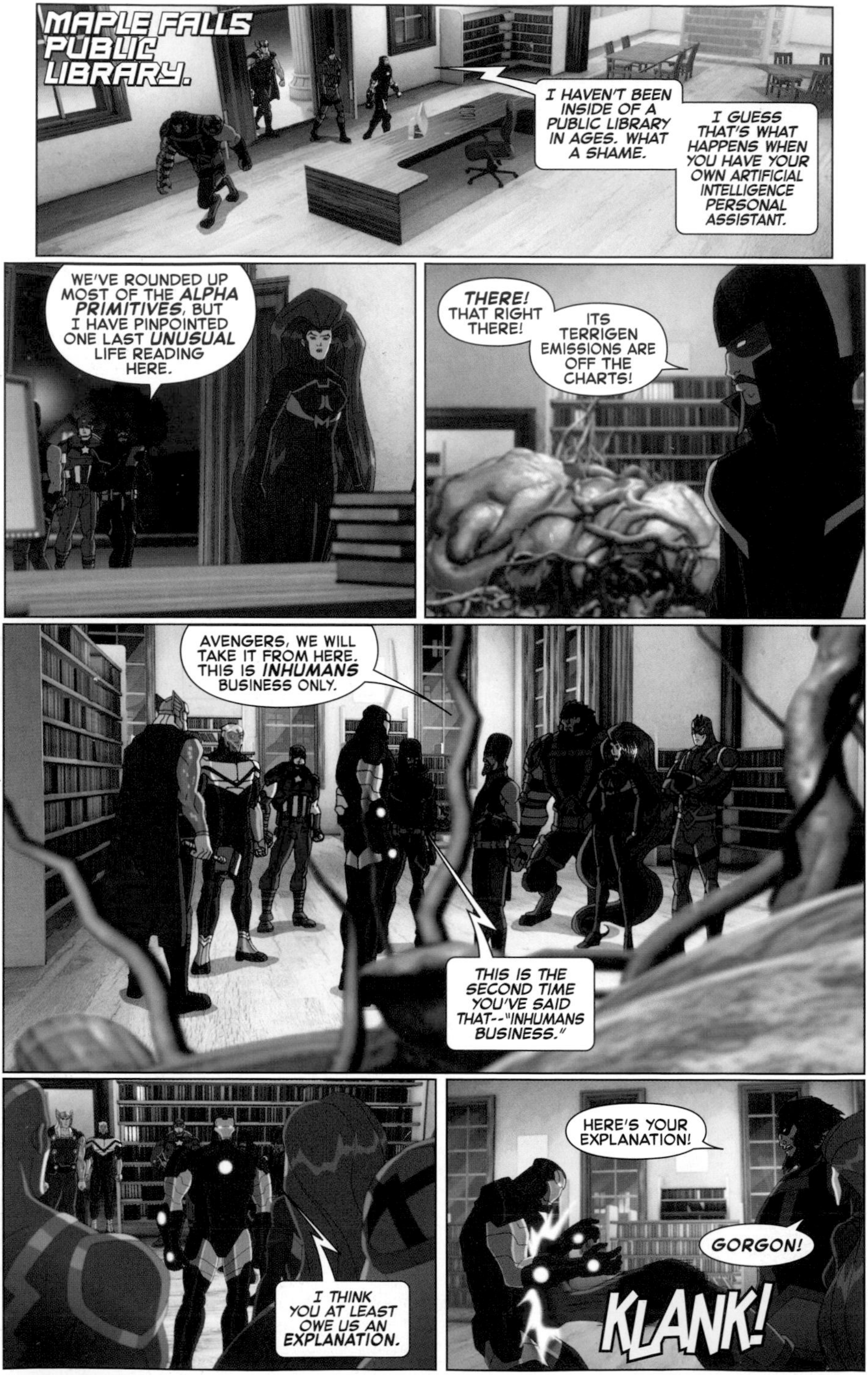
MAPLE FALLS PUBLIC LIBRARY.
I HAVEN'T BEEN INSIDE OF A PUBLIC LIBRARY IN AGES. WHAT A SHAME.
I GUESS THAT'S WHAT HAPPENS WHEN YOU HAVE YOUR OWN ARTIFICIAL INTELLIGENCE PERSONAL ASSISTANT.
WE'VE ROUNDED UP MOST OF THE ALPHA PRIMITIVES, BUT I HAVE PINPOINTED ONE LAST UNUSUAL LIFE READING HERE.
THERE! THAT RIGHT THERE!
ITS TERRIGEN EMISSIONS ARE OFF THE CHARTS!
AVENGERS, WE WILL TAKE IT FROM HERE. THIS IS INHUMANS BUSINESS ONLY.
THIS IS THE SECOND TIME YOU'VE SAID THAT--"INHUMANS BUSINESS."
I THINK YOU AT LEAST OWE US AN EXPLANATION.
HERE'S YOUR EXPLANATION!
GORGON!
KLANK!

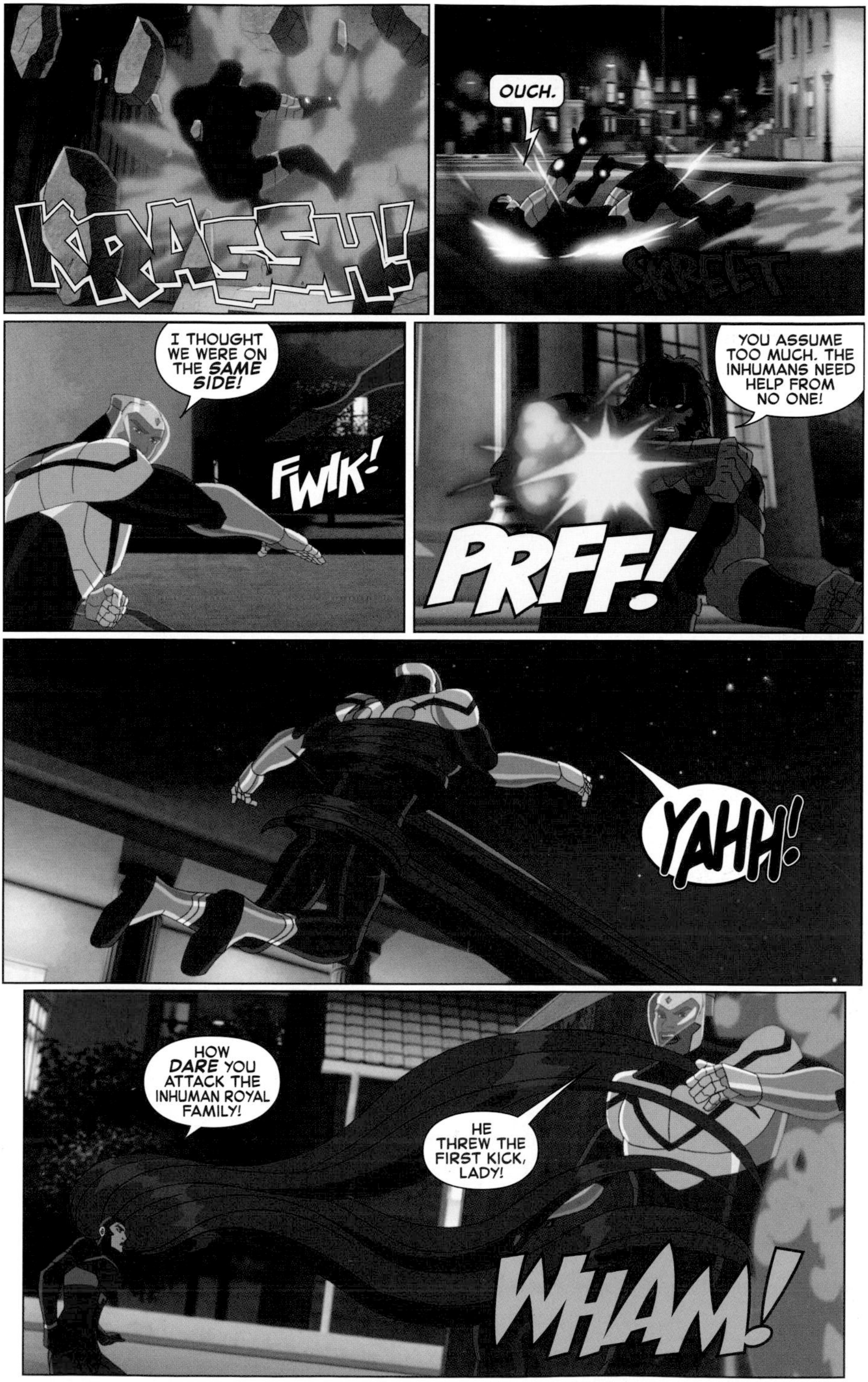
KRASSH!
OUCH.
SKREEET
I THOUGHT WE WERE ON THE SAME SIDE!
FWIK!
YOU ASSUME TOO MUCH. THE INHUMANS NEED HELP FROM NO ONE!
PRFF!
YAHH!
HOW DARE YOU ATTACK THE INHUMAN ROYAL FAMILY!
HE THREW THE FIRST KICK, LADY!
WHAM!

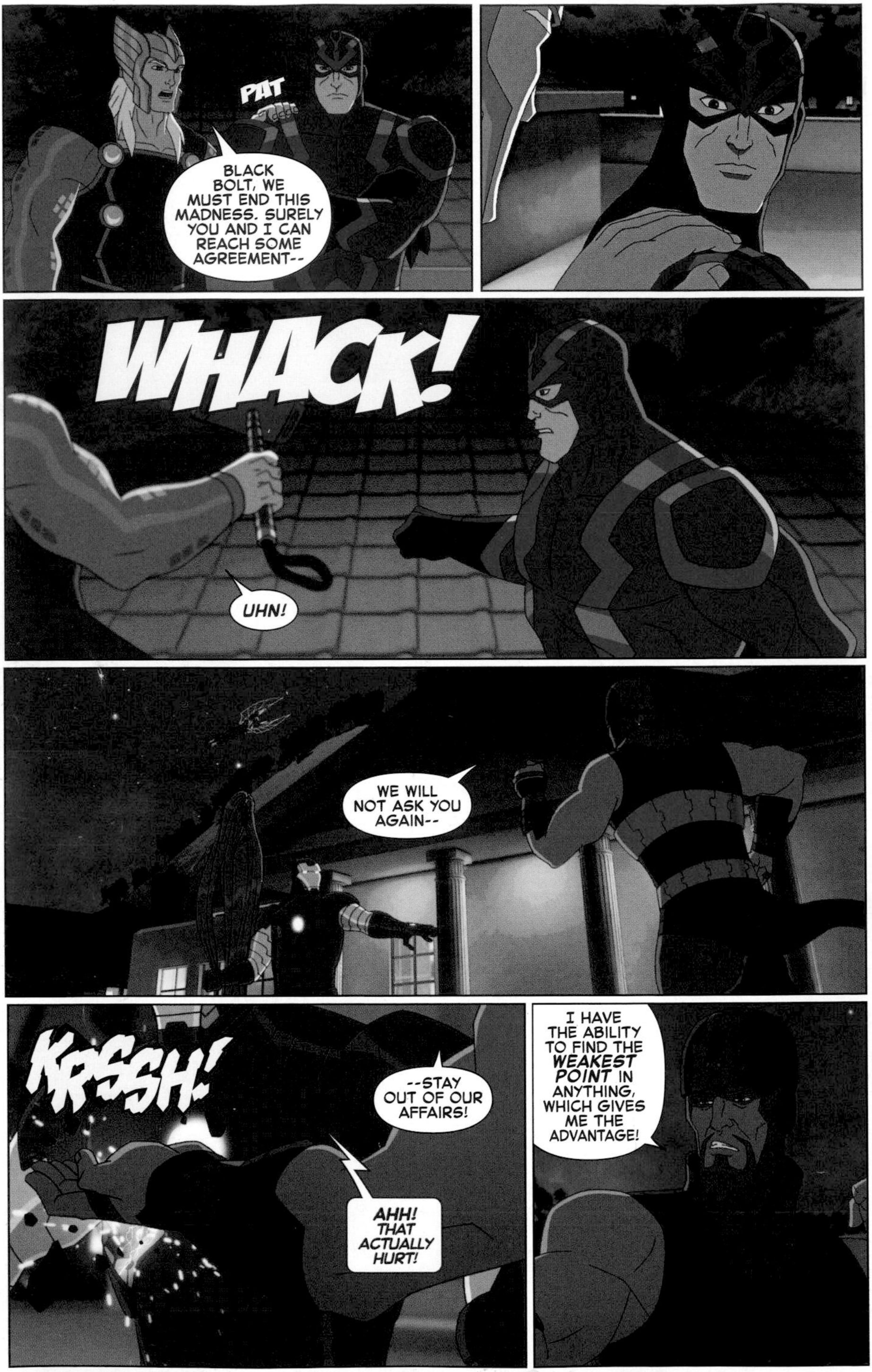
PAT
BLACK BOLT, WE MUST END THIS MADNESS. SURELY YOU AND I CAN REACH SOME AGREEMENT--
WHACK!
UHN!
WE WILL NOT ASK YOU AGAIN--
KRSSH!
--STAY OUT OF OUR AFFAIRS!
AHH! THAT ACTUALLY HURT!
I HAVE THE ABILITY TO FIND THE *WEAKEST POINT* IN ANYTHING, WHICH GIVES ME THE ADVANTAGE!

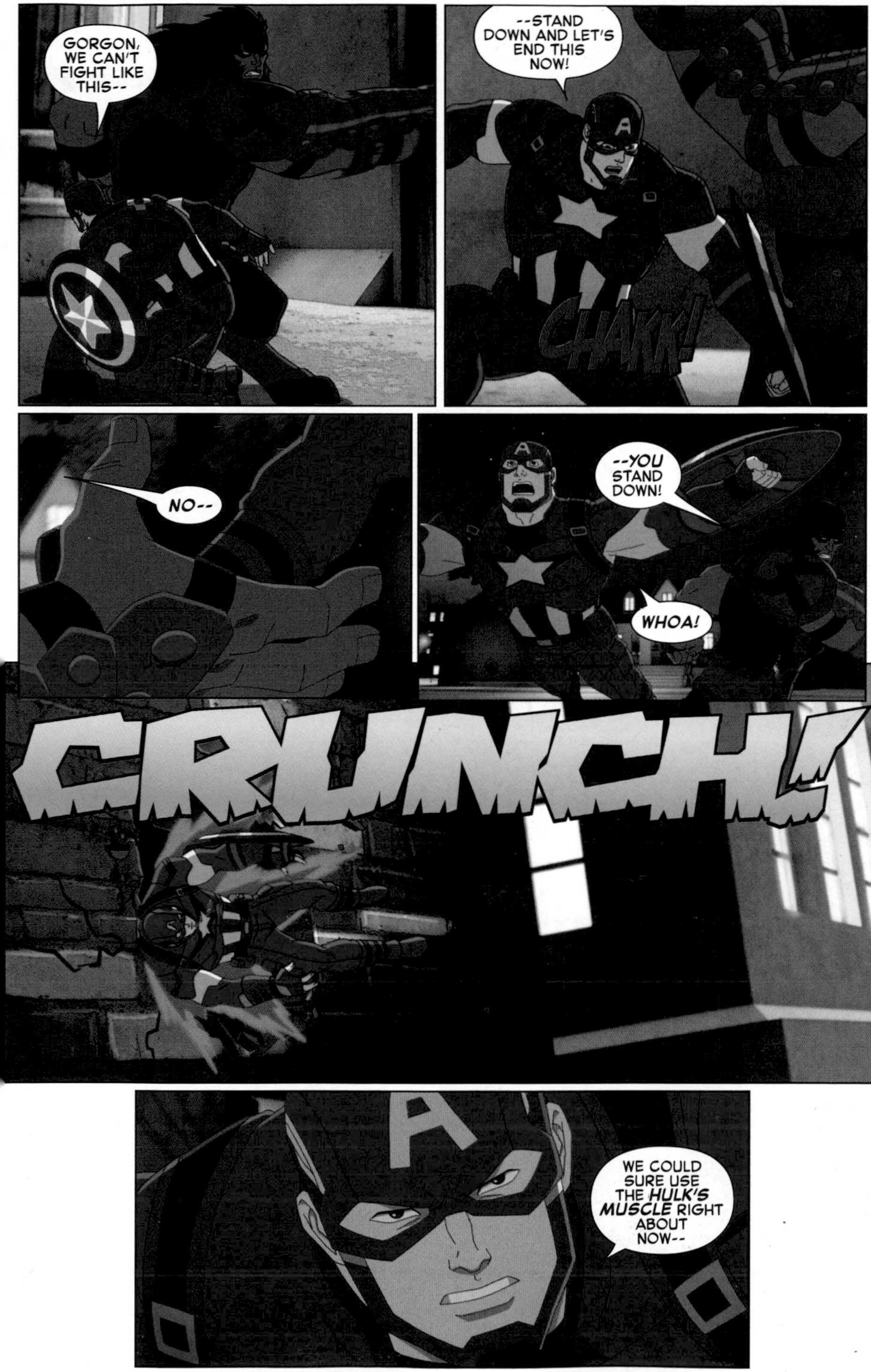
GORGON, WE CAN'T FIGHT LIKE THIS--
--STAND DOWN AND LET'S END THIS NOW!
CHAKK!
NO--
--YOU STAND DOWN!
WHOA!
CRUNCH!
WE COULD SURE USE THE HULK'S MUSCLE RIGHT ABOUT NOW--

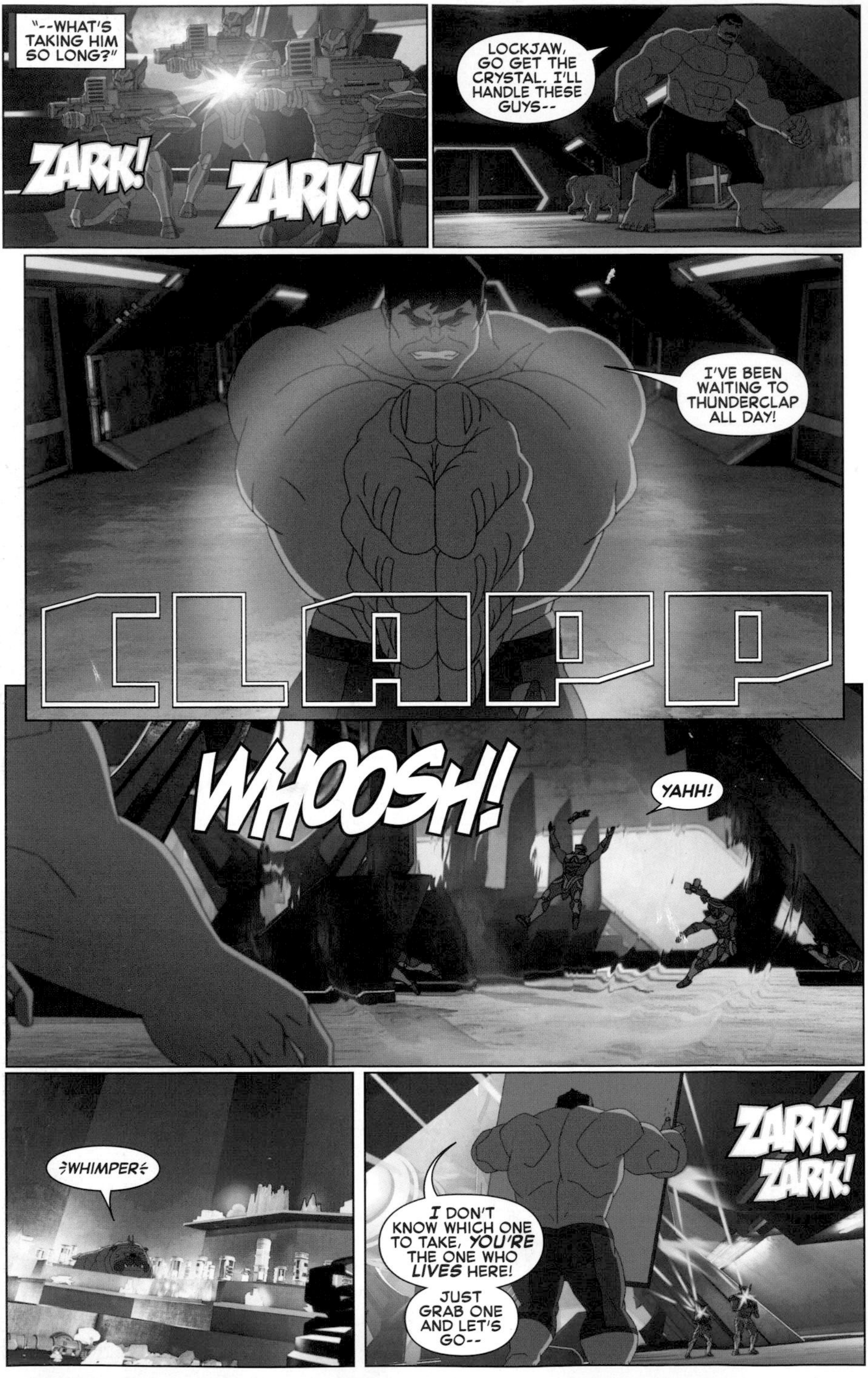
"--WHAT'S TAKING HIM SO LONG?"
ZARK!
ZARK!
LOCKJAW, GO GET THE CRYSTAL. I'LL HANDLE THESE GUYS--
I'VE BEEN WAITING TO THUNDERCLAP ALL DAY!
CLAPP
WHOOSH!
YAHH!
WHIMPER
I DON'T KNOW WHICH ONE TO TAKE, YOU'RE THE ONE WHO LIVES HERE!
JUST GRAB ONE AND LET'S GO--
ZARK!
ZARK!

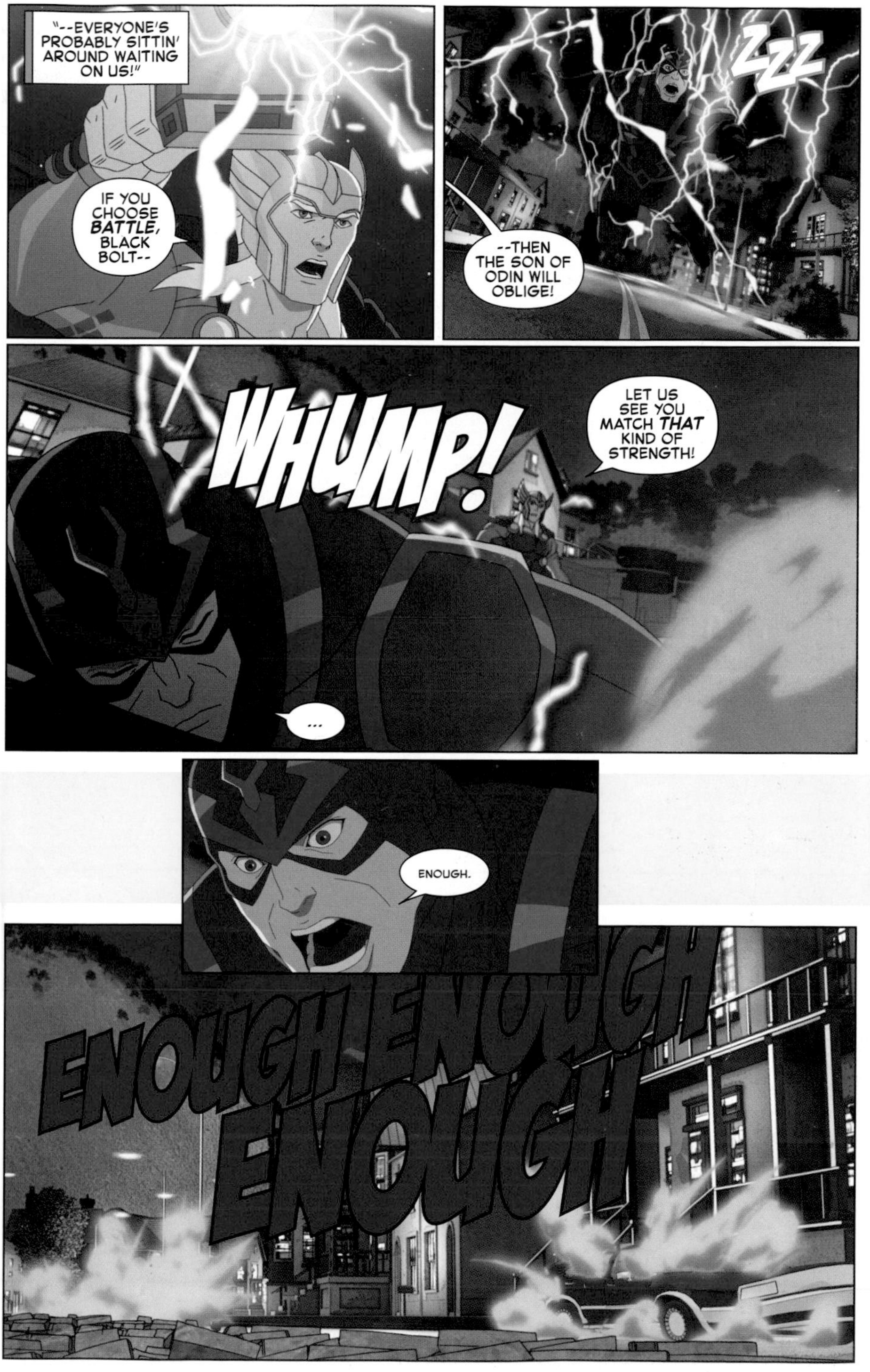
"--EVERYONE'S PROBABLY SITTIN' AROUND WAITING ON US!"
IF YOU CHOOSE *BATTLE*, BLACK BOLT--
ZZZ
--THEN THE SON OF ODIN WILL OBLIGE!
WHUMP!
LET US SEE YOU MATCH *THAT* KIND OF STRENGTH!
...
ENOUGH.
ENOUGH ENOUGH ENOUGH

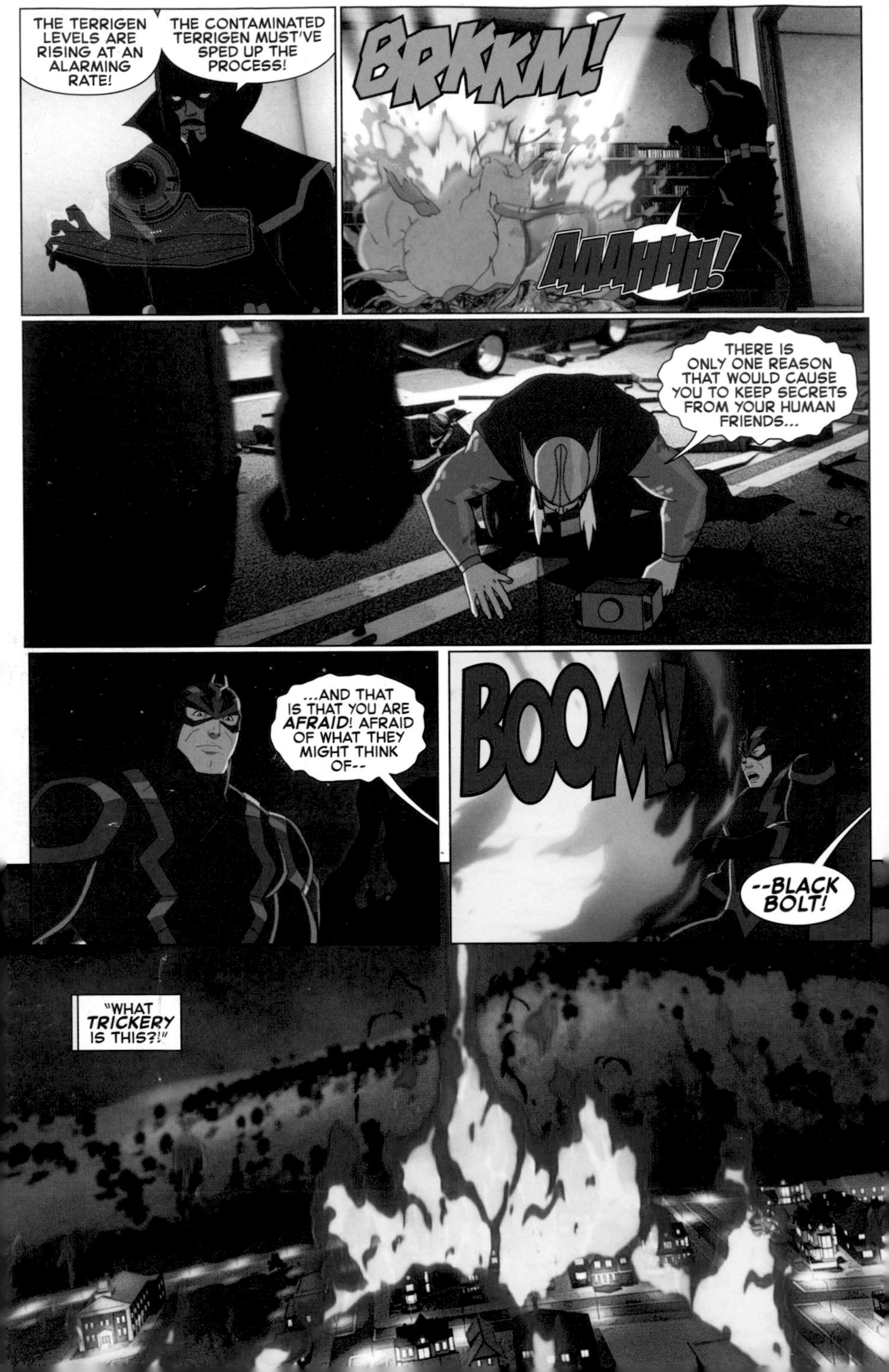
THE TERRIGEN LEVELS ARE RISING AT AN ALARMING RATE!
THE CONTAMINATED TERRIGEN MUST'VE SPED UP THE PROCESS!
BRKKM!
AAAHHH!
THERE IS ONLY ONE REASON THAT WOULD CAUSE YOU TO KEEP SECRETS FROM YOUR HUMAN FRIENDS...
...AND THAT IS THAT YOU ARE AFRAID! AFRAID OF WHAT THEY MIGHT THINK OF--
BOOM!
--BLACK BOLT!
"WHAT TRICKERY IS THIS?!"

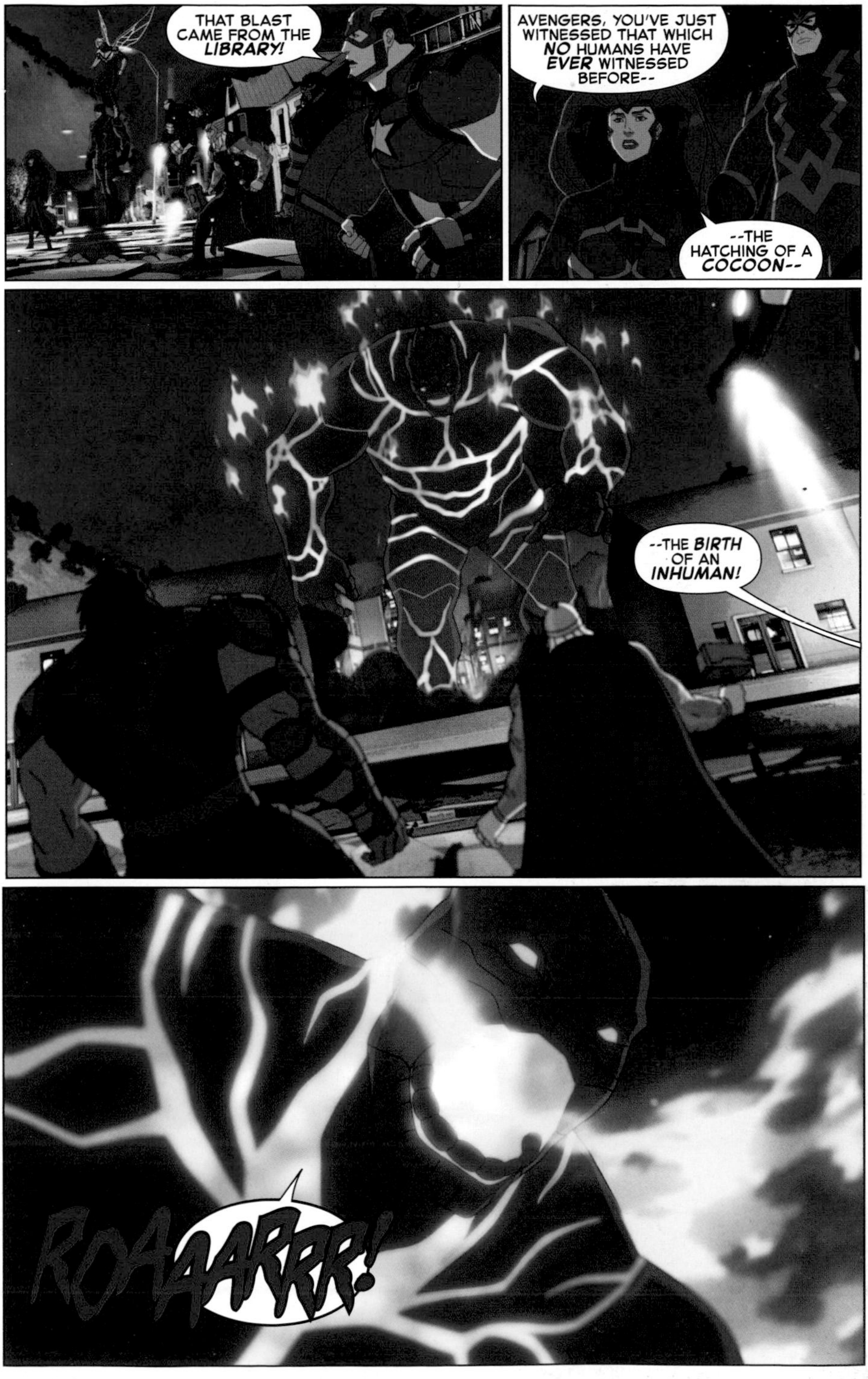
THAT BLAST CAME FROM THE LIBRARY!
AVENGERS, YOU'VE JUST WITNESSED THAT WHICH NO HUMANS HAVE EVER WITNESSED BEFORE--
--THE HATCHING OF A COCOON--
--THE BIRTH OF AN INHUMAN!
ROAAARRR!

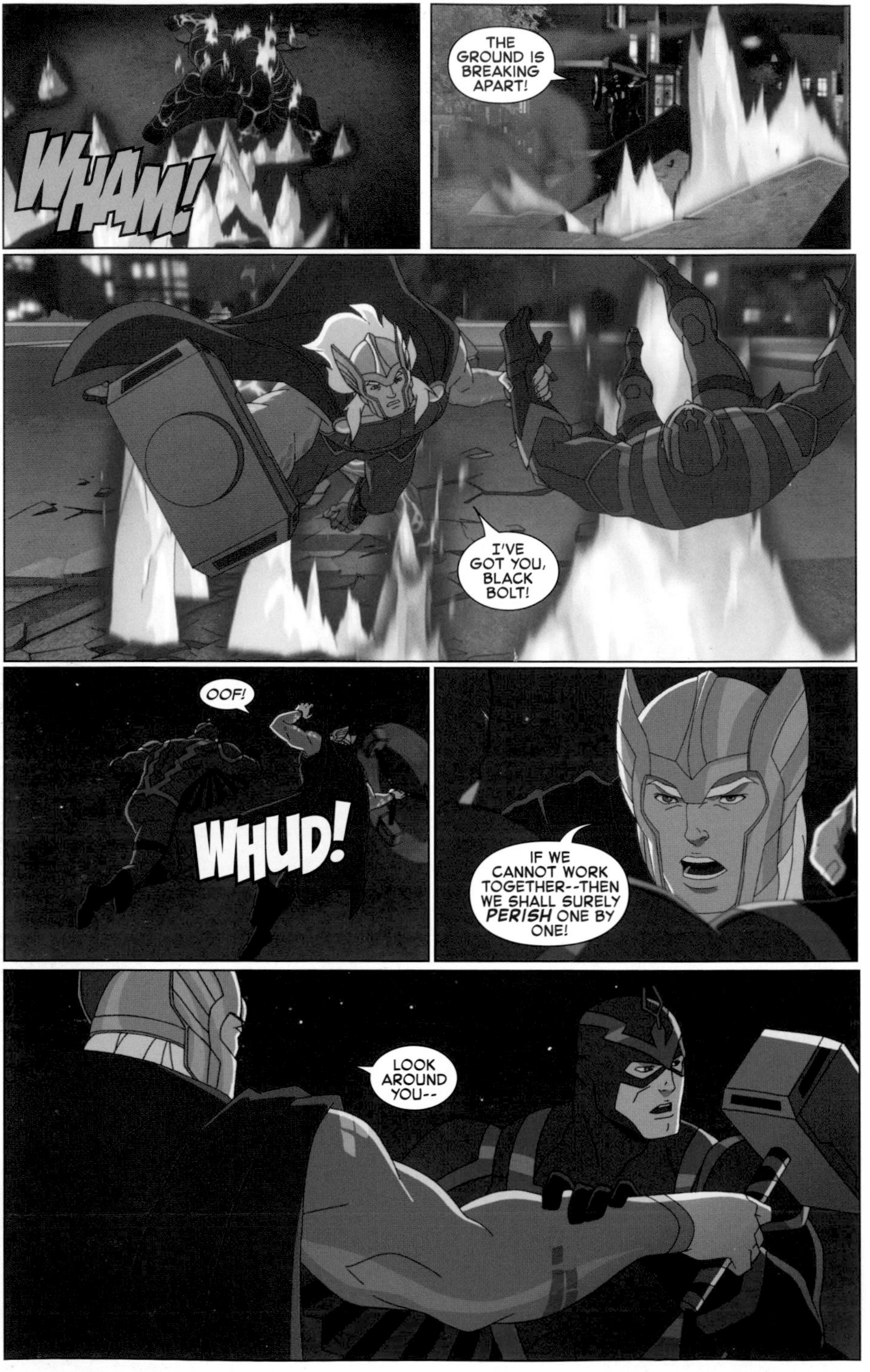
WHAM!
THE GROUND IS BREAKING APART!
I'VE GOT YOU, BLACK BOLT!
OOF!
WHUD!
IF WE CANNOT WORK TOGETHER--THEN WE SHALL SURELY *PERISH* ONE BY ONE!
LOOK AROUND YOU--

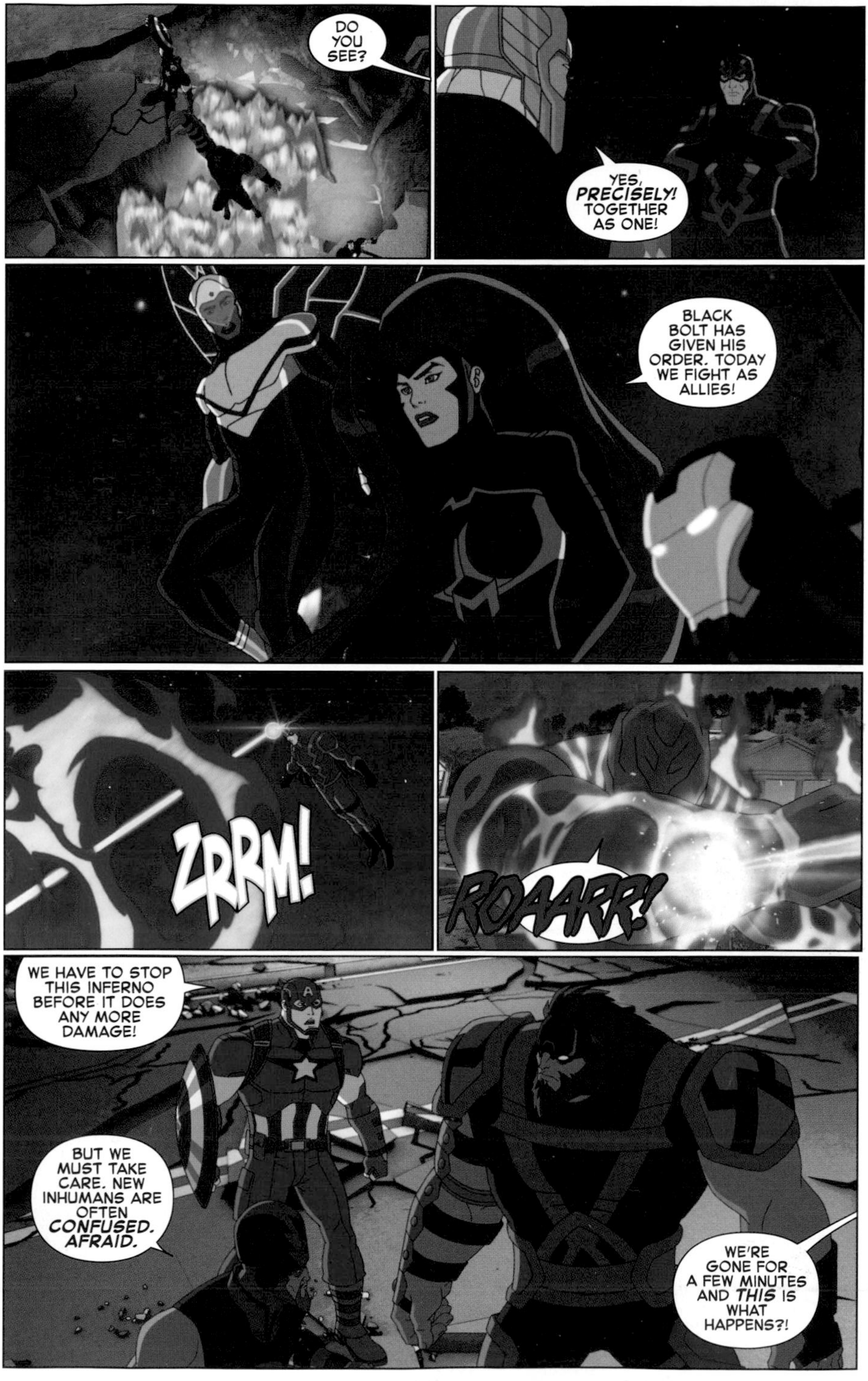
DO YOU SEE?
YES, PRECISELY! TOGETHER AS ONE!
BLACK BOLT HAS GIVEN HIS ORDER. TODAY WE FIGHT AS ALLIES!
ZRRM!
ROAARR!
WE HAVE TO STOP THIS INFERNO BEFORE IT DOES ANY MORE DAMAGE!
BUT WE MUST TAKE CARE. NEW INHUMANS ARE OFTEN CONFUSED. AFRAID.
WE'RE GONE FOR A FEW MINUTES AND THIS IS WHAT HAPPENS?!

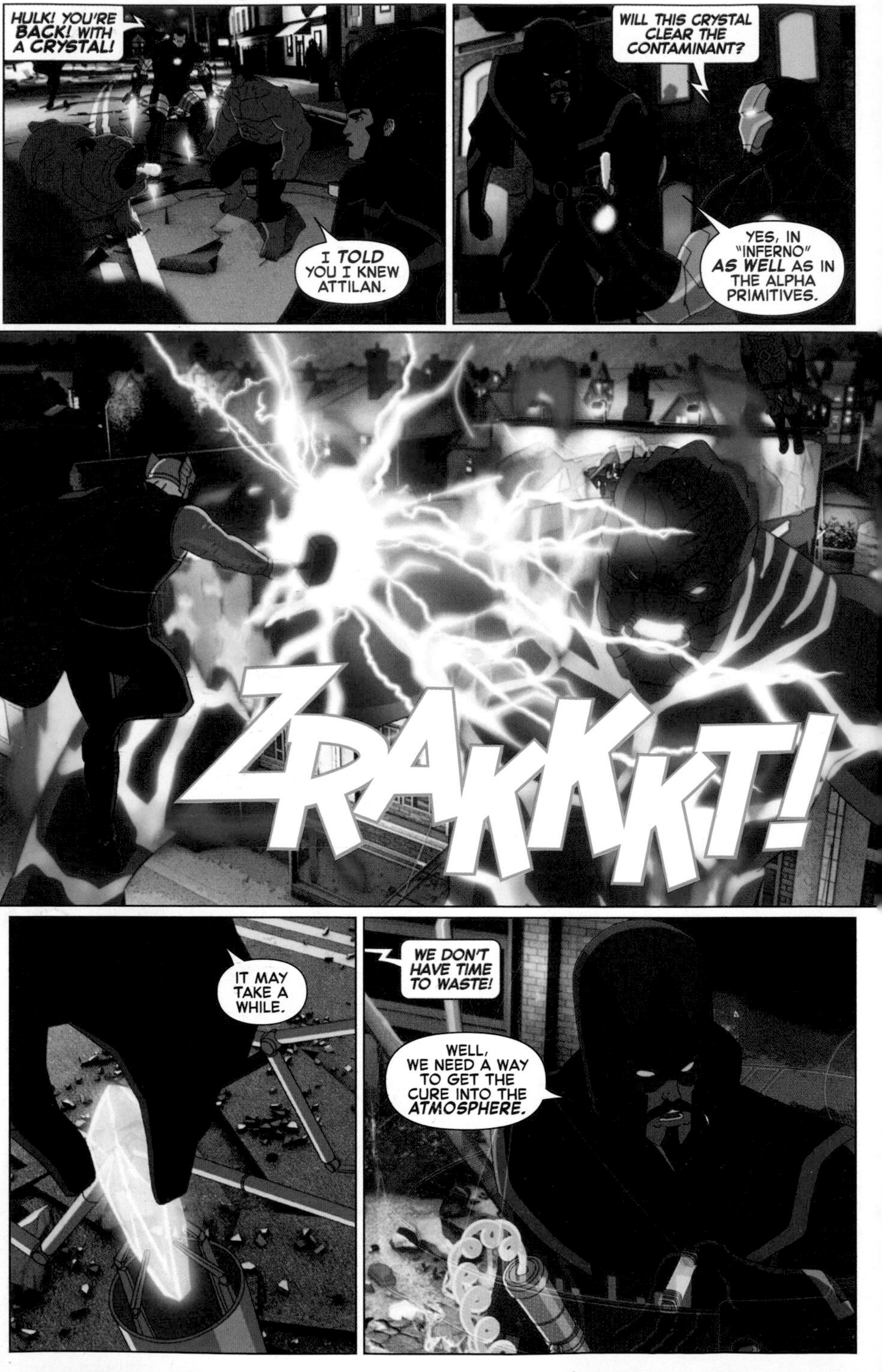
HULK! YOU'RE BACK! WITH A CRYSTAL!
I TOLD YOU I KNEW ATTILAN.
WILL THIS CRYSTAL CLEAR THE CONTAMINANT?
YES, IN "INFERNO" AS WELL AS IN THE ALPHA PRIMITIVES.
ZRAKKKT!
IT MAY TAKE A WHILE.
WE DON'T HAVE TIME TO WASTE!
WELL, WE NEED A WAY TO GET THE CURE INTO THE ATMOSPHERE.

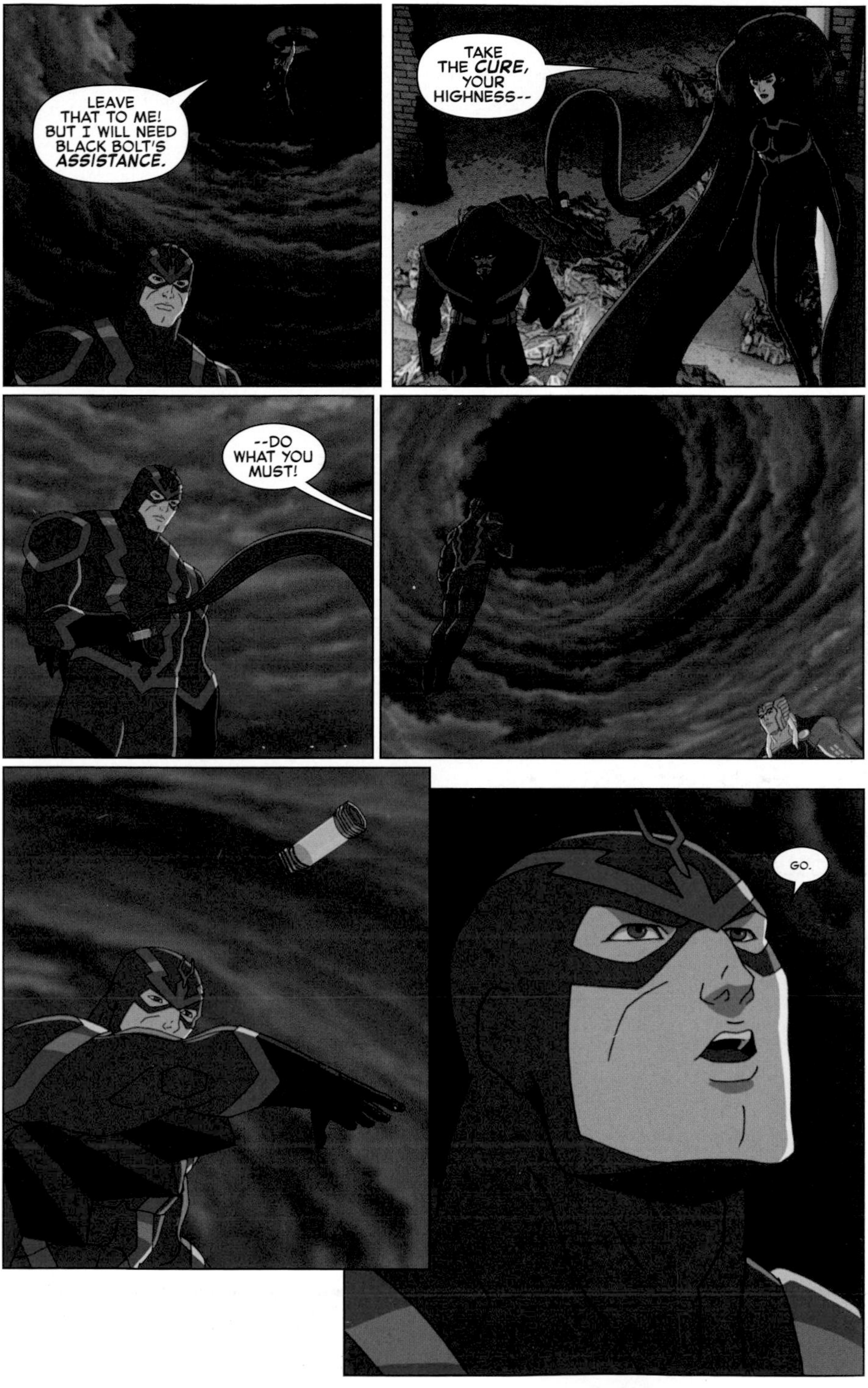
LEAVE THAT TO ME! BUT I WILL NEED BLACK BOLT'S ASSISTANCE.
TAKE THE CURE, YOUR HIGHNESS--
--DO WHAT YOU MUST!
GO.

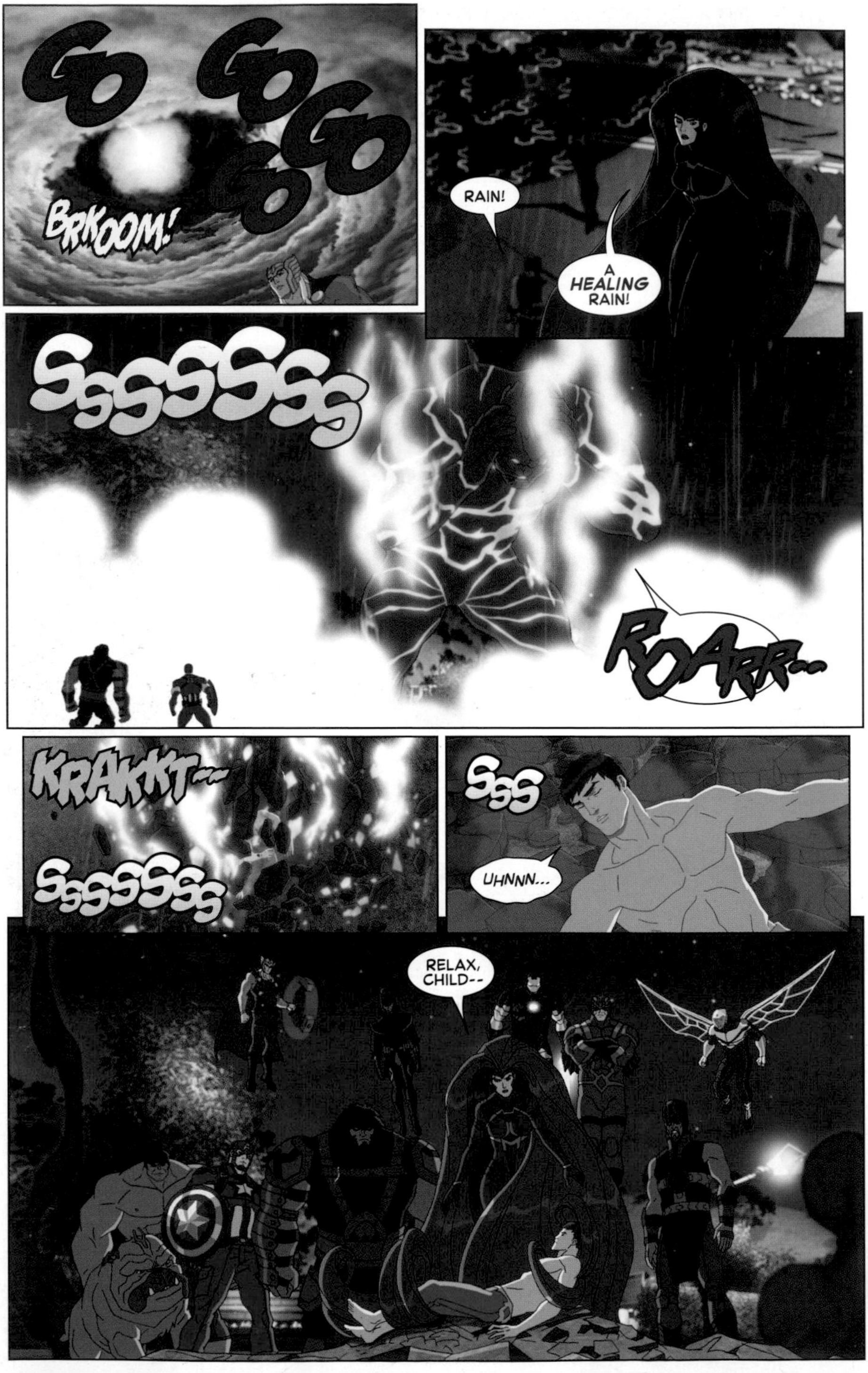
GO GO GO GO GO
BRKOOM!
RAIN!
A HEALING RAIN!
SSSSSSSS
ROARR--
KRAKKT--
SSSSSSSS
SSS
UHNNN...
RELAX, CHILD--

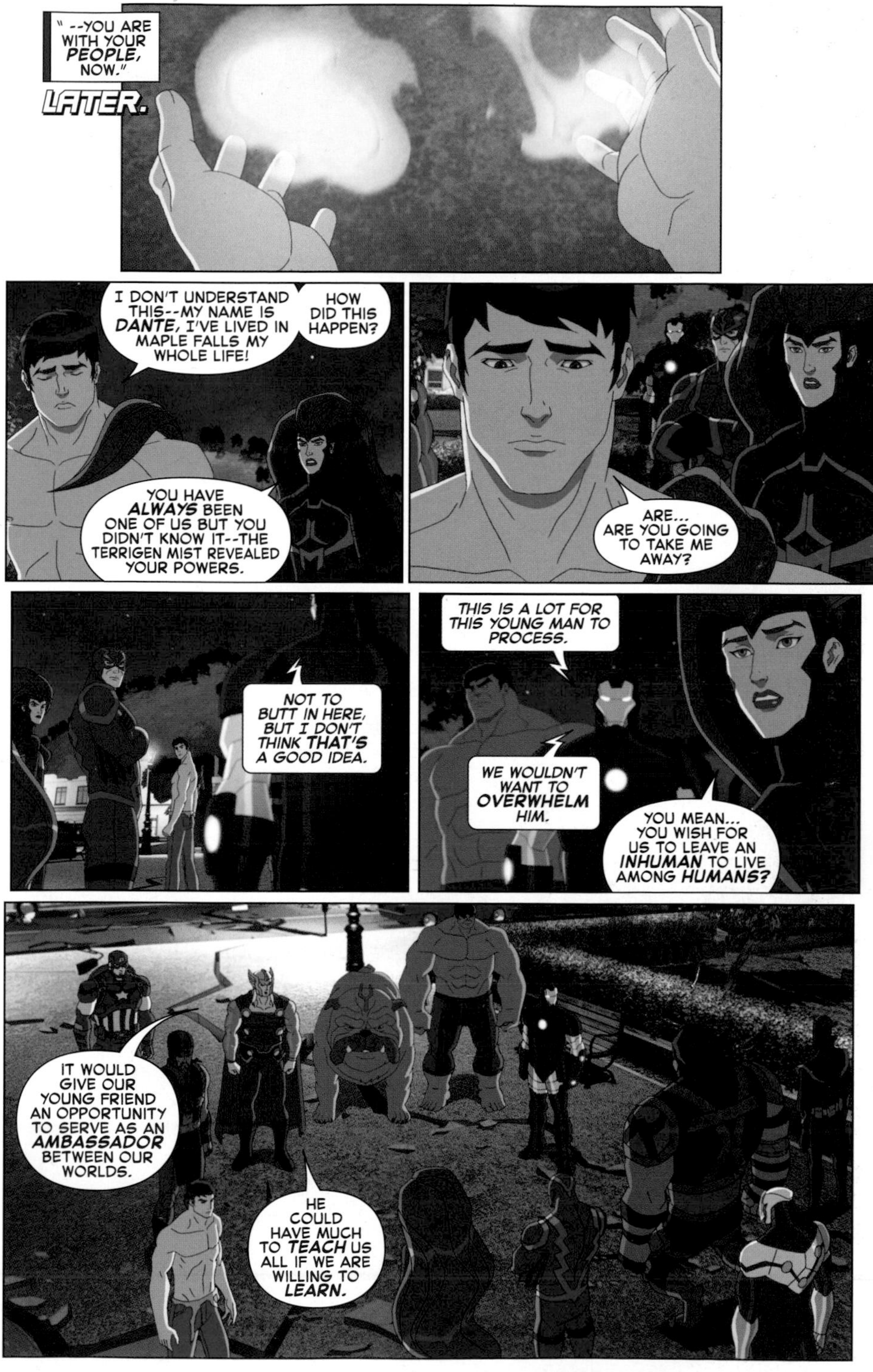
" --YOU ARE WITH YOUR PEOPLE, NOW."
LATER.
I DON'T UNDERSTAND THIS--MY NAME IS DANTE, I'VE LIVED IN MAPLE FALLS MY WHOLE LIFE!
HOW DID THIS HAPPEN?
YOU HAVE ALWAYS BEEN ONE OF US BUT YOU DIDN'T KNOW IT--THE TERRIGEN MIST REVEALED YOUR POWERS.
ARE... ARE YOU GOING TO TAKE ME AWAY?
NOT TO BUTT IN HERE, BUT I DON'T THINK THAT'S A GOOD IDEA.
THIS IS A LOT FOR THIS YOUNG MAN TO PROCESS.
WE WOULDN'T WANT TO OVERWHELM HIM.
YOU MEAN... YOU WISH FOR US TO LEAVE AN INHUMAN TO LIVE AMONG HUMANS?
IT WOULD GIVE OUR YOUNG FRIEND AN OPPORTUNITY TO SERVE AS AN AMBASSADOR BETWEEN OUR WORLDS.
HE COULD HAVE MUCH TO TEACH US ALL IF WE ARE WILLING TO LEARN.

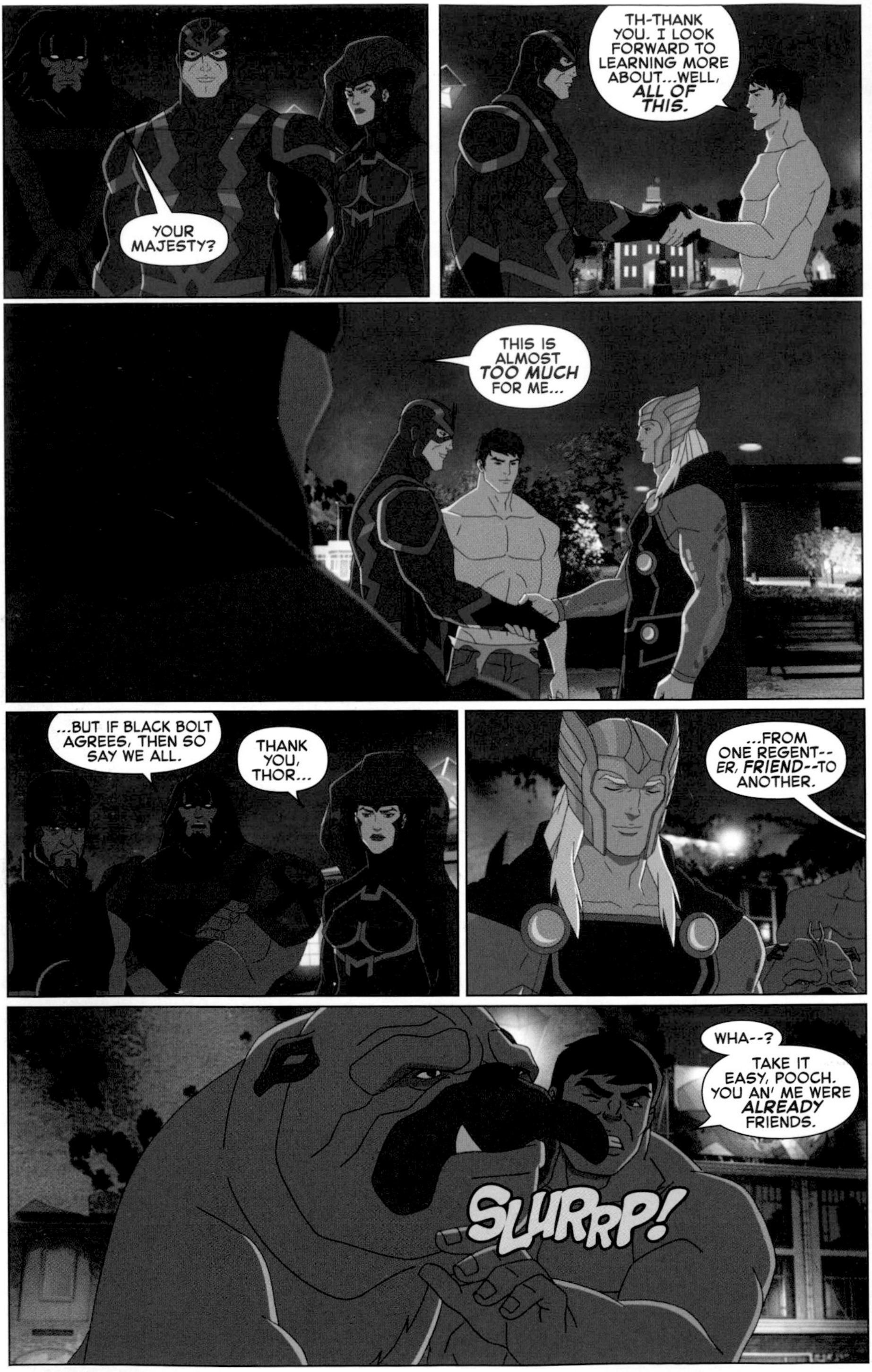
YOUR MAJESTY?
TH-THANK YOU. I LOOK FORWARD TO LEARNING MORE ABOUT...WELL, ALL OF THIS.
THIS IS ALMOST TOO MUCH FOR ME...
...BUT IF BLACK BOLT AGREES, THEN SO SAY WE ALL.
THANK YOU, THOR...
...FROM ONE REGENT-- ER, FRIEND--TO ANOTHER.
WHA--?
TAKE IT EASY, POOCH. YOU AN' ME WERE ALREADY FRIENDS.
SLURRP!

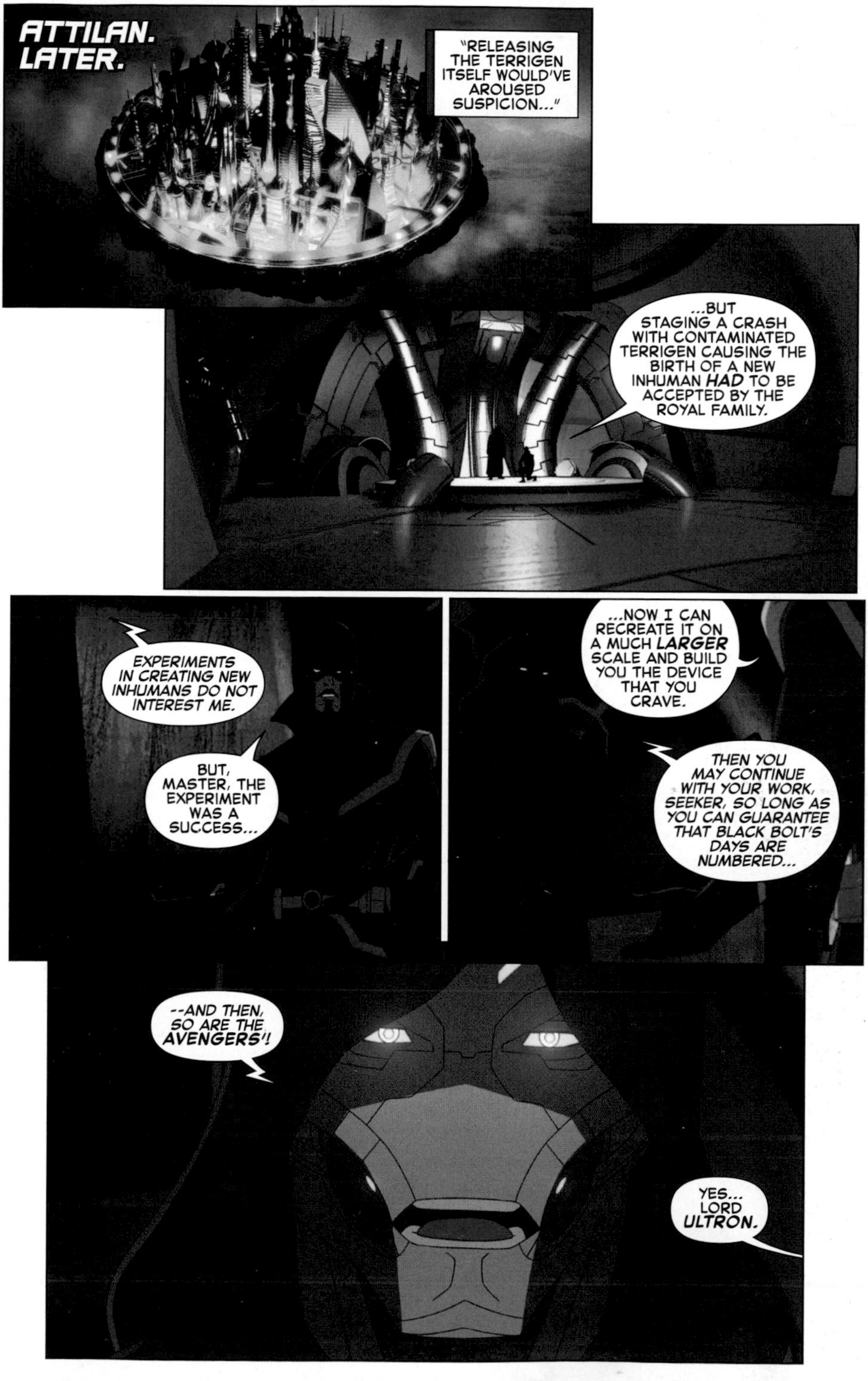
ATTILAN. LATER.
"RELEASING THE TERRIGEN ITSELF WOULD'VE AROUSED SUSPICION..."
...BUT STAGING A CRASH WITH CONTAMINATED TERRIGEN CAUSING THE BIRTH OF A NEW INHUMAN HAD TO BE ACCEPTED BY THE ROYAL FAMILY.
EXPERIMENTS IN CREATING NEW INHUMANS DO NOT INTEREST ME.
BUT, MASTER, THE EXPERIMENT WAS A SUCCESS...
...NOW I CAN RECREATE IT ON A MUCH LARGER SCALE AND BUILD YOU THE DEVICE THAT YOU CRAVE.
THEN YOU MAY CONTINUE WITH YOUR WORK, SEEKER, SO LONG AS YOU CAN GUARANTEE THAT BLACK BOLT'S DAYS ARE NUMBERED...
--AND THEN, SO ARE THE AVENGERS'!
YES... LORD ULTRON.

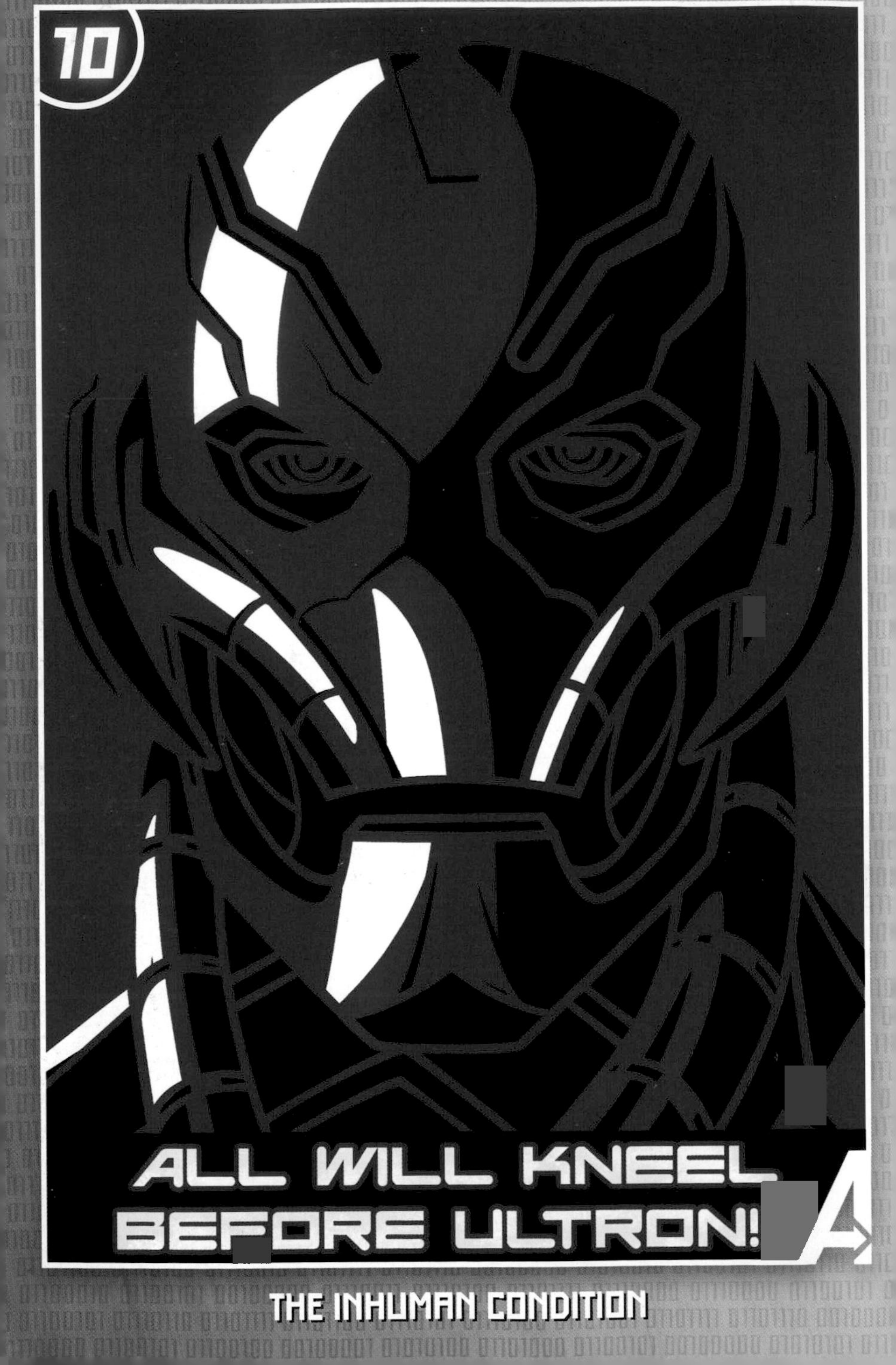
10
ALL WILL KNEEL
BEFORE ULTRON!

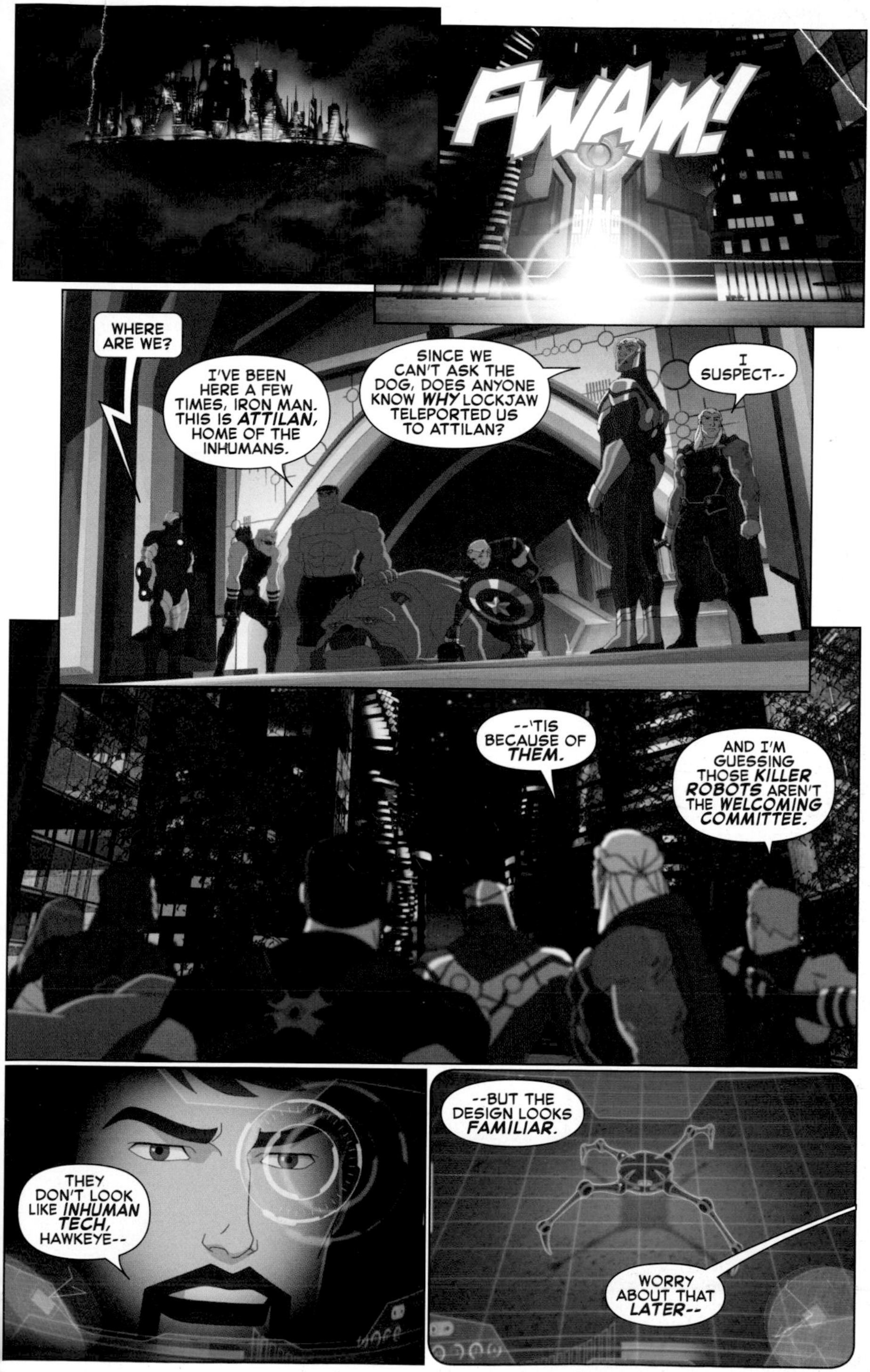
FWAM!
WHERE ARE WE?
I'VE BEEN HERE A FEW TIMES, IRON MAN. THIS IS ATTILAN, HOME OF THE INHUMANS.
SINCE WE CAN'T ASK THE DOG, DOES ANYONE KNOW WHY LOCKJAW TELEPORTED US TO ATTILAN?
I SUSPECT--
--'TIS BECAUSE OF THEM.
AND I'M GUESSING THOSE KILLER ROBOTS AREN'T THE WELCOMING COMMITTEE.
THEY DON'T LOOK LIKE INHUMAN TECH, HAWKEYE--
--BUT THE DESIGN LOOKS FAMILIAR.
WORRY ABOUT THAT LATER--

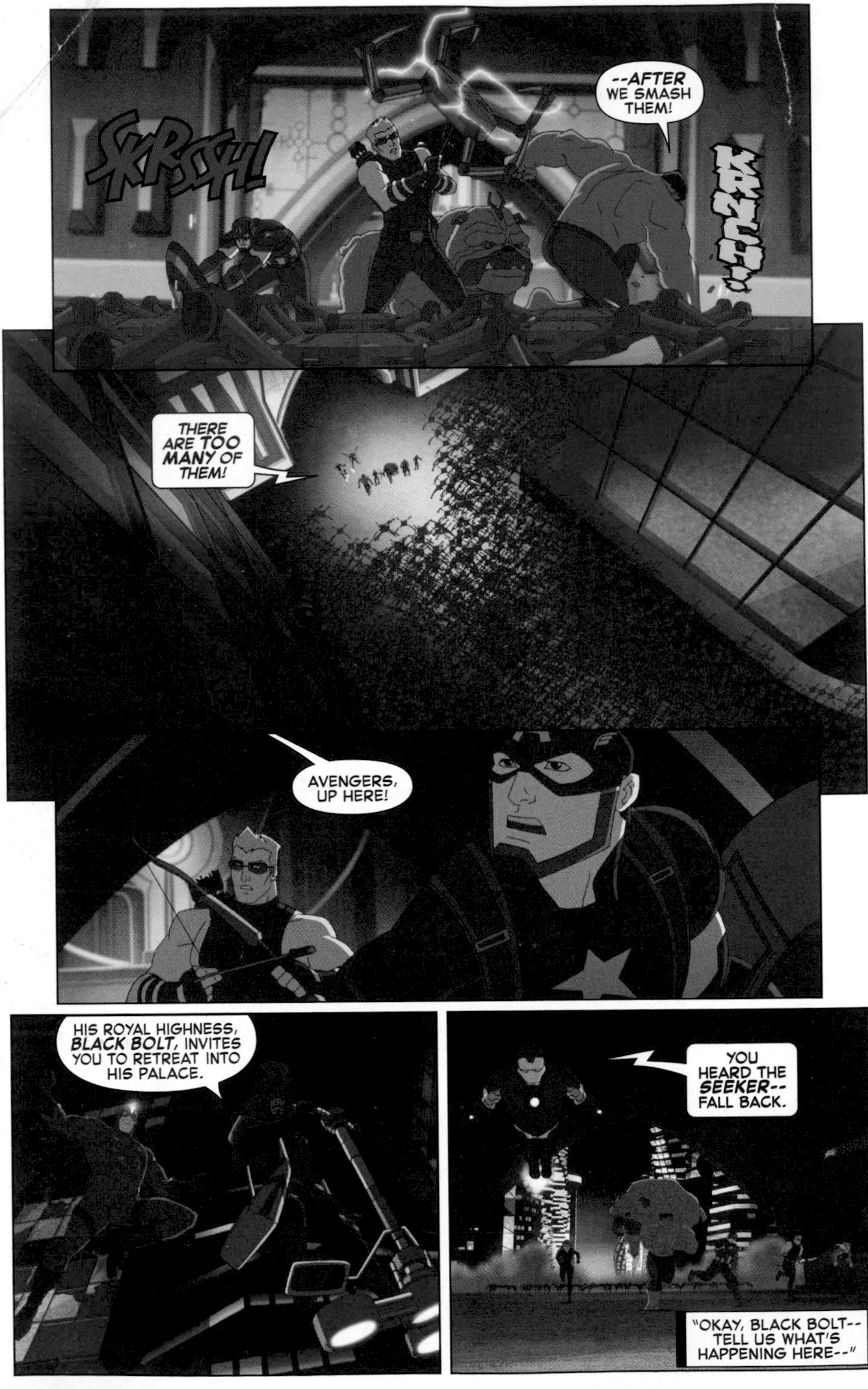
SKRSSH!
--AFTER WE SMASH THEM!
KRNCH!
THERE ARE TOO MANY OF THEM!
AVENGERS, UP HERE!
HIS ROYAL HIGHNESS, BLACK BOLT, INVITES YOU TO RETREAT INTO HIS PALACE.
YOU HEARD THE SEEKER-- FALL BACK.
"OKAY, BLACK BOLT-- TELL US WHAT'S HAPPENING HERE--"

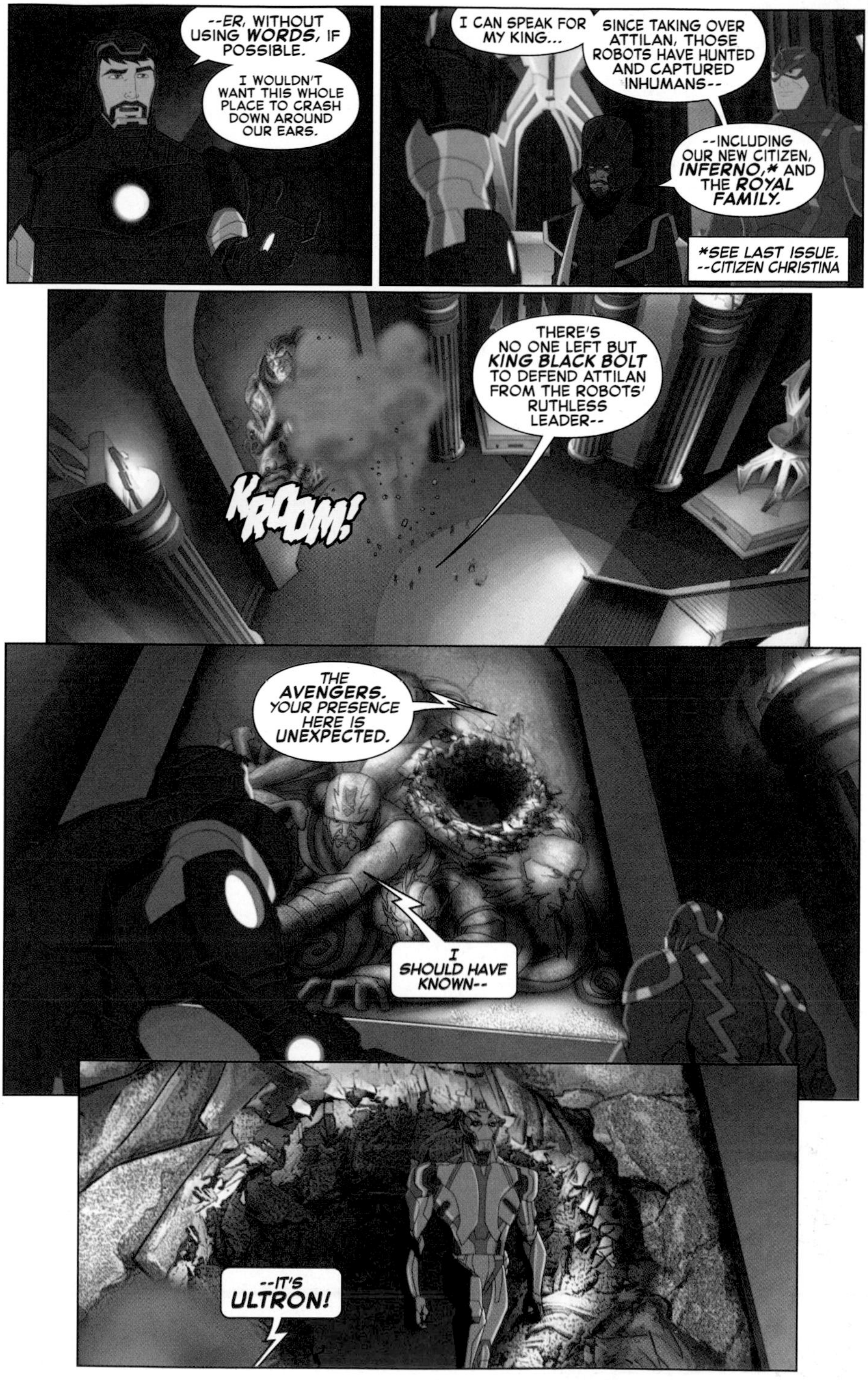
--ER, WITHOUT USING WORDS, IF POSSIBLE.
I WOULDN'T WANT THIS WHOLE PLACE TO CRASH DOWN AROUND OUR EARS.
I CAN SPEAK FOR MY KING...
SINCE TAKING OVER ATTILAN, THOSE ROBOTS HAVE HUNTED AND CAPTURED INHUMANS--
--INCLUDING OUR NEW CITIZEN, INFERNO,* AND THE ROYAL FAMILY.
*SEE LAST ISSUE. --CITIZEN CHRISTINA
THERE'S NO ONE LEFT BUT KING BLACK BOLT TO DEFEND ATTILAN FROM THE ROBOTS' RUTHLESS LEADER--
KROOM!
THE AVENGERS. YOUR PRESENCE HERE IS UNEXPECTED.
I SHOULD HAVE KNOWN--
--IT'S ULTRON!

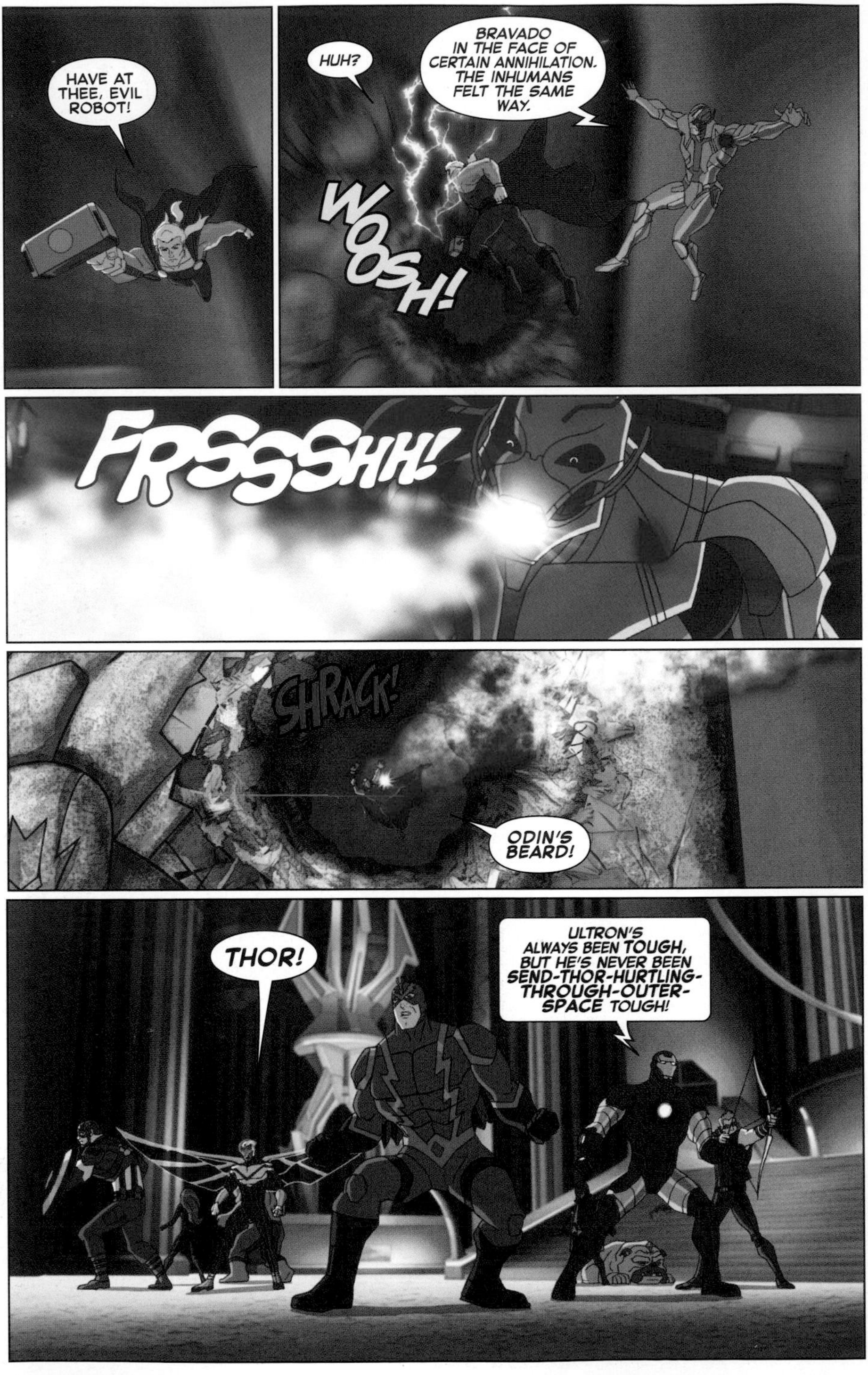
HAVE AT THEE, EVIL ROBOT!
HUH?
BRAVADO IN THE FACE OF CERTAIN ANNIHILATION. THE INHUMANS FELT THE SAME WAY.
WOOSH!
FRSSSHH!
SHRACK!
ODIN'S BEARD!
THOR!
ULTRON'S ALWAYS BEEN TOUGH, BUT HE'S NEVER BEEN SEND-THOR-HURTLING-THROUGH-OUTER-SPACE TOUGH!

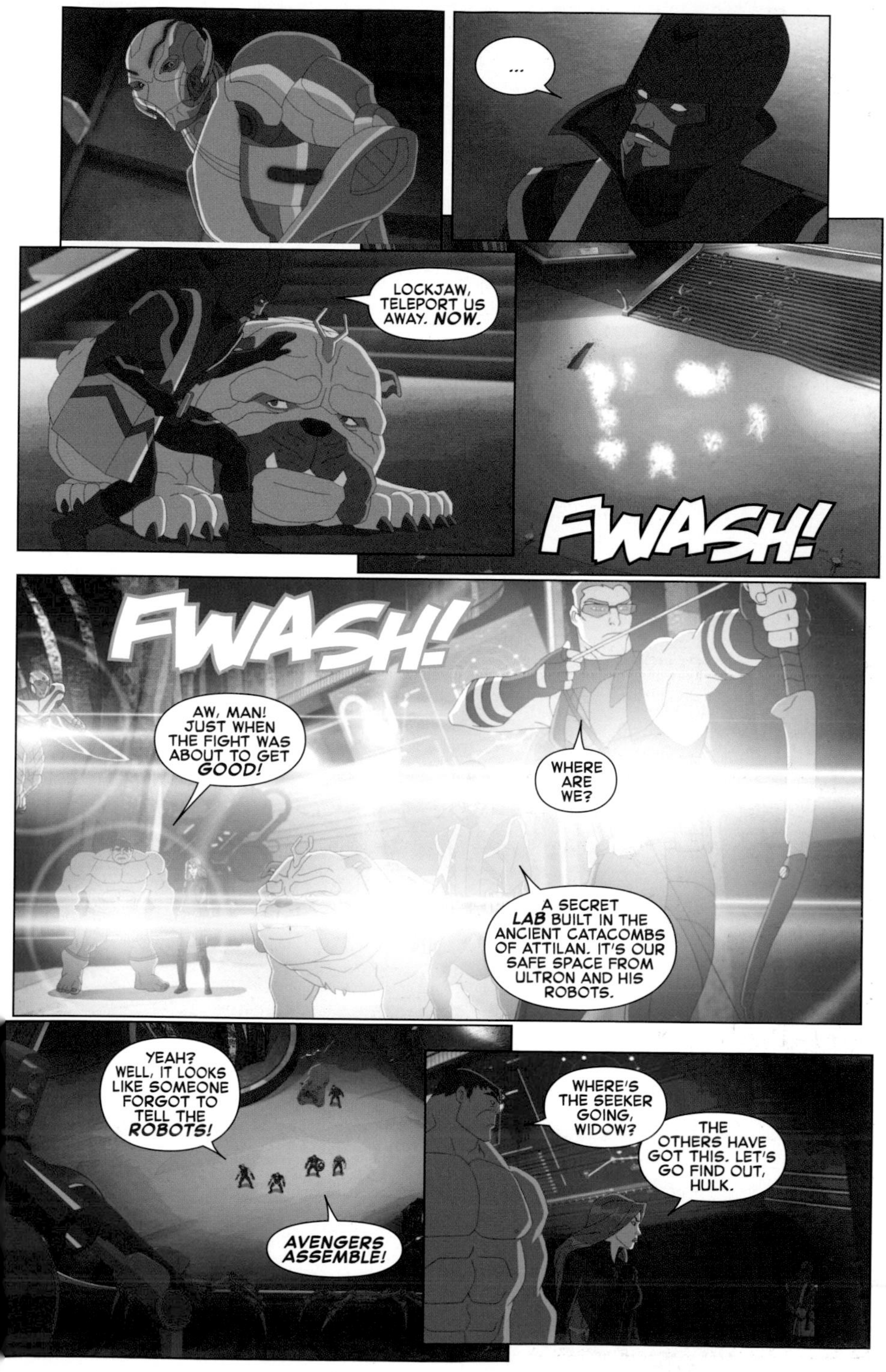
...
LOCKJAW, TELEPORT US AWAY. NOW.
FWASH!
FWASH!
AW, MAN! JUST WHEN THE FIGHT WAS ABOUT TO GET GOOD!
WHERE ARE WE?
A SECRET LAB BUILT IN THE ANCIENT CATACOMBS OF ATTILAN. IT'S OUR SAFE SPACE FROM ULTRON AND HIS ROBOTS.
YEAH? WELL, IT LOOKS LIKE SOMEONE FORGOT TO TELL THE ROBOTS!
AVENGERS ASSEMBLE!
WHERE'S THE SEEKER GOING, WIDOW?
THE OTHERS HAVE GOT THIS. LET'S GO FIND OUT, HULK.

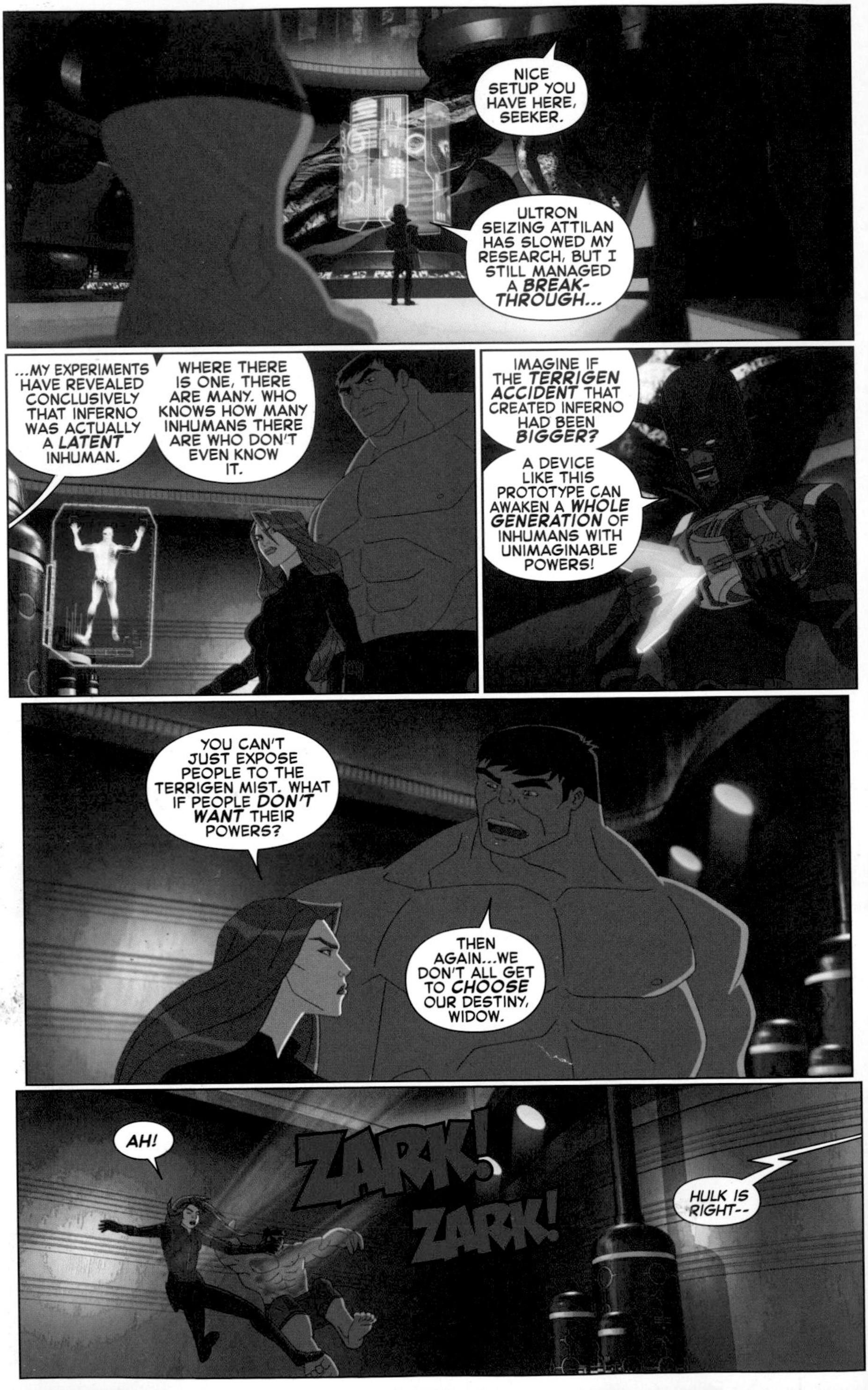
NICE SETUP YOU HAVE HERE, SEEKER.
ULTRON SEIZING ATTILAN HAS SLOWED MY RESEARCH, BUT I STILL MANAGED A BREAKTHROUGH...
...MY EXPERIMENTS HAVE REVEALED CONCLUSIVELY THAT INFERNO WAS ACTUALLY A LATENT INHUMAN.
WHERE THERE IS ONE, THERE ARE MANY. WHO KNOWS HOW MANY INHUMANS THERE ARE WHO DON'T EVEN KNOW IT.
IMAGINE IF THE TERRIGEN ACCIDENT THAT CREATED INFERNO HAD BEEN BIGGER?
A DEVICE LIKE THIS PROTOTYPE CAN AWAKEN A WHOLE GENERATION OF INHUMANS WITH UNIMAGINABLE POWERS!
YOU CAN'T JUST EXPOSE PEOPLE TO THE TERRIGEN MIST. WHAT IF PEOPLE DON'T WANT THEIR POWERS?
THEN AGAIN...WE DON'T ALL GET TO CHOOSE OUR DESTINY, WIDOW.
AH!
ZARK!
ZARK!
HULK IS RIGHT--

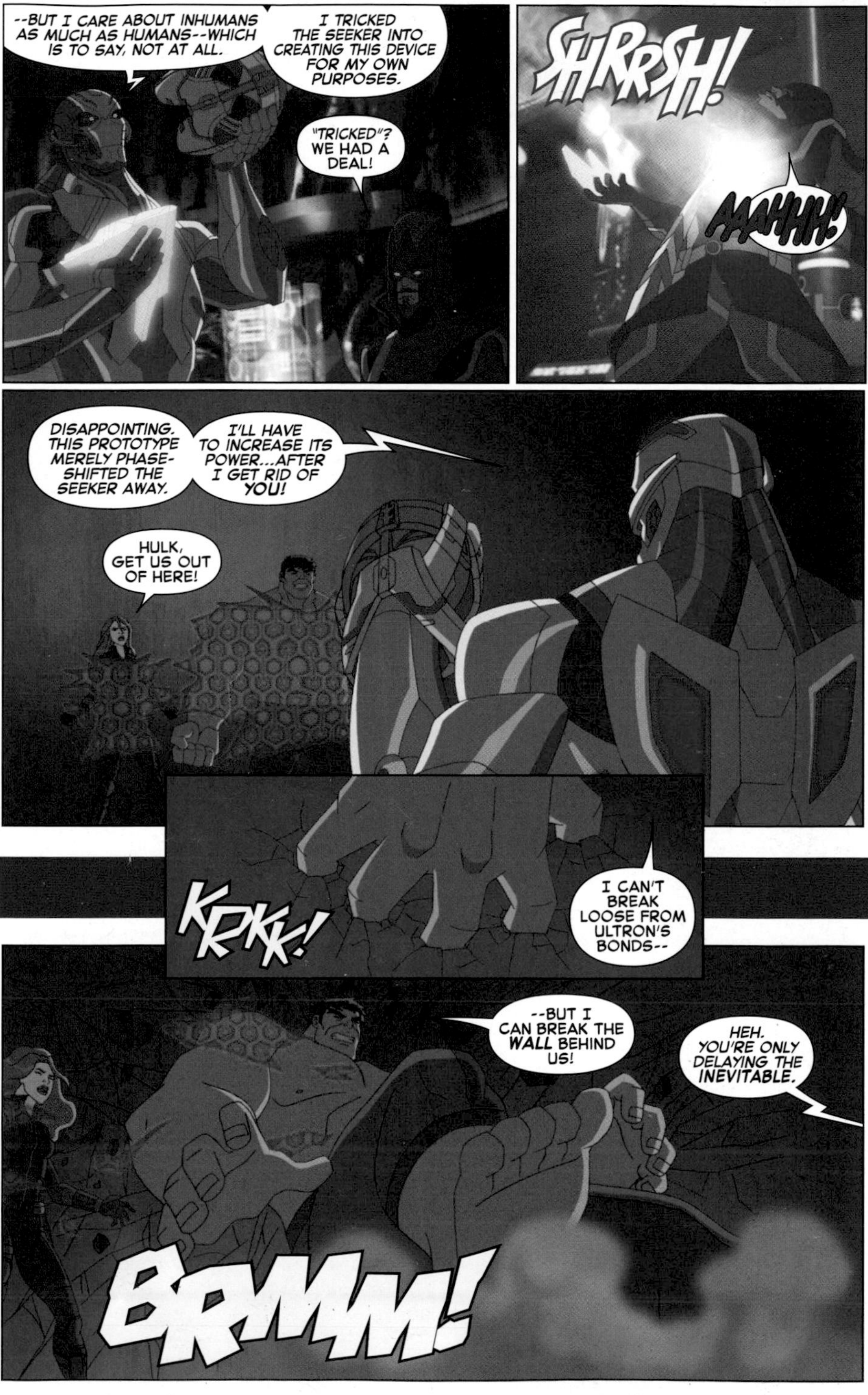
--BUT I CARE ABOUT INHUMANS AS MUCH AS HUMANS--WHICH IS TO SAY, NOT AT ALL.
I TRICKED THE SEEKER INTO CREATING THIS DEVICE FOR MY OWN PURPOSES.
"TRICKED"? WE HAD A DEAL!
SHRRSH!
AAAHHH!
DISAPPOINTING. THIS PROTOTYPE MERELY PHASE-SHIFTED THE SEEKER AWAY.
I'LL HAVE TO INCREASE ITS POWER...AFTER I GET RID OF YOU!
HULK, GET US OUT OF HERE!
KRKK!
I CAN'T BREAK LOOSE FROM ULTRON'S BONDS--
--BUT I CAN BREAK THE WALL BEHIND US!
HEH. YOU'RE ONLY DELAYING THE INEVITABLE.
BRMMM!

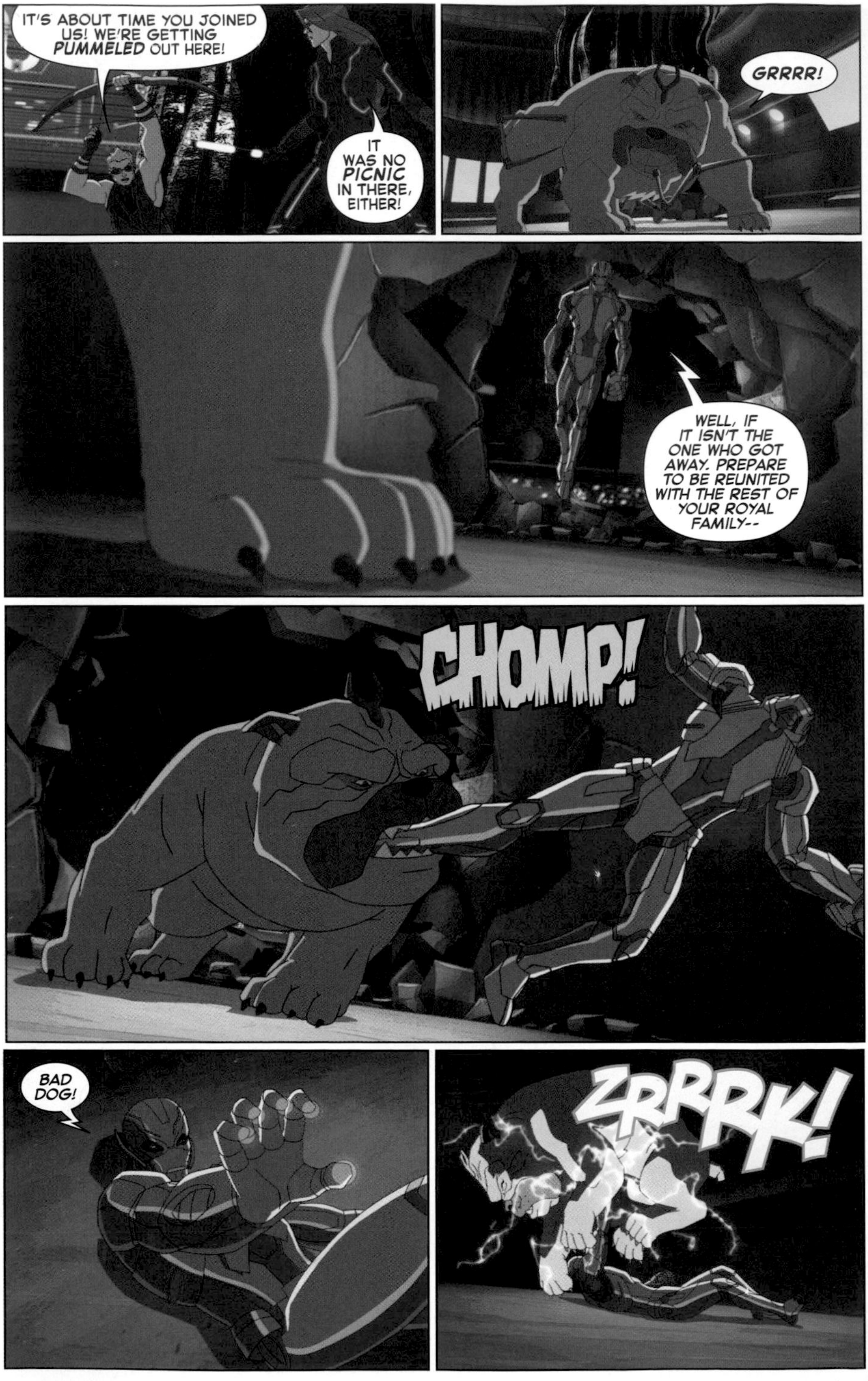
IT'S ABOUT TIME YOU JOINED US! WE'RE GETTING PUMMELED OUT HERE!
IT WAS NO PICNIC IN THERE, EITHER!
GRRRR!
WELL, IF IT ISN'T THE ONE WHO GOT AWAY. PREPARE TO BE REUNITED WITH THE REST OF YOUR ROYAL FAMILY--
CHOMP!
BAD DOG!
ZRRRK!

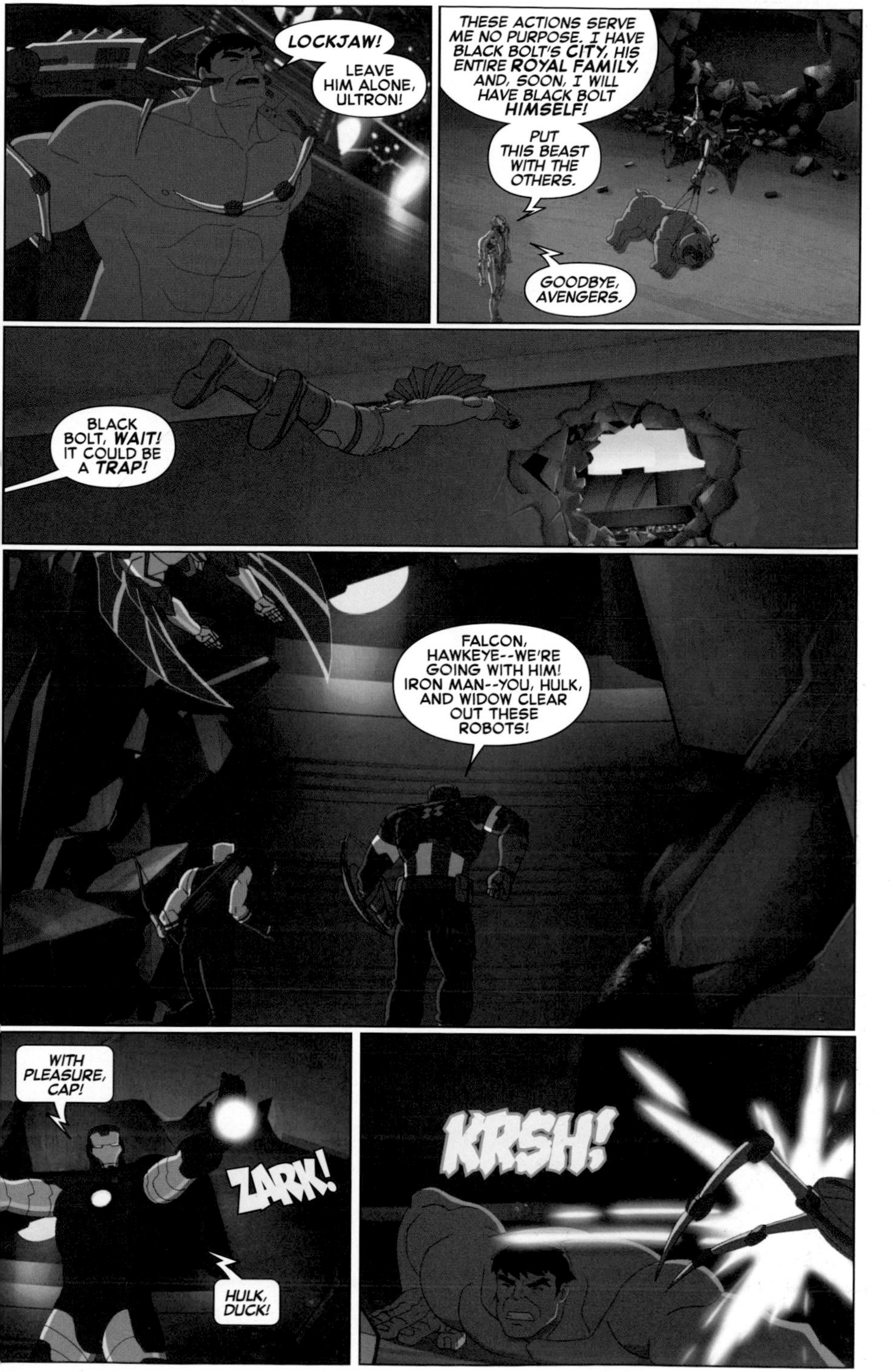
LOCKJAW!
LEAVE HIM ALONE, ULTRON!
THESE ACTIONS SERVE ME NO PURPOSE. I HAVE BLACK BOLT'S CITY, HIS ENTIRE ROYAL FAMILY, AND, SOON, I WILL HAVE BLACK BOLT HIMSELF!
PUT THIS BEAST WITH THE OTHERS.
GOODBYE, AVENGERS.
BLACK BOLT, WAIT! IT COULD BE A TRAP!
FALCON, HAWKEYE--WE'RE GOING WITH HIM! IRON MAN--YOU, HULK, AND WIDOW CLEAR OUT THESE ROBOTS!
WITH PLEASURE, CAP!
ZARK!
HULK, DUCK!
KRSH!

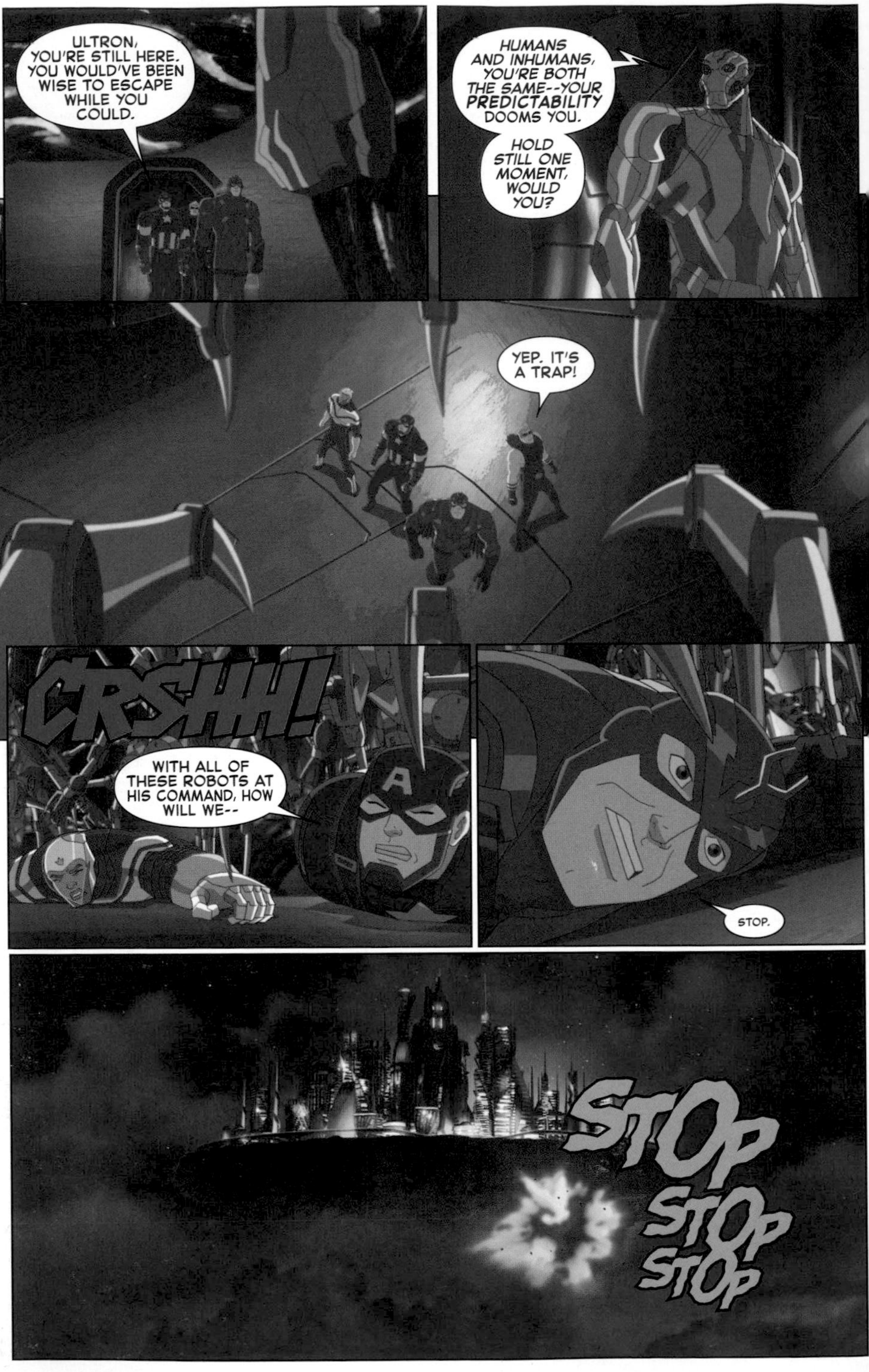
ULTRON, YOU'RE STILL HERE. YOU WOULD'VE BEEN WISE TO ESCAPE WHILE YOU COULD.
HUMANS AND INHUMANS, YOU'RE BOTH THE SAME--YOUR PREDICTABILITY DOOMS YOU.
HOLD STILL ONE MOMENT, WOULD YOU?
YEP. IT'S A TRAP!
CRSHHH!
WITH ALL OF THESE ROBOTS AT HIS COMMAND, HOW WILL WE--
STOP.
STOP
STOP
STOP

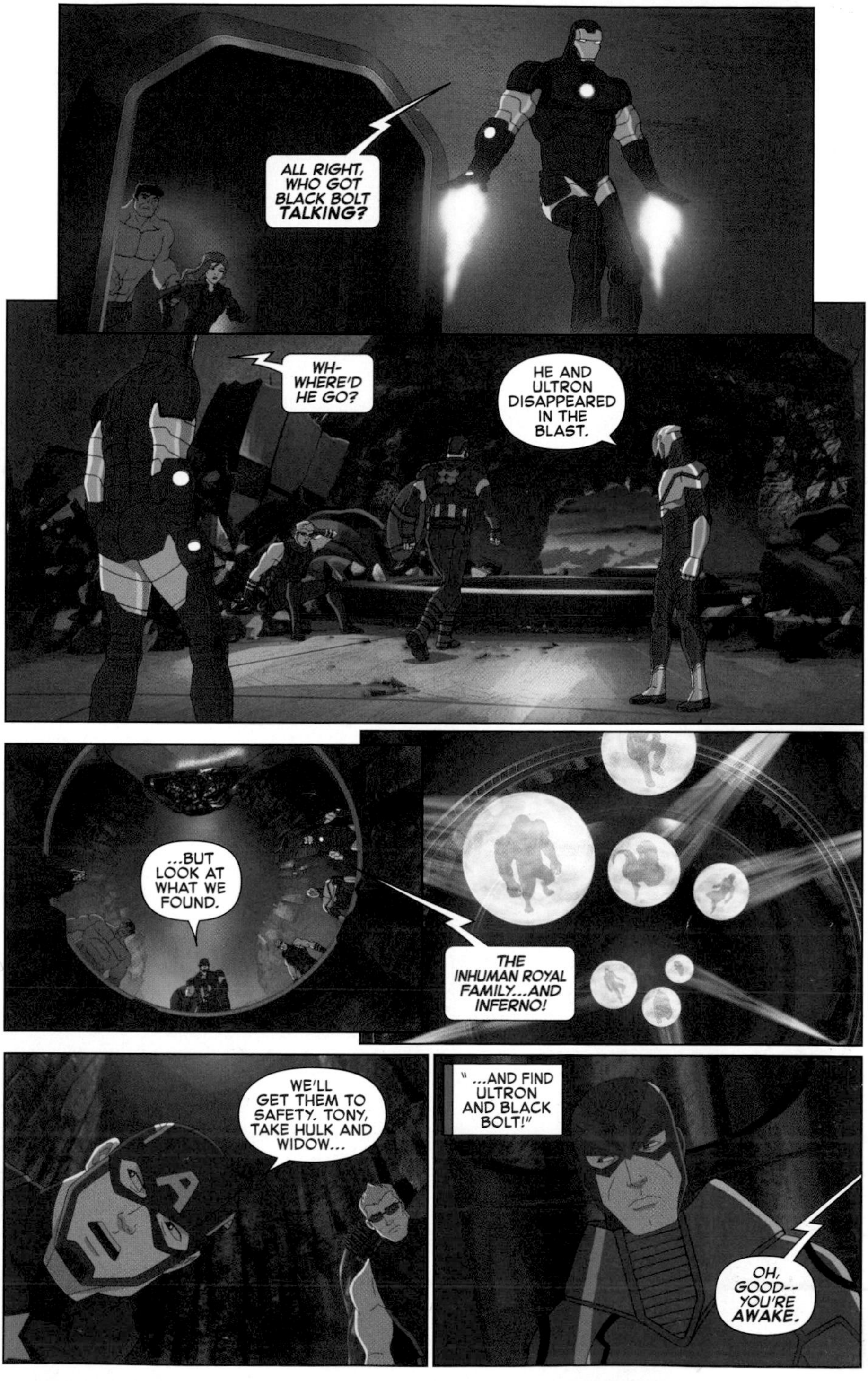
ALL RIGHT, WHO GOT BLACK BOLT TALKING?
WH-WHERE'D HE GO?
HE AND ULTRON DISAPPEARED IN THE BLAST.
...BUT LOOK AT WHAT WE FOUND.
THE INHUMAN ROYAL FAMILY...AND INFERNO!
WE'LL GET THEM TO SAFETY. TONY, TAKE HULK AND WIDOW...
"...AND FIND ULTRON AND BLACK BOLT!"
OH, GOOD--YOU'RE AWAKE.

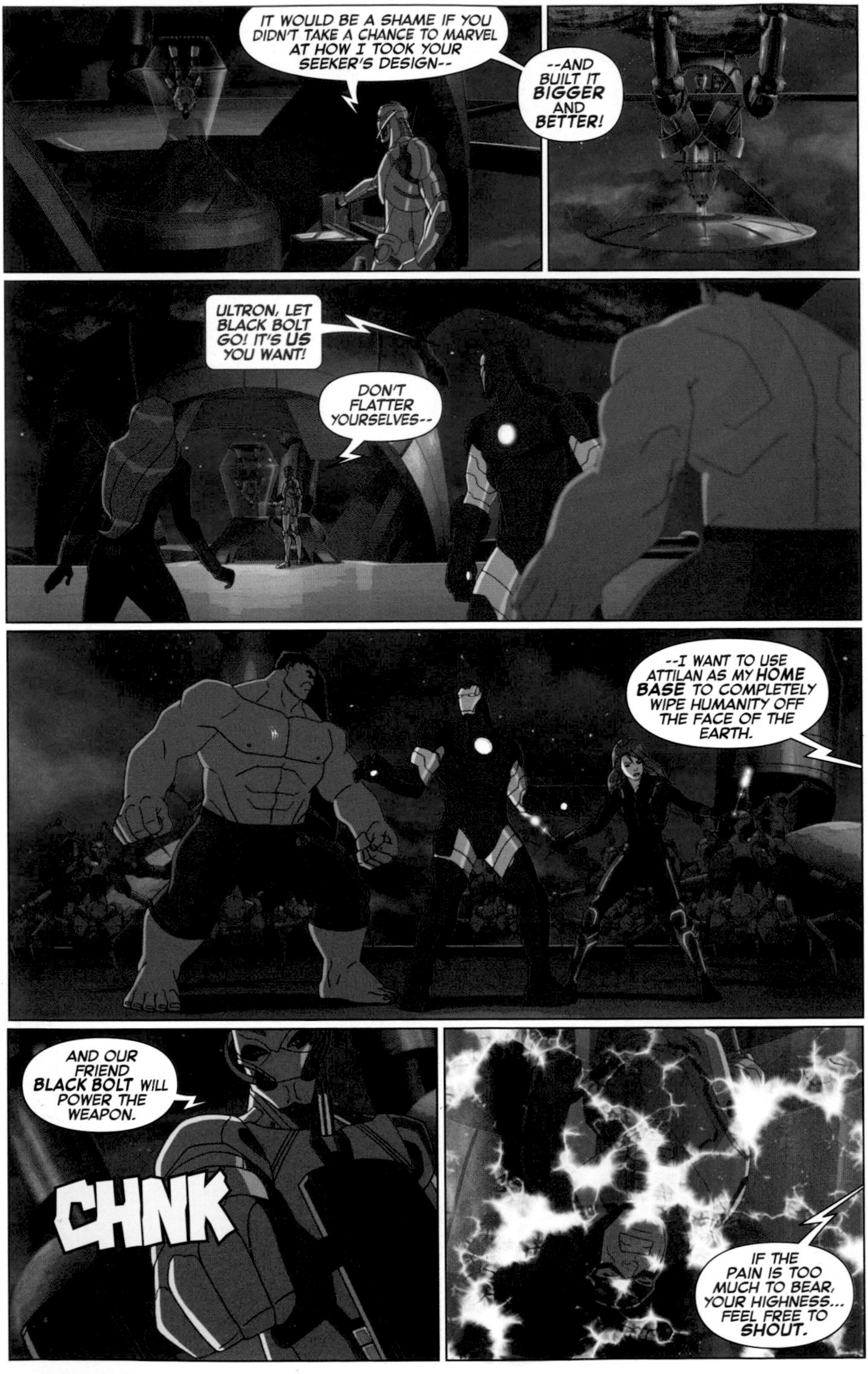
IT WOULD BE A SHAME IF YOU DIDN'T TAKE A CHANCE TO MARVEL AT HOW I TOOK YOUR SEEKER'S DESIGN--
--AND BUILT IT BIGGER AND BETTER!
ULTRON, LET BLACK BOLT GO! IT'S US YOU WANT!
DON'T FLATTER YOURSELVES--
--I WANT TO USE ATTILAN AS MY HOME BASE TO COMPLETELY WIPE HUMANITY OFF THE FACE OF THE EARTH.
AND OUR FRIEND BLACK BOLT WILL POWER THE WEAPON.
CHNK
IF THE PAIN IS TOO MUCH TO BEAR, YOUR HIGHNESS... FEEL FREE TO SHOUT.

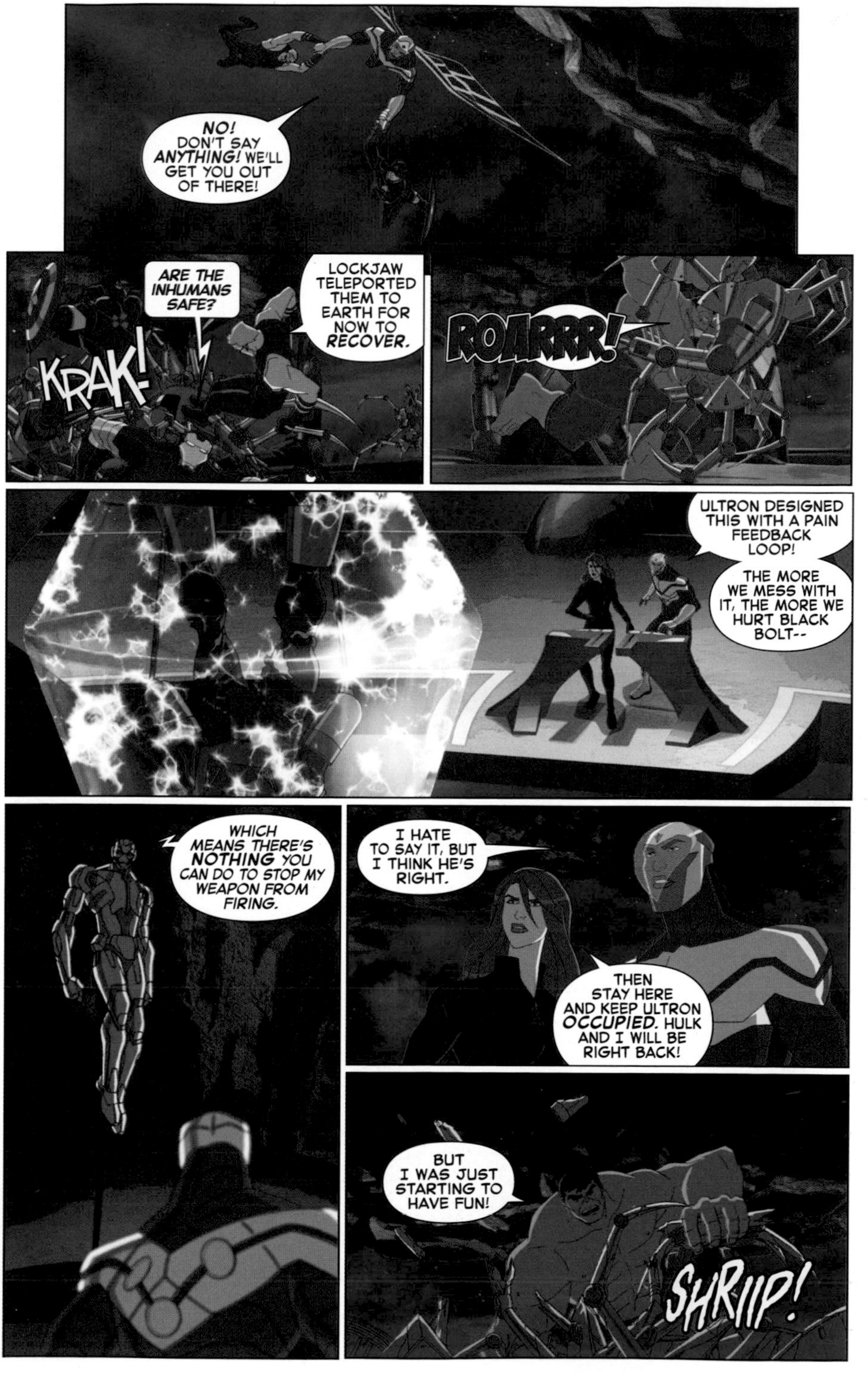

NO! DON'T SAY ANYTHING! WE'LL GET YOU OUT OF THERE!
ARE THE INHUMANS SAFE?
LOCKJAW TELEPORTED THEM TO EARTH FOR NOW TO RECOVER.
KRAK!
ROARRR!
ULTRON DESIGNED THIS WITH A PAIN FEEDBACK LOOP!
THE MORE WE MESS WITH IT, THE MORE WE HURT BLACK BOLT--
WHICH MEANS THERE'S NOTHING YOU CAN DO TO STOP MY WEAPON FROM FIRING.
I HATE TO SAY IT, BUT I THINK HE'S RIGHT.
THEN STAY HERE AND KEEP ULTRON OCCUPIED. HULK AND I WILL BE RIGHT BACK!
BUT I WAS JUST STARTING TO HAVE FUN!
SHRIIP!

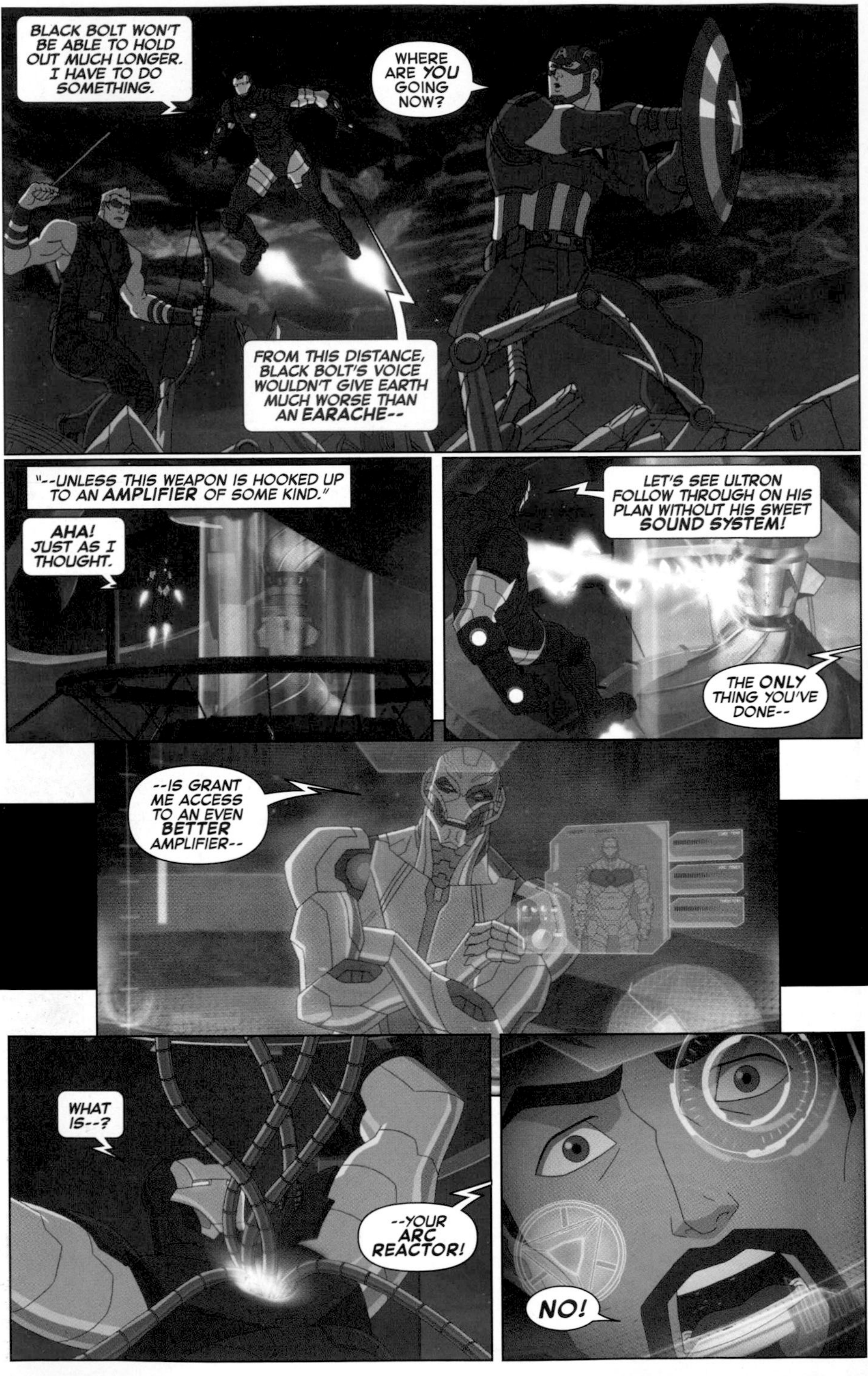
BLACK BOLT WON'T BE ABLE TO HOLD OUT MUCH LONGER. I HAVE TO DO SOMETHING.
WHERE ARE YOU GOING NOW?
FROM THIS DISTANCE, BLACK BOLT'S VOICE WOULDN'T GIVE EARTH MUCH WORSE THAN AN EARACHE--
"--UNLESS THIS WEAPON IS HOOKED UP TO AN AMPLIFIER OF SOME KIND."
AHA! JUST AS I THOUGHT.
LET'S SEE ULTRON FOLLOW THROUGH ON HIS PLAN WITHOUT HIS SWEET SOUND SYSTEM!
THE ONLY THING YOU'VE DONE--
--IS GRANT ME ACCESS TO AN EVEN BETTER AMPLIFIER--
WHAT IS--?
--YOUR ARC REACTOR!
NO!

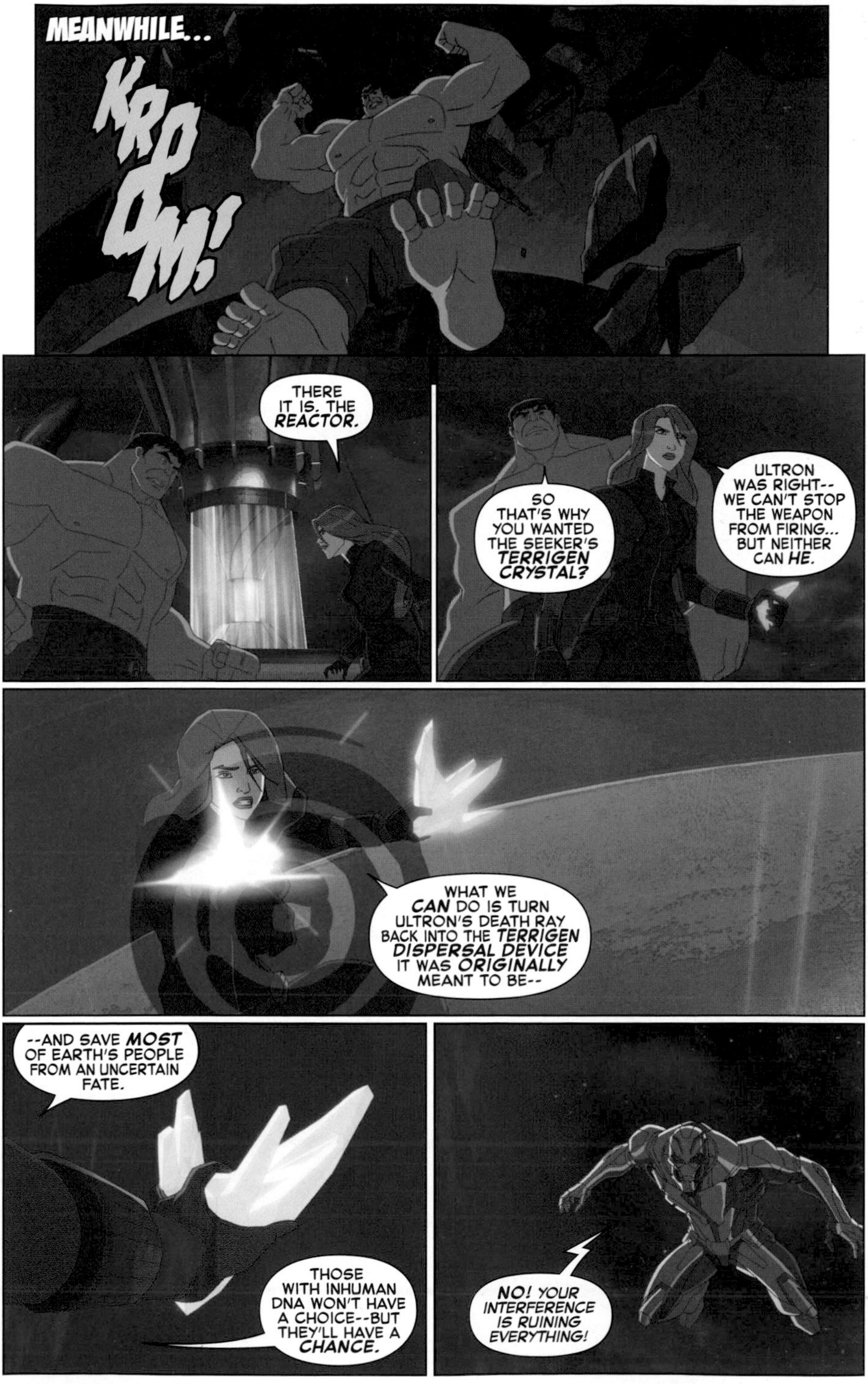
MEANWHILE...
KRROOM!
THERE IT IS. THE REACTOR.
SO THAT'S WHY YOU WANTED THE SEEKER'S TERRIGEN CRYSTAL?
ULTRON WAS RIGHT-- WE CAN'T STOP THE WEAPON FROM FIRING... BUT NEITHER CAN HE.
WHAT WE CAN DO IS TURN ULTRON'S DEATH RAY BACK INTO THE TERRIGEN DISPERSAL DEVICE IT WAS ORIGINALLY MEANT TO BE--
--AND SAVE MOST OF EARTH'S PEOPLE FROM AN UNCERTAIN FATE.
THOSE WITH INHUMAN DNA WON'T HAVE A CHOICE--BUT THEY'LL HAVE A CHANCE.
NO! YOUR INTERFERENCE IS RUINING EVERYTHING!

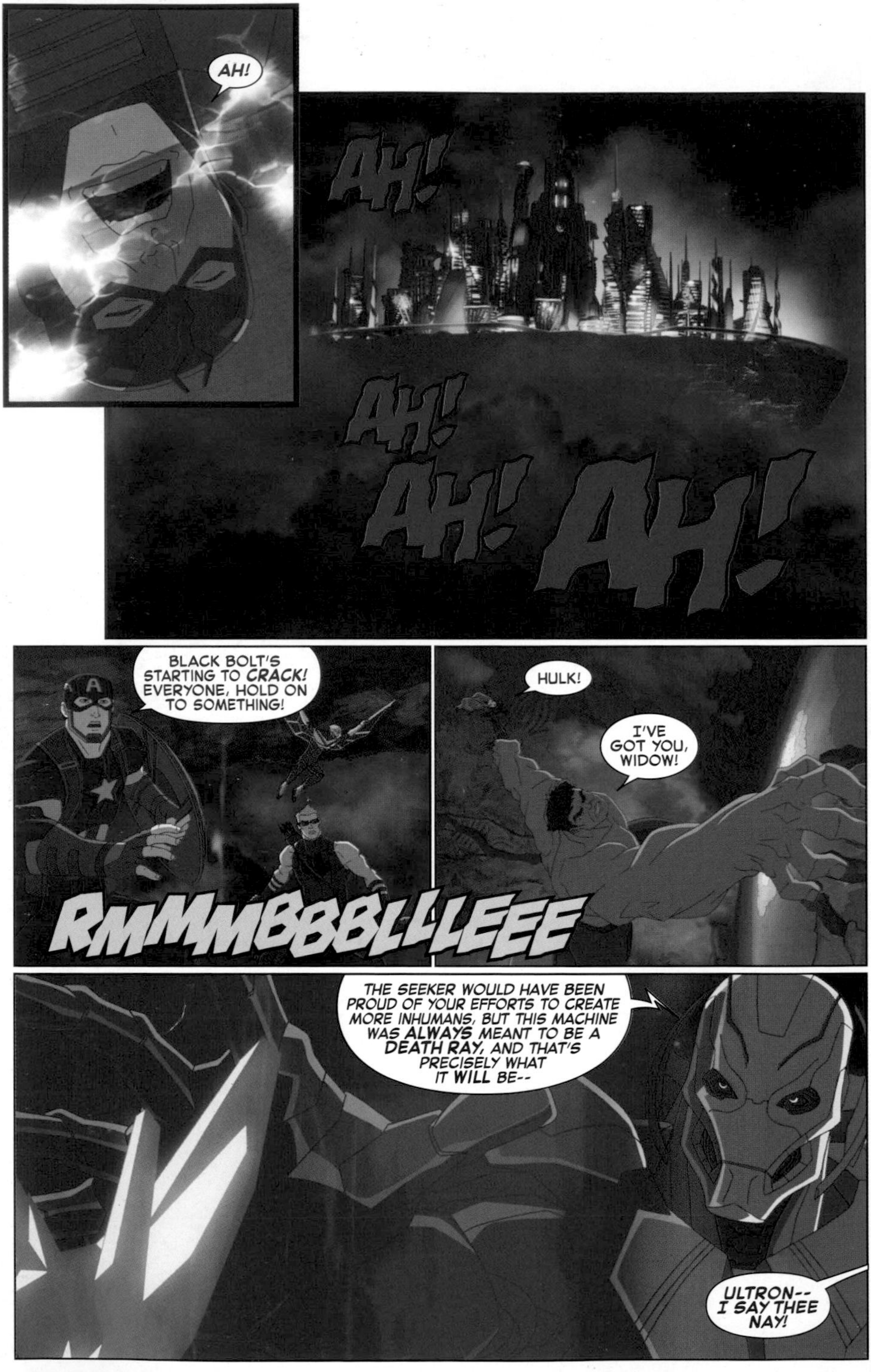
AH!
AH!
AH!
AH!
AH!
BLACK BOLT'S STARTING TO CRACK! EVERYONE, HOLD ON TO SOMETHING!
RMMMMBBBLLLLEEE
HULK!
I'VE GOT YOU, WIDOW!
THE SEEKER WOULD HAVE BEEN PROUD OF YOUR EFFORTS TO CREATE MORE INHUMANS, BUT THIS MACHINE WAS ALWAYS MEANT TO BE A DEATH RAY, AND THAT'S PRECISELY WHAT IT WILL BE--
ULTRON-- I SAY THEE NAY!

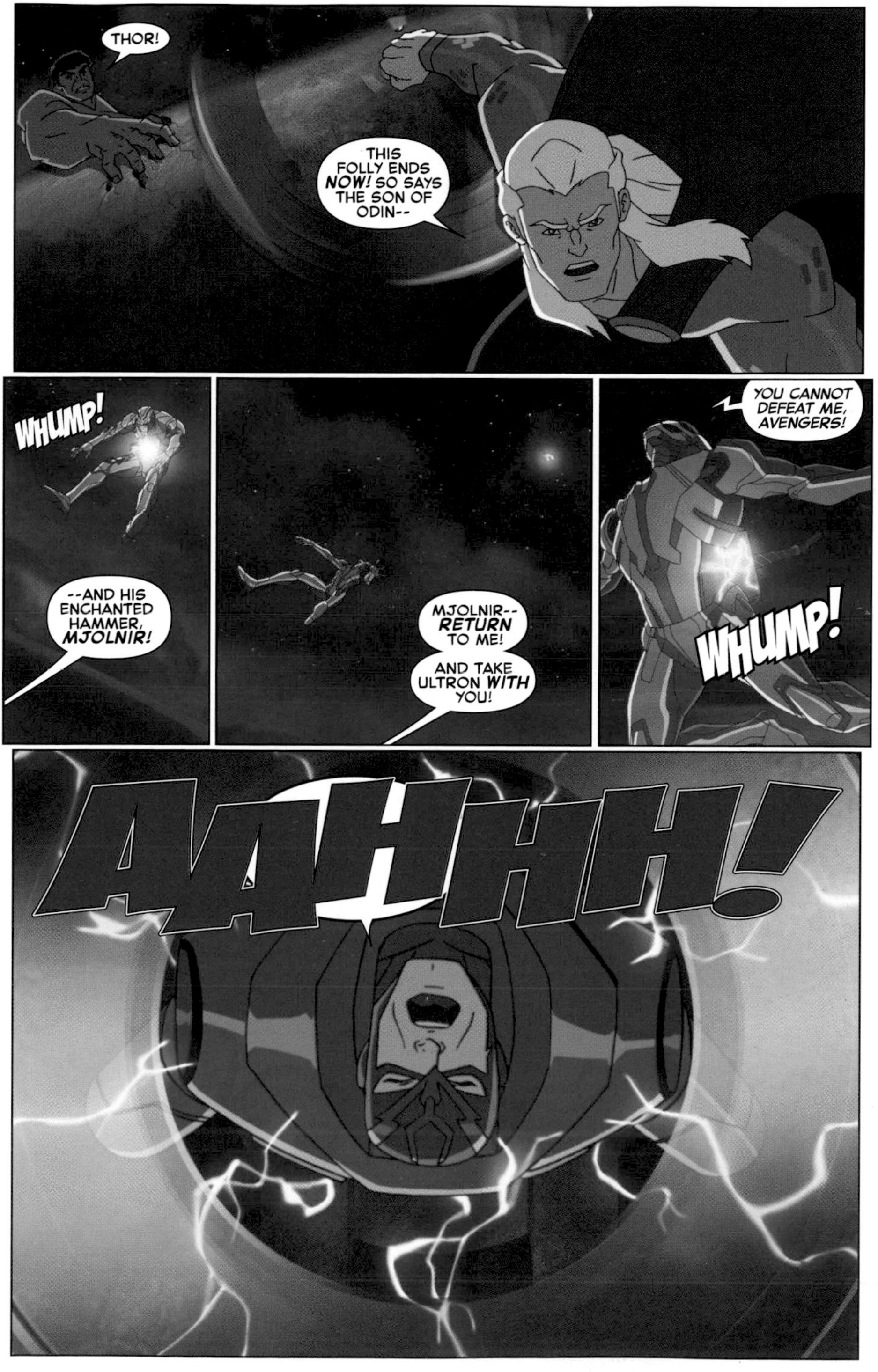
THOR!
THIS FOLLY ENDS NOW! SO SAYS THE SON OF ODIN--
WHUMP!
--AND HIS ENCHANTED HAMMER, MJOLNIR!
MJOLNIR--RETURN TO ME!
AND TAKE ULTRON WITH YOU!
YOU CANNOT DEFEAT ME, AVENGERS!
WHUMP!
AAHHH!

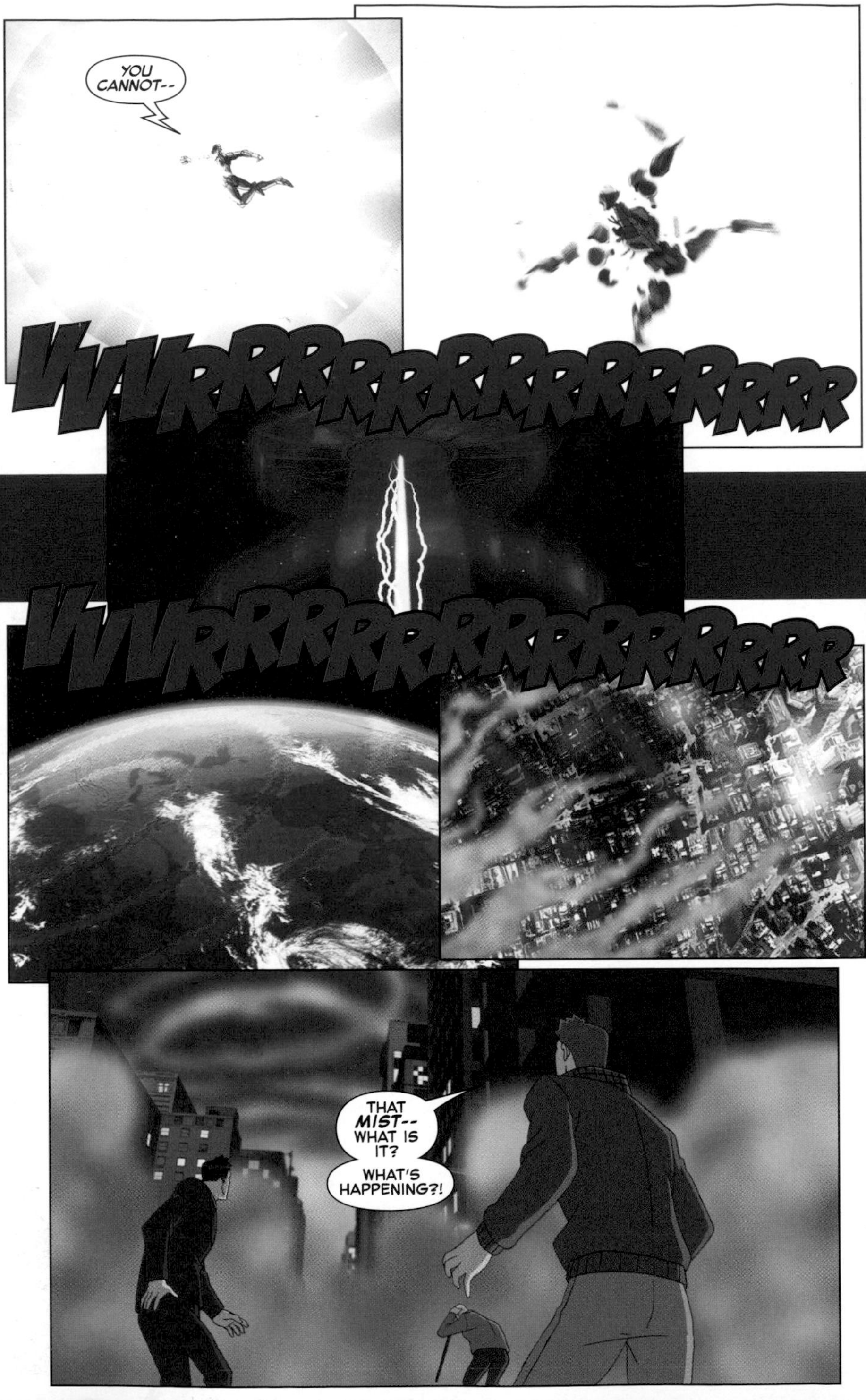
YOU CANNOT--
VVVRRRRRRRRRRRRRRRRR
VVVRRRRRRRRRRRRRRRRR
THAT MIST-- WHAT IS IT?
WHAT'S HAPPENING?!

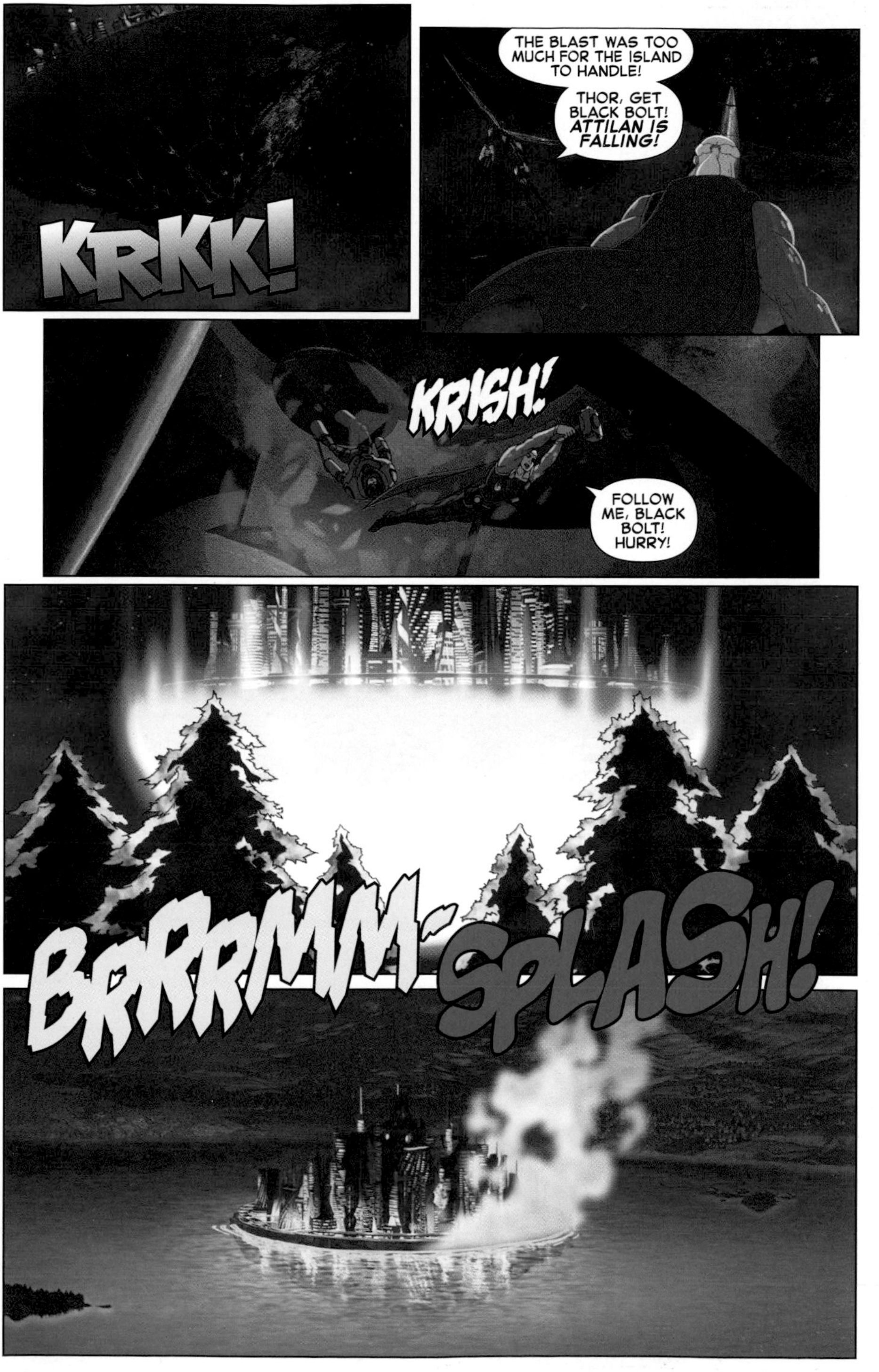
KRKK!
THE BLAST WAS TOO MUCH FOR THE ISLAND TO HANDLE!
THOR, GET BLACK BOLT! ATTILAN IS FALLING!
KRISH!
FOLLOW ME, BLACK BOLT! HURRY!
BRRRMM-SPLASH!

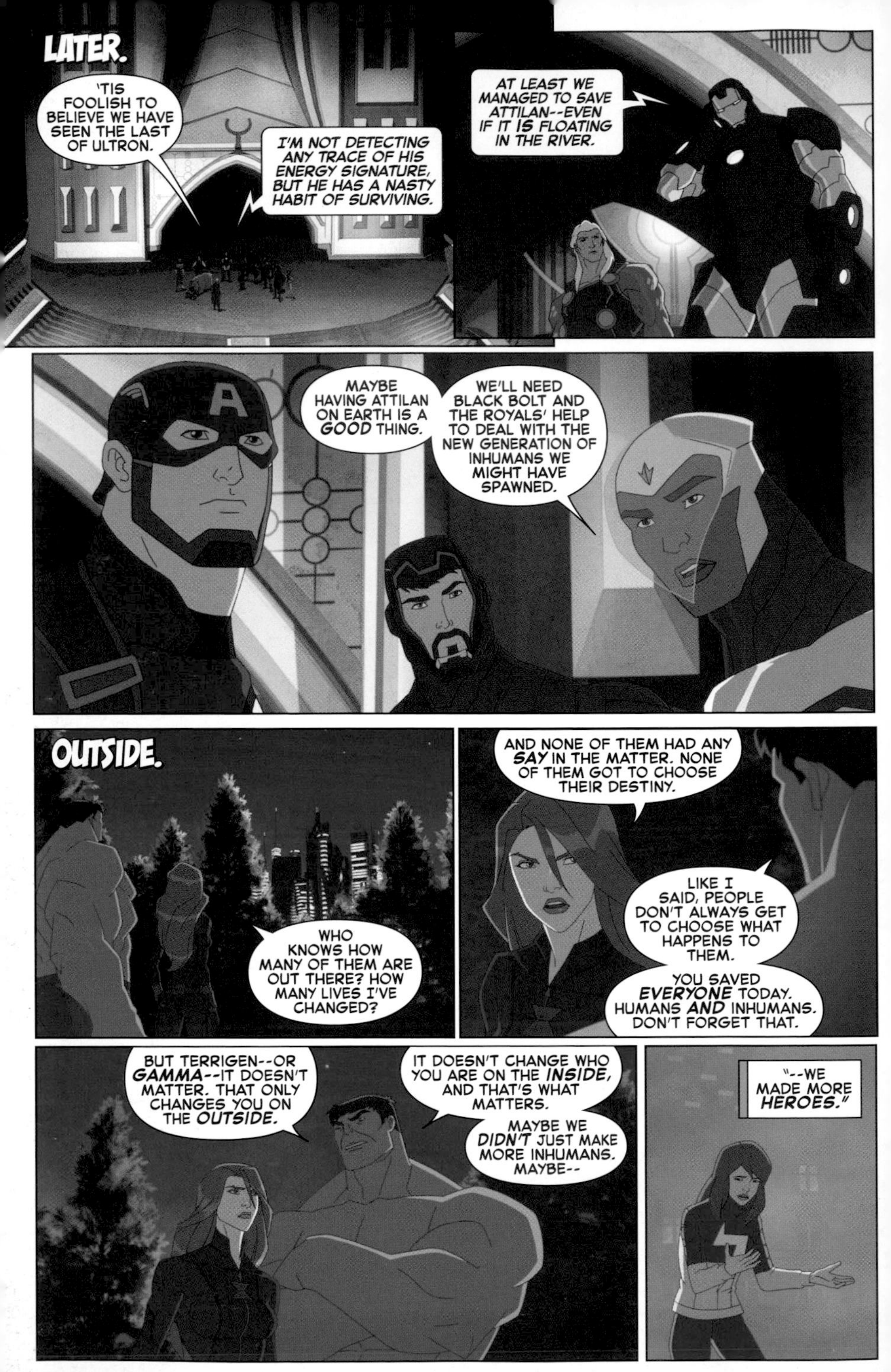

LATER.
'TIS FOOLISH TO BELIEVE WE HAVE SEEN THE LAST OF ULTRON.
I'M NOT DETECTING ANY TRACE OF HIS ENERGY SIGNATURE, BUT HE HAS A NASTY HABIT OF SURVIVING.
AT LEAST WE MANAGED TO SAVE ATTILAN--EVEN IF IT IS FLOATING IN THE RIVER.
MAYBE HAVING ATTILAN ON EARTH IS A GOOD THING.
WE'LL NEED BLACK BOLT AND THE ROYALS' HELP TO DEAL WITH THE NEW GENERATION OF INHUMANS WE MIGHT HAVE SPAWNED.
OUTSIDE.
WHO KNOWS HOW MANY OF THEM ARE OUT THERE? HOW MANY LIVES I'VE CHANGED?
AND NONE OF THEM HAD ANY SAY IN THE MATTER. NONE OF THEM GOT TO CHOOSE THEIR DESTINY.
LIKE I SAID, PEOPLE DON'T ALWAYS GET TO CHOOSE WHAT HAPPENS TO THEM.
YOU SAVED EVERYONE TODAY. HUMANS AND INHUMANS. DON'T FORGET THAT.
BUT TERRIGEN--OR GAMMA--IT DOESN'T MATTER. THAT ONLY CHANGES YOU ON THE OUTSIDE.
IT DOESN'T CHANGE WHO YOU ARE ON THE INSIDE, AND THAT'S WHAT MATTERS.
MAYBE WE DIDN'T JUST MAKE MORE INHUMANS. MAYBE--
"--WE MADE MORE HEROES."

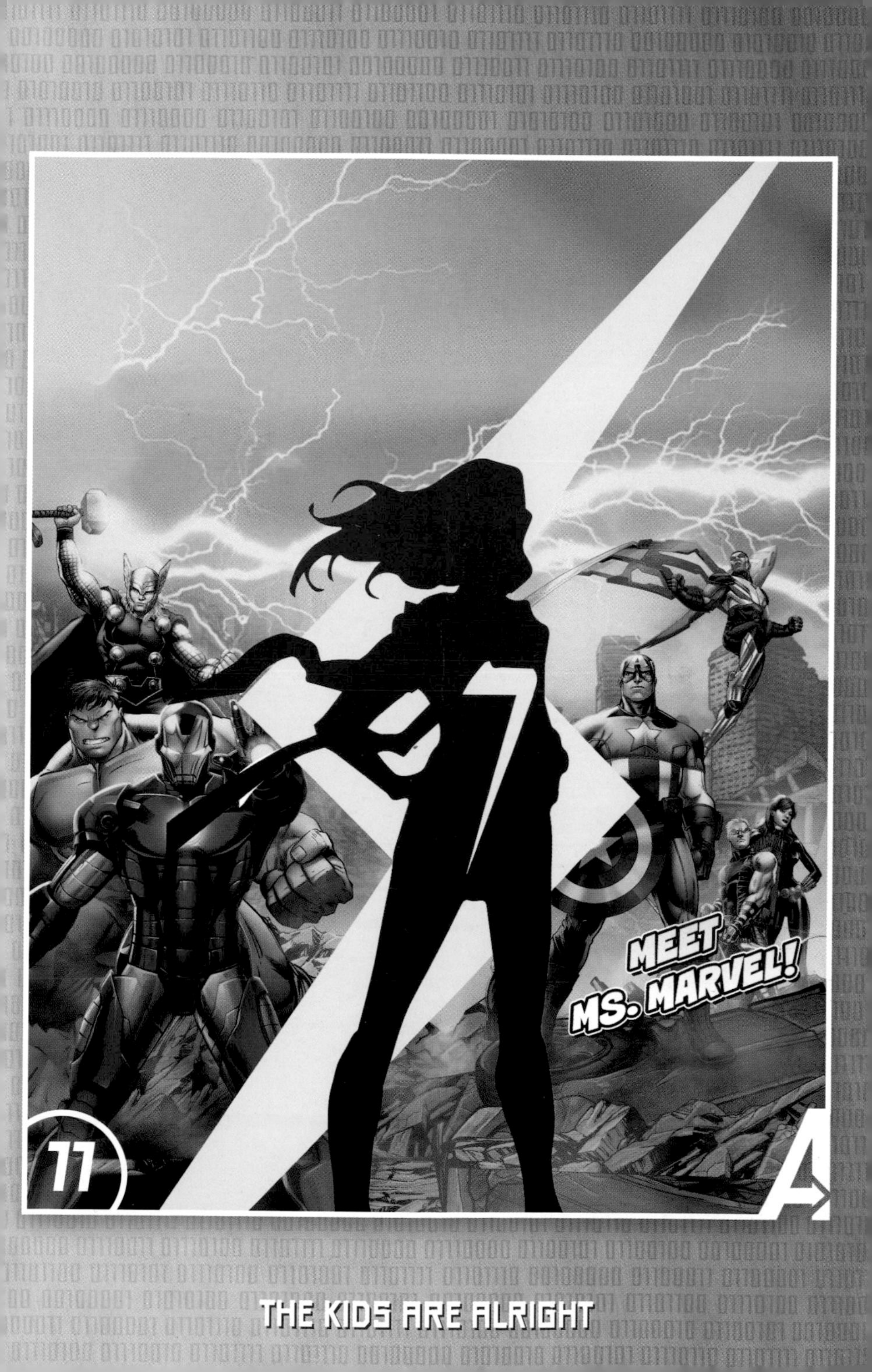
MEET
MS. MARVEL!
77

THE KIDS ARE ALRIGHT

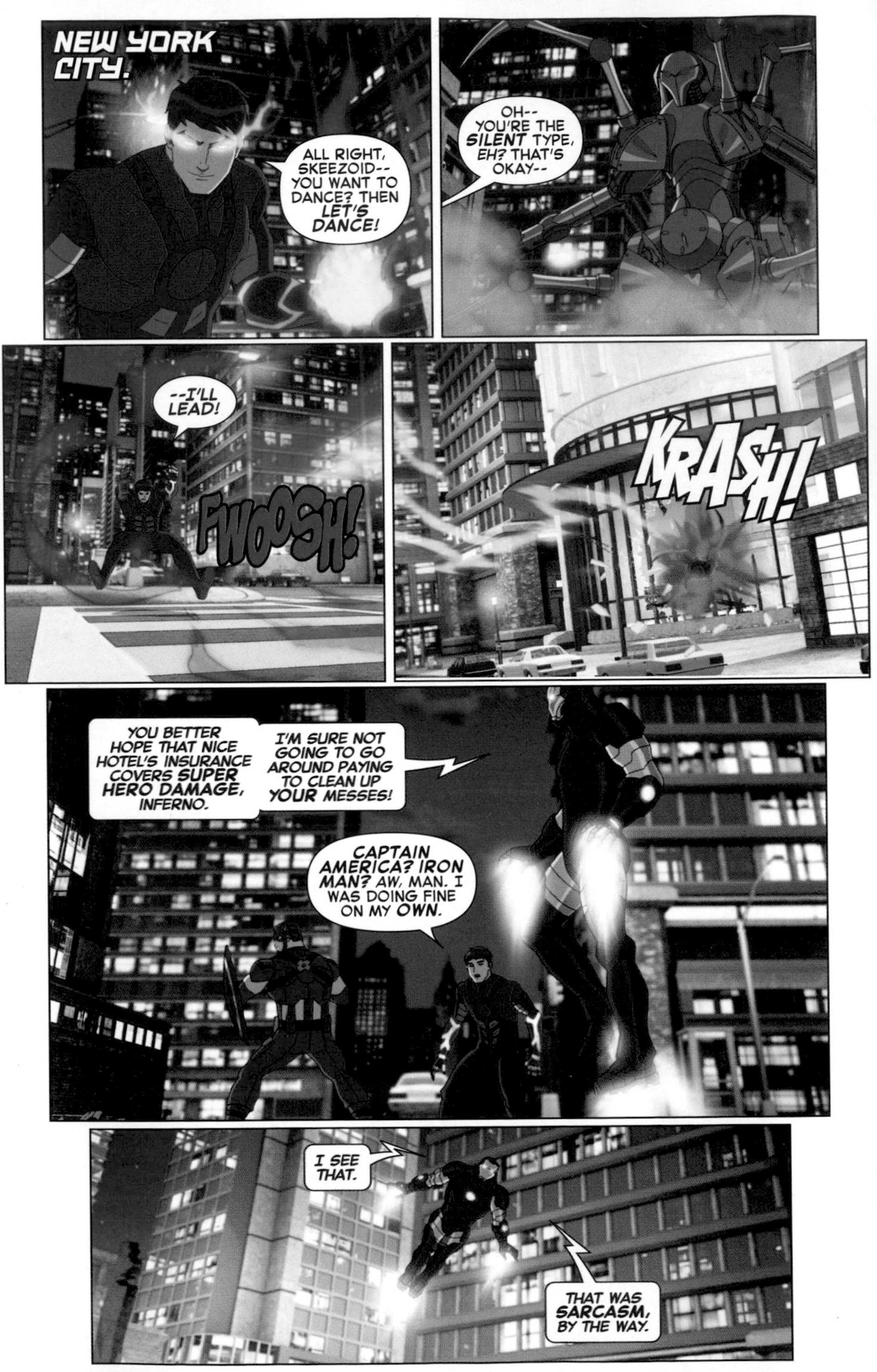
NEW YORK CITY.
ALL RIGHT, SKEEZOID-- YOU WANT TO DANCE? THEN LET'S DANCE!
OH-- YOU'RE THE SILENT TYPE, EH? THAT'S OKAY--
--I'LL LEAD!
FWOOSH!
KRASH!
YOU BETTER HOPE THAT NICE HOTEL'S INSURANCE COVERS SUPER HERO DAMAGE, INFERNO.
I'M SURE NOT GOING TO GO AROUND PAYING TO CLEAN UP YOUR MESSES!
CAPTAIN AMERICA? IRON MAN? AW, MAN. I WAS DOING FINE ON MY OWN.
I SEE THAT.
THAT WAS SARCASM, BY THE WAY.

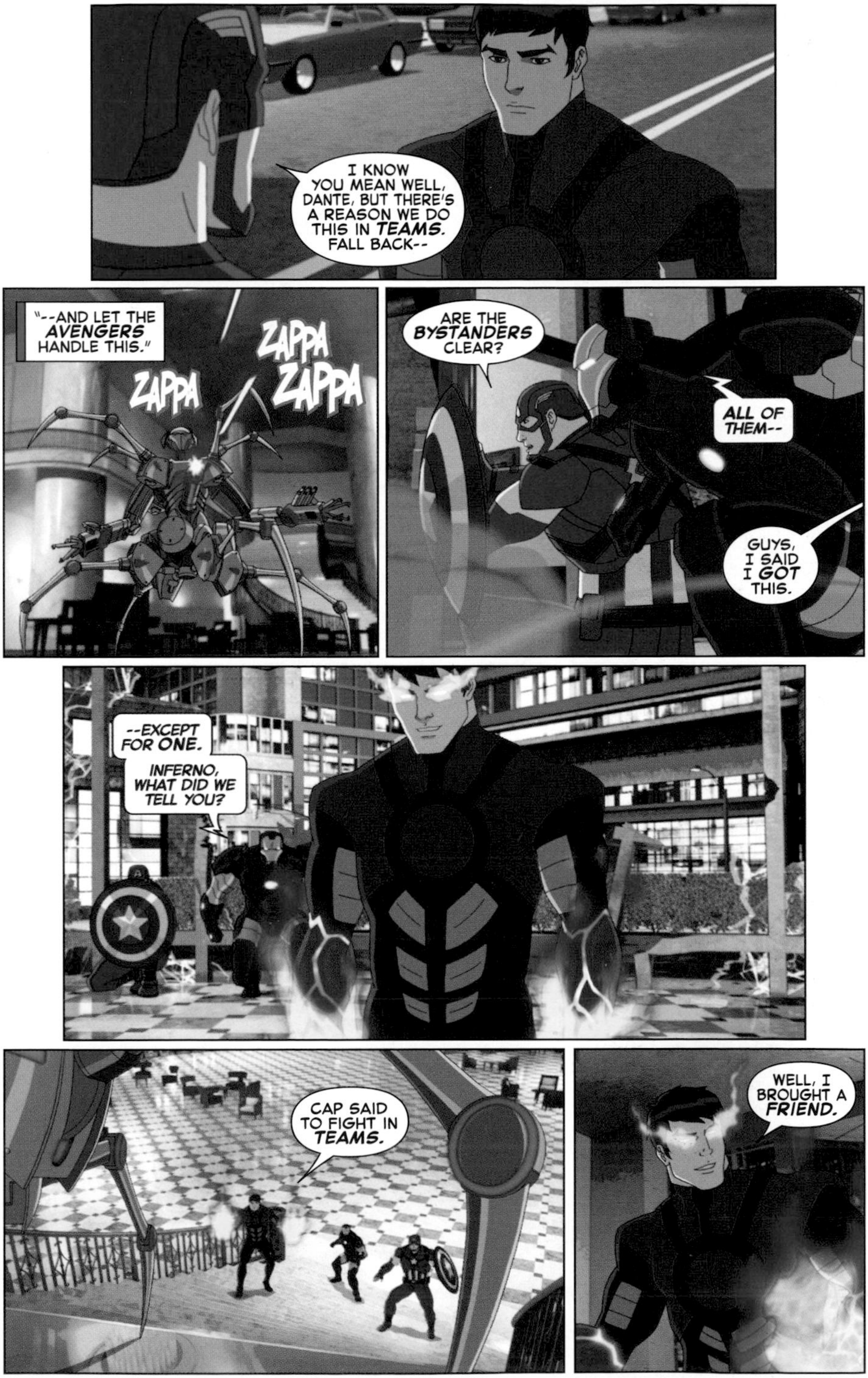
I KNOW YOU MEAN WELL, DANTE, BUT THERE'S A REASON WE DO THIS IN TEAMS. FALL BACK--
"--AND LET THE AVENGERS HANDLE THIS."
ZAPPA
ZAPPA ZAPPA
ARE THE BYSTANDERS CLEAR?
ALL OF THEM--
GUYS, I SAID I GOT THIS.
--EXCEPT FOR ONE.
INFERNO, WHAT DID WE TELL YOU?
CAP SAID TO FIGHT IN TEAMS.
WELL, I BROUGHT A FRIEND.

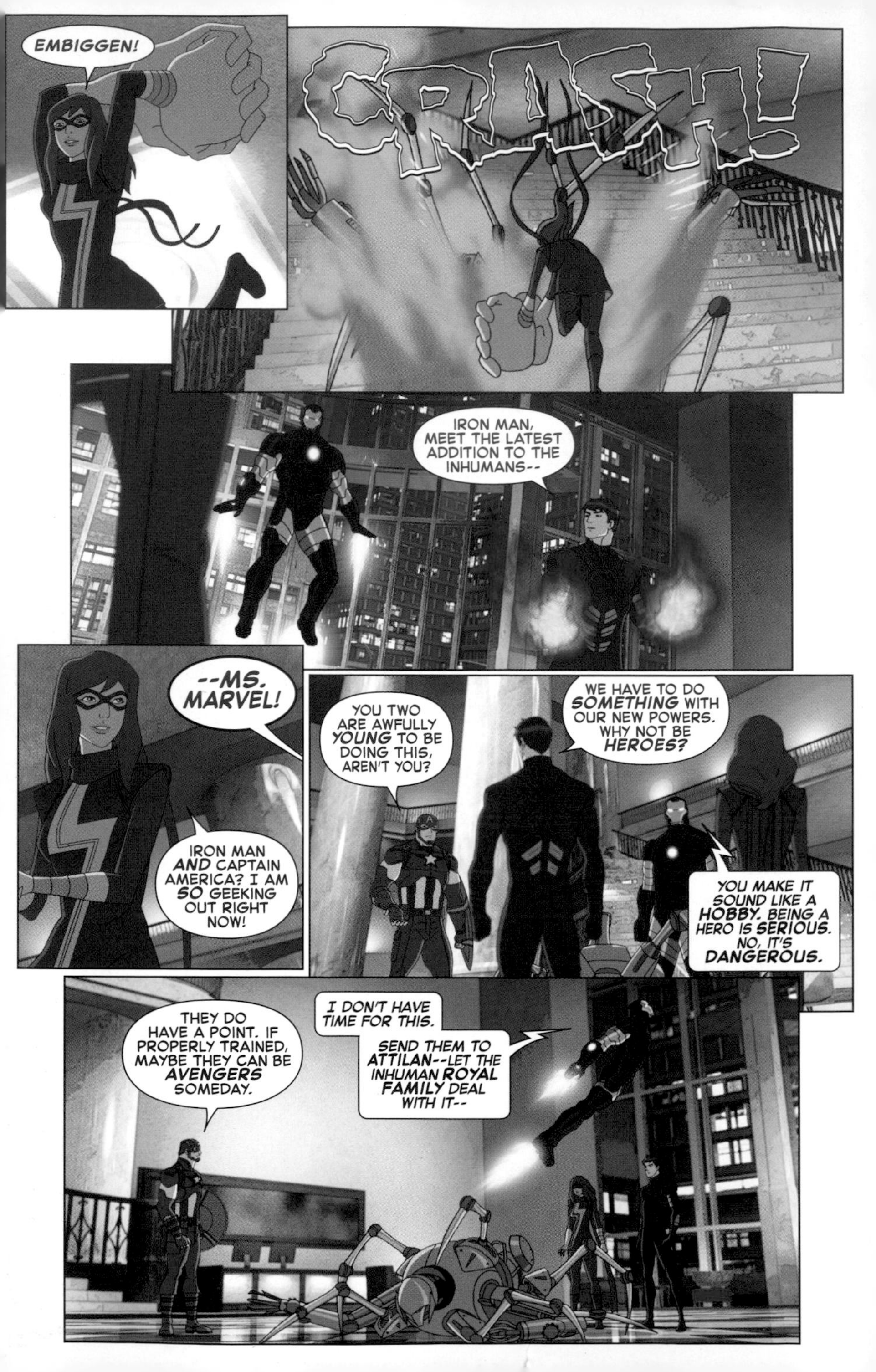
EMBIGGEN!
CRASH!
IRON MAN, MEET THE LATEST ADDITION TO THE INHUMANS--
--MS. MARVEL!
IRON MAN AND CAPTAIN AMERICA? I AM SO GEEKING OUT RIGHT NOW!
YOU TWO ARE AWFULLY YOUNG TO BE DOING THIS, AREN'T YOU?
WE HAVE TO DO SOMETHING WITH OUR NEW POWERS. WHY NOT BE HEROES?
YOU MAKE IT SOUND LIKE A HOBBY. BEING A HERO IS SERIOUS. NO, IT'S DANGEROUS.
THEY DO HAVE A POINT. IF PROPERLY TRAINED, MAYBE THEY CAN BE AVENGERS SOMEDAY.
I DON'T HAVE TIME FOR THIS.
SEND THEM TO ATTILAN--LET THE INHUMAN ROYAL FAMILY DEAL WITH IT--

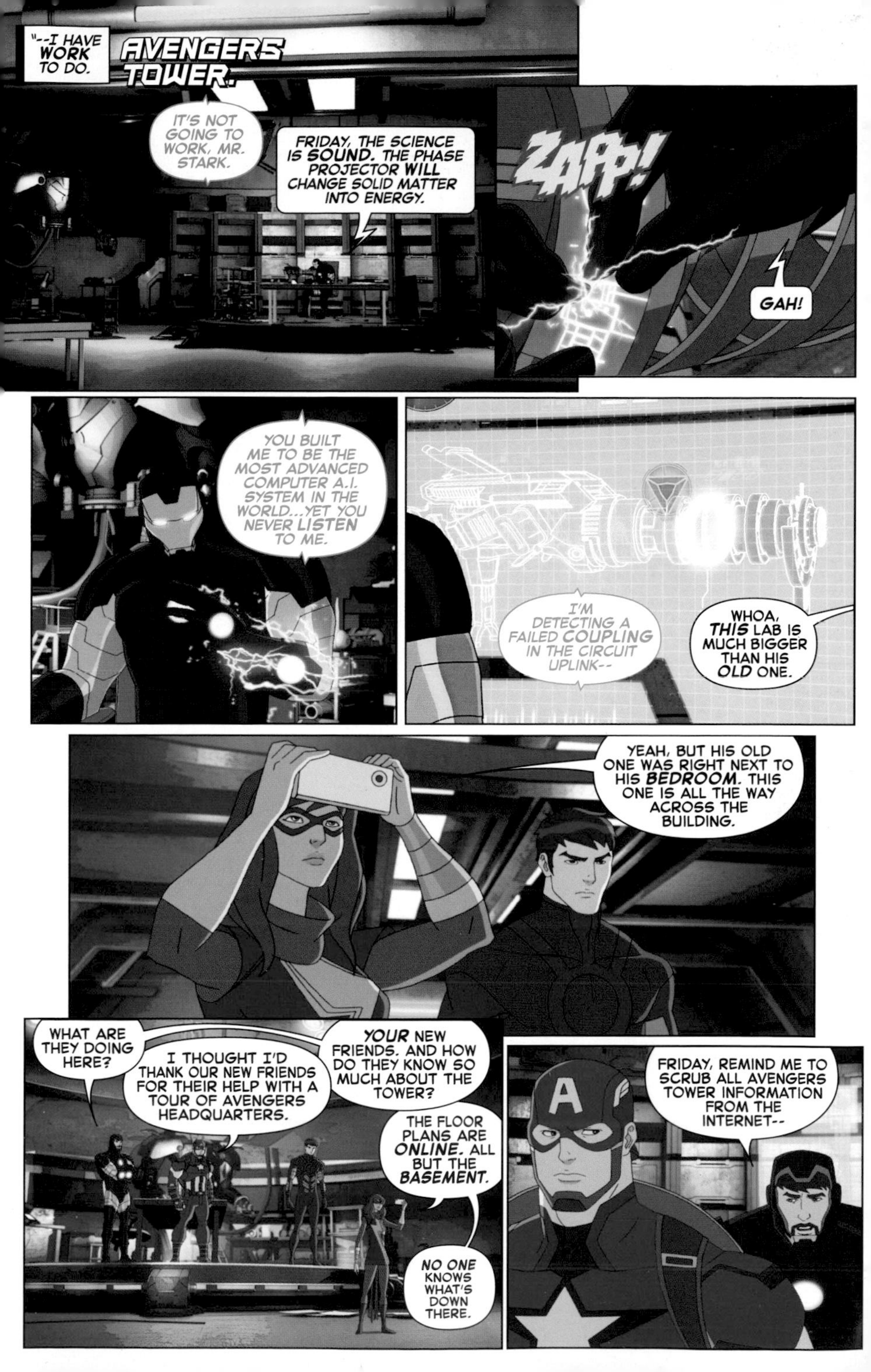
"--I HAVE WORK TO DO.
AVENGERS TOWER.
IT'S NOT GOING TO WORK, MR. STARK.
FRIDAY, THE SCIENCE IS SOUND. THE PHASE PROJECTOR WILL CHANGE SOLID MATTER INTO ENERGY.
ZAPP!
GAH!
YOU BUILT ME TO BE THE MOST ADVANCED COMPUTER A.I. SYSTEM IN THE WORLD...YET YOU NEVER LISTEN TO ME.
I'M DETECTING A FAILED COUPLING IN THE CIRCUIT UPLINK--
WHOA, THIS LAB IS MUCH BIGGER THAN HIS OLD ONE.
YEAH, BUT HIS OLD ONE WAS RIGHT NEXT TO HIS BEDROOM. THIS ONE IS ALL THE WAY ACROSS THE BUILDING.
WHAT ARE THEY DOING HERE?
I THOUGHT I'D THANK OUR NEW FRIENDS FOR THEIR HELP WITH A TOUR OF AVENGERS HEADQUARTERS.
YOUR NEW FRIENDS. AND HOW DO THEY KNOW SO MUCH ABOUT THE TOWER?
THE FLOOR PLANS ARE ONLINE. ALL BUT THE BASEMENT.
NO ONE KNOWS WHAT'S DOWN THERE.
FRIDAY, REMIND ME TO SCRUB ALL AVENGERS TOWER INFORMATION FROM THE INTERNET--

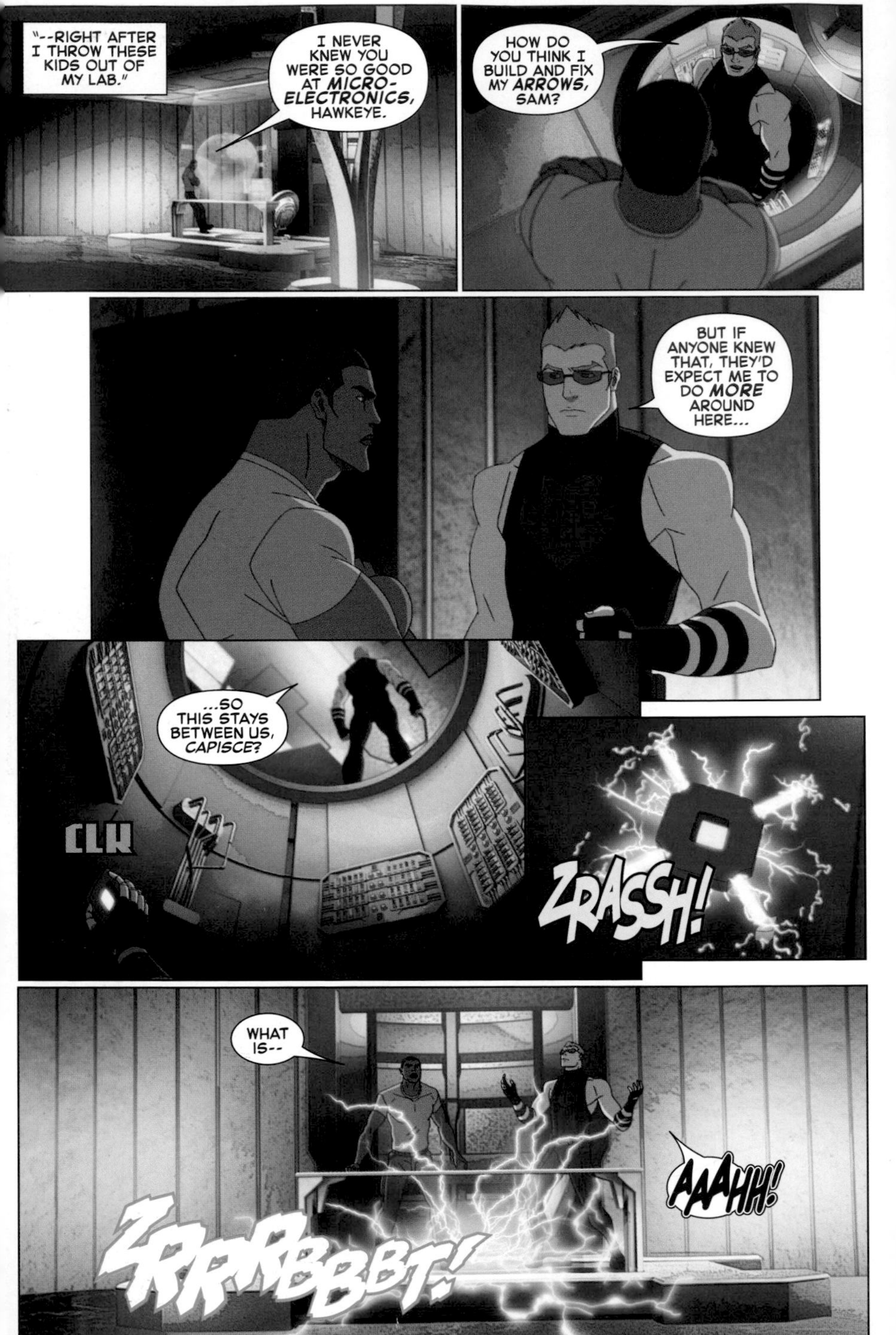
"--RIGHT AFTER I THROW THESE KIDS OUT OF MY LAB."
I NEVER KNEW YOU WERE SO GOOD AT *MICRO-ELECTRONICS,* HAWKEYE.
HOW DO YOU THINK I BUILD AND FIX MY *ARROWS,* SAM?
BUT IF ANYONE KNEW THAT, THEY'D EXPECT ME TO DO *MORE* AROUND HERE...
...SO THIS STAYS BETWEEN US, *CAPISCE?*
CLK
ZRASSH!
WHAT IS--
AAAHH!
ZRRRBBBT!

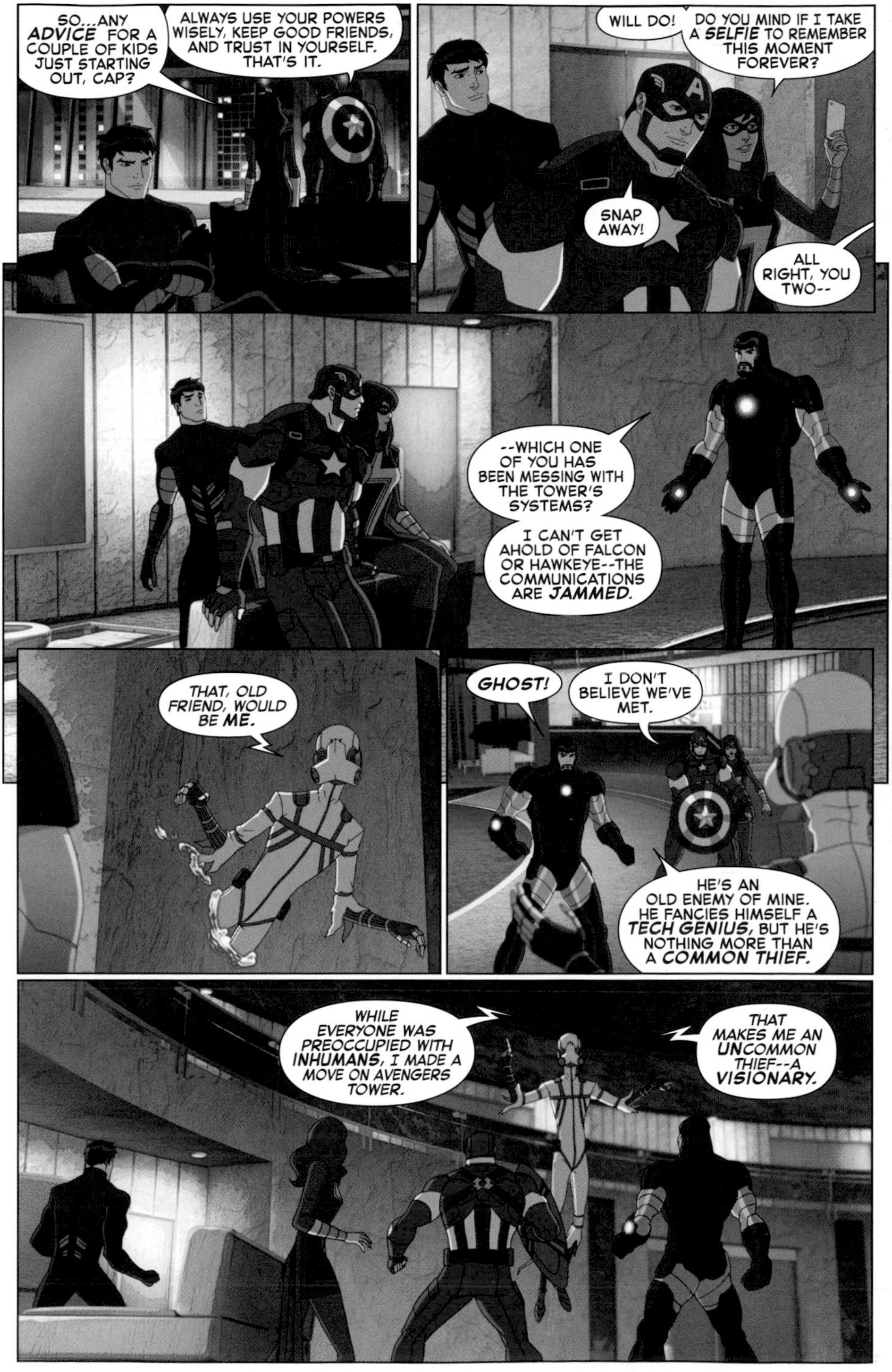
SO...ANY ADVICE FOR A COUPLE OF KIDS JUST STARTING OUT, CAP?
ALWAYS USE YOUR POWERS WISELY, KEEP GOOD FRIENDS, AND TRUST IN YOURSELF. THAT'S IT.
WILL DO!
DO YOU MIND IF I TAKE A SELFIE TO REMEMBER THIS MOMENT FOREVER?
SNAP AWAY!
ALL RIGHT, YOU TWO--
--WHICH ONE OF YOU HAS BEEN MESSING WITH THE TOWER'S SYSTEMS?
I CAN'T GET AHOLD OF FALCON OR HAWKEYE--THE COMMUNICATIONS ARE JAMMED.
THAT, OLD FRIEND, WOULD BE ME.
GHOST!
I DON'T BELIEVE WE'VE MET.
HE'S AN OLD ENEMY OF MINE. HE FANCIES HIMSELF A TECH GENIUS, BUT HE'S NOTHING MORE THAN A COMMON THIEF.
WHILE EVERYONE WAS PREOCCUPIED WITH INHUMANS, I MADE A MOVE ON AVENGERS TOWER.
THAT MAKES ME AN UNCOMMON THIEF--A VISIONARY.

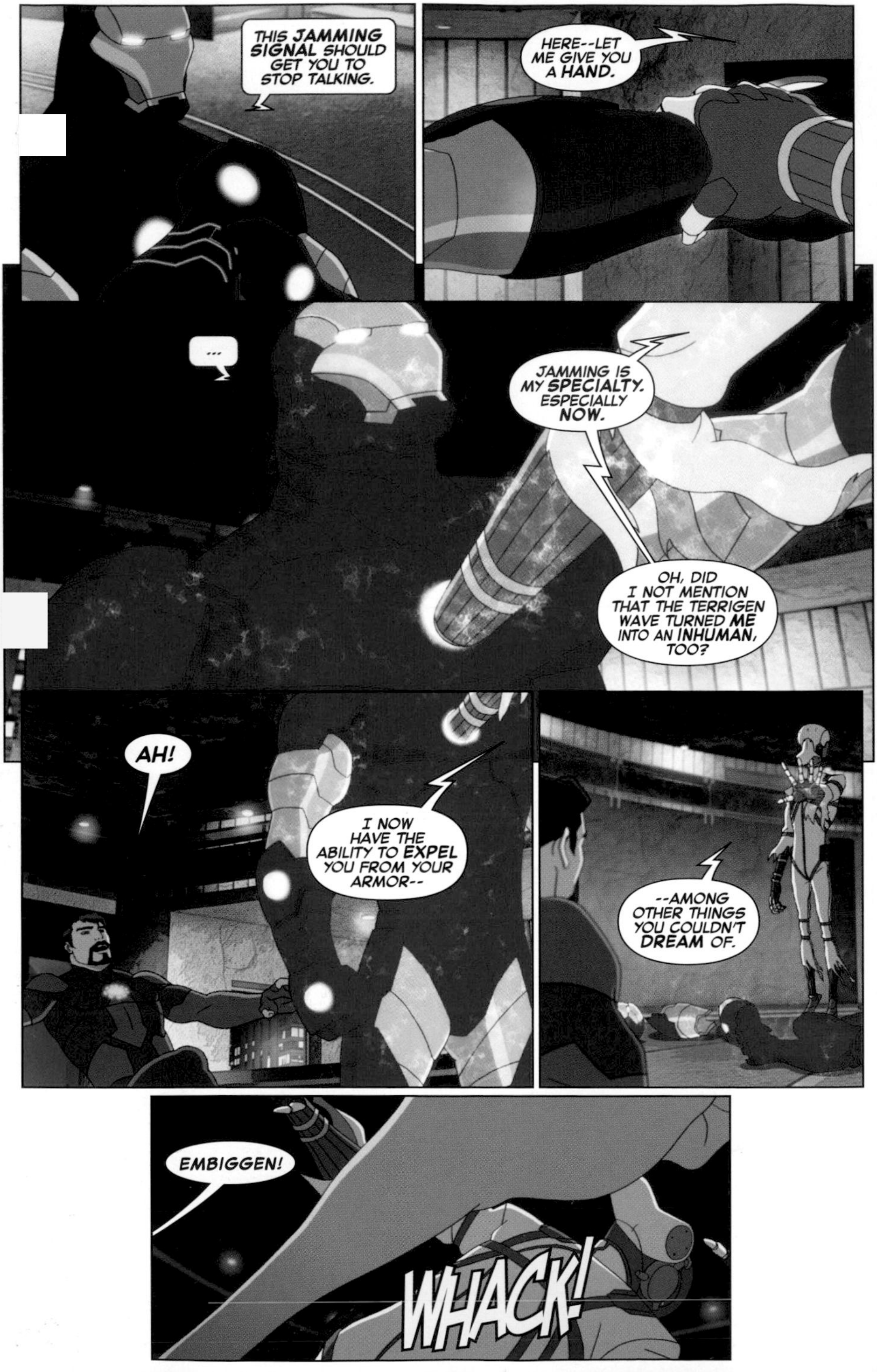
THIS JAMMING SIGNAL SHOULD GET YOU TO STOP TALKING.
HERE--LET ME GIVE YOU A HAND.
...
JAMMING IS MY SPECIALTY. ESPECIALLY NOW.
OH, DID I NOT MENTION THAT THE TERRIGEN WAVE TURNED ME INTO AN INHUMAN, TOO?
AH!
I NOW HAVE THE ABILITY TO EXPEL YOU FROM YOUR ARMOR--
--AMONG OTHER THINGS YOU COULDN'T DREAM OF.
EMBIGGEN!
WHACK!

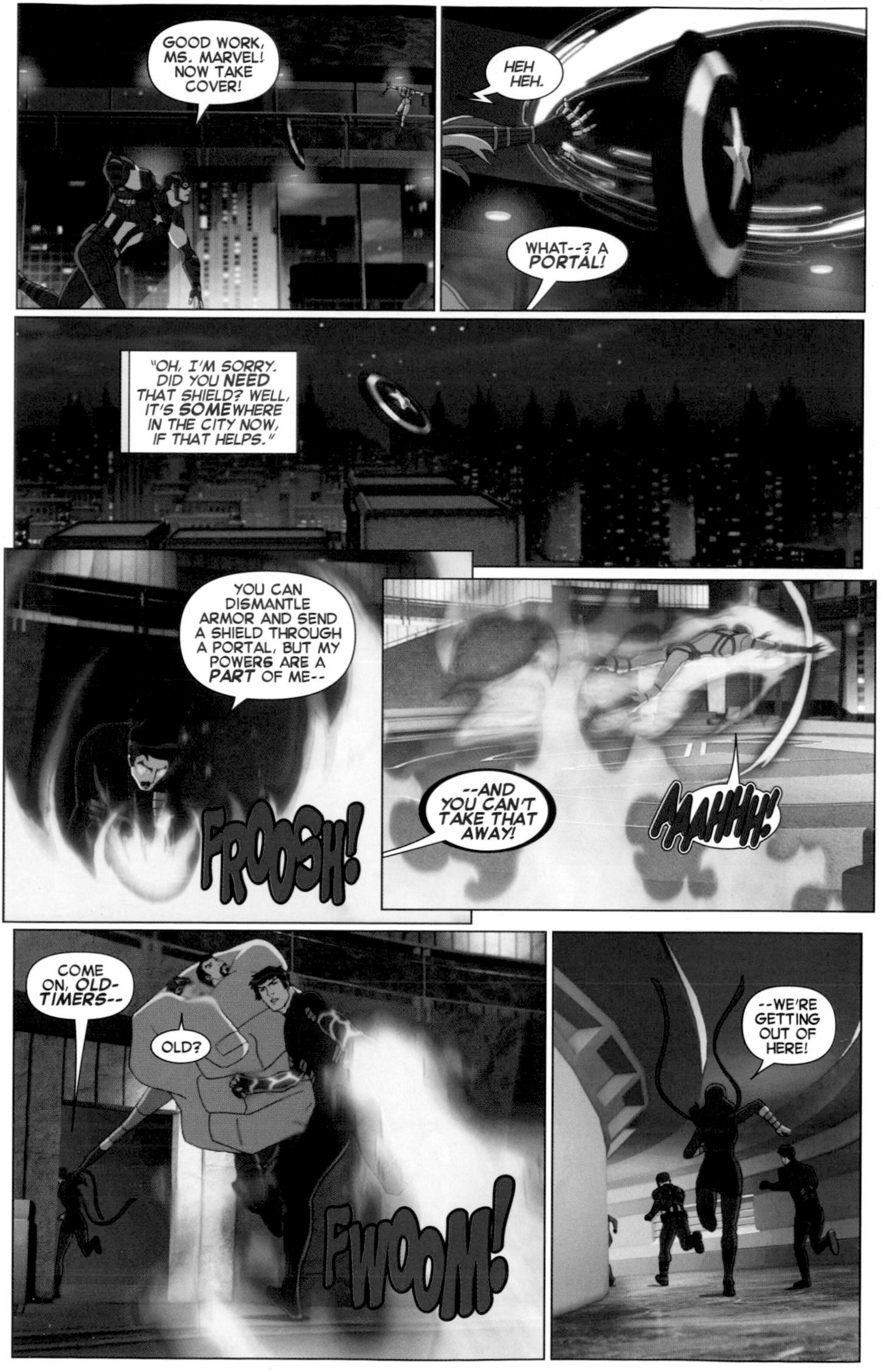
GOOD WORK, MS. MARVEL! NOW TAKE COVER!
HEH HEH.
WHAT--? A PORTAL!
"OH, I'M SORRY. DID YOU NEED THAT SHIELD? WELL, IT'S SOMEWHERE IN THE CITY NOW, IF THAT HELPS."
YOU CAN DISMANTLE ARMOR AND SEND A SHIELD THROUGH A PORTAL, BUT MY POWERS ARE A PART OF ME--
FROOSH!
--AND YOU CAN'T TAKE THAT AWAY!
AAAHHH!
COME ON, OLD-TIMERS--
OLD?
FWOOM!
--WE'RE GETTING OUT OF HERE!

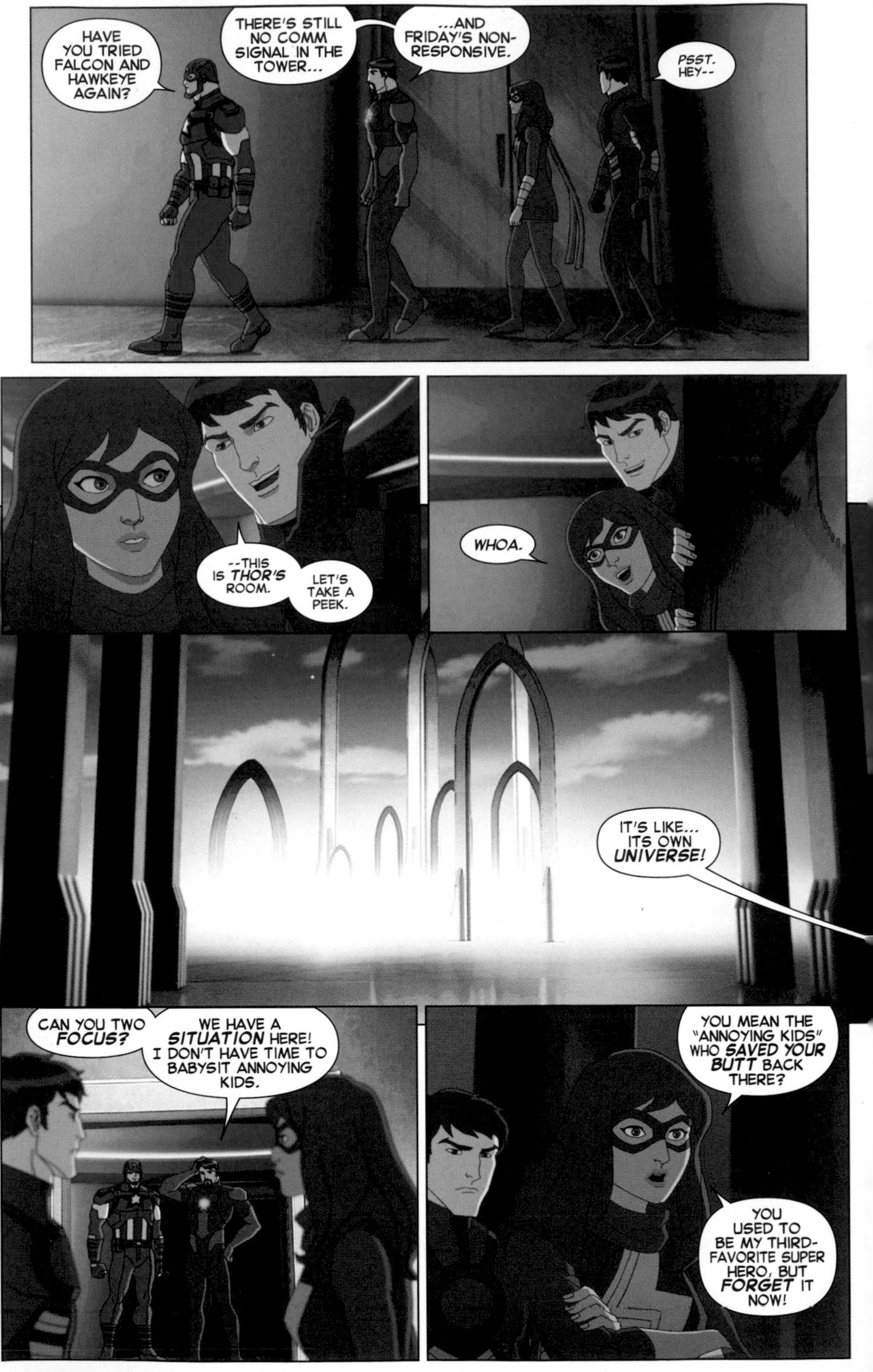

HAVE YOU TRIED FALCON AND HAWKEYE AGAIN?
THERE'S STILL NO COMM SIGNAL IN THE TOWER...
...AND FRIDAY'S NON-RESPONSIVE.
PSST. HEY--
--THIS IS THOR'S ROOM.
LET'S TAKE A PEEK.
WHOA.
IT'S LIKE... ITS OWN UNIVERSE!
CAN YOU TWO FOCUS?
WE HAVE A SITUATION HERE! I DON'T HAVE TIME TO BABYSIT ANNOYING KIDS.
YOU MEAN THE "ANNOYING KIDS" WHO SAVED YOUR BUTT BACK THERE?
YOU USED TO BE MY THIRD-FAVORITE SUPER HERO, BUT FORGET IT NOW!

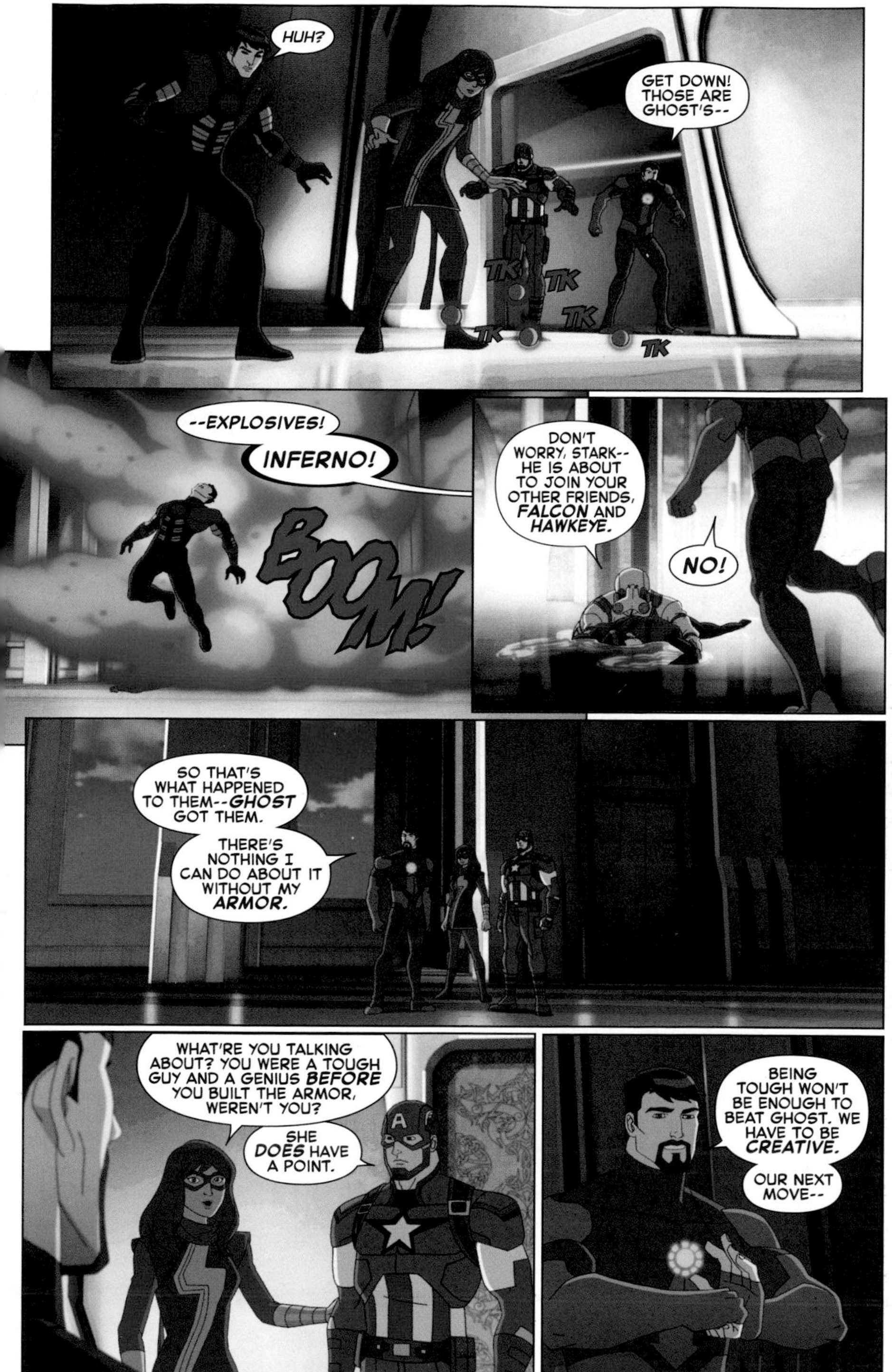
HUH?
GET DOWN! THOSE ARE GHOST'S--
TK
TK
TK
TK
TK
--EXPLOSIVES!
INFERNO!
BOOM!
DON'T WORRY, STARK-- HE IS ABOUT TO JOIN YOUR OTHER FRIENDS, FALCON AND HAWKEYE.
NO!
SO THAT'S WHAT HAPPENED TO THEM--GHOST GOT THEM.
THERE'S NOTHING I CAN DO ABOUT IT WITHOUT MY ARMOR.
WHAT'RE YOU TALKING ABOUT? YOU WERE A TOUGH GUY AND A GENIUS BEFORE YOU BUILT THE ARMOR, WEREN'T YOU?
SHE DOES HAVE A POINT.
BEING TOUGH WON'T BE ENOUGH TO BEAT GHOST. WE HAVE TO BE CREATIVE.
OUR NEXT MOVE--

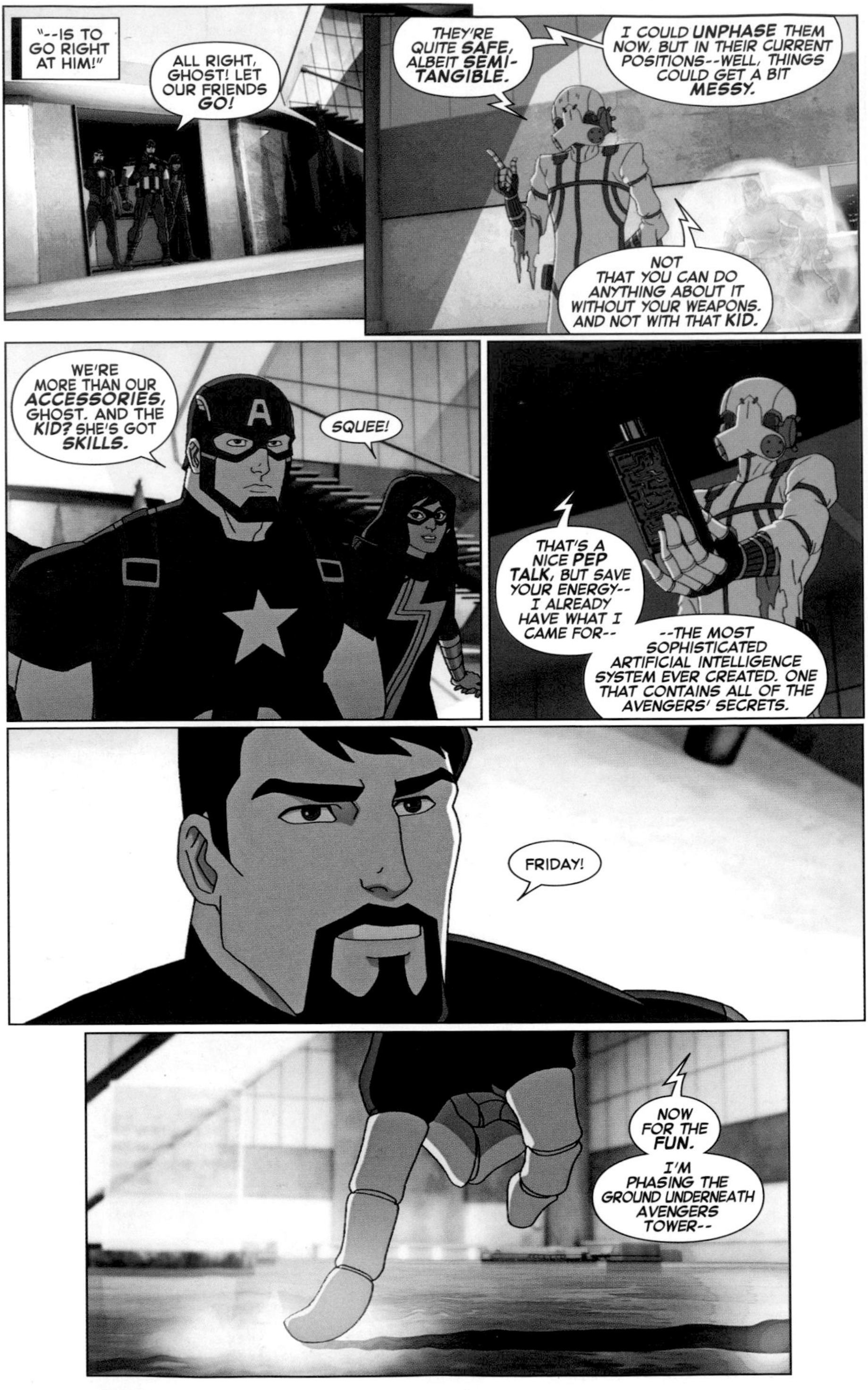
"--IS TO GO RIGHT AT HIM!"
ALL RIGHT, GHOST! LET OUR FRIENDS GO!
THEY'RE QUITE SAFE, ALBEIT SEMI-TANGIBLE.
I COULD UNPHASE THEM NOW, BUT IN THEIR CURRENT POSITIONS--WELL, THINGS COULD GET A BIT MESSY.
NOT THAT YOU CAN DO ANYTHING ABOUT IT WITHOUT YOUR WEAPONS. AND NOT WITH THAT KID.
WE'RE MORE THAN OUR ACCESSORIES, GHOST. AND THE KID? SHE'S GOT SKILLS.
SQUEE!
THAT'S A NICE PEP TALK, BUT SAVE YOUR ENERGY-- I ALREADY HAVE WHAT I CAME FOR--
--THE MOST SOPHISTICATED ARTIFICIAL INTELLIGENCE SYSTEM EVER CREATED. ONE THAT CONTAINS ALL OF THE AVENGERS' SECRETS.
FRIDAY!
NOW FOR THE FUN.
I'M PHASING THE GROUND UNDERNEATH AVENGERS TOWER--

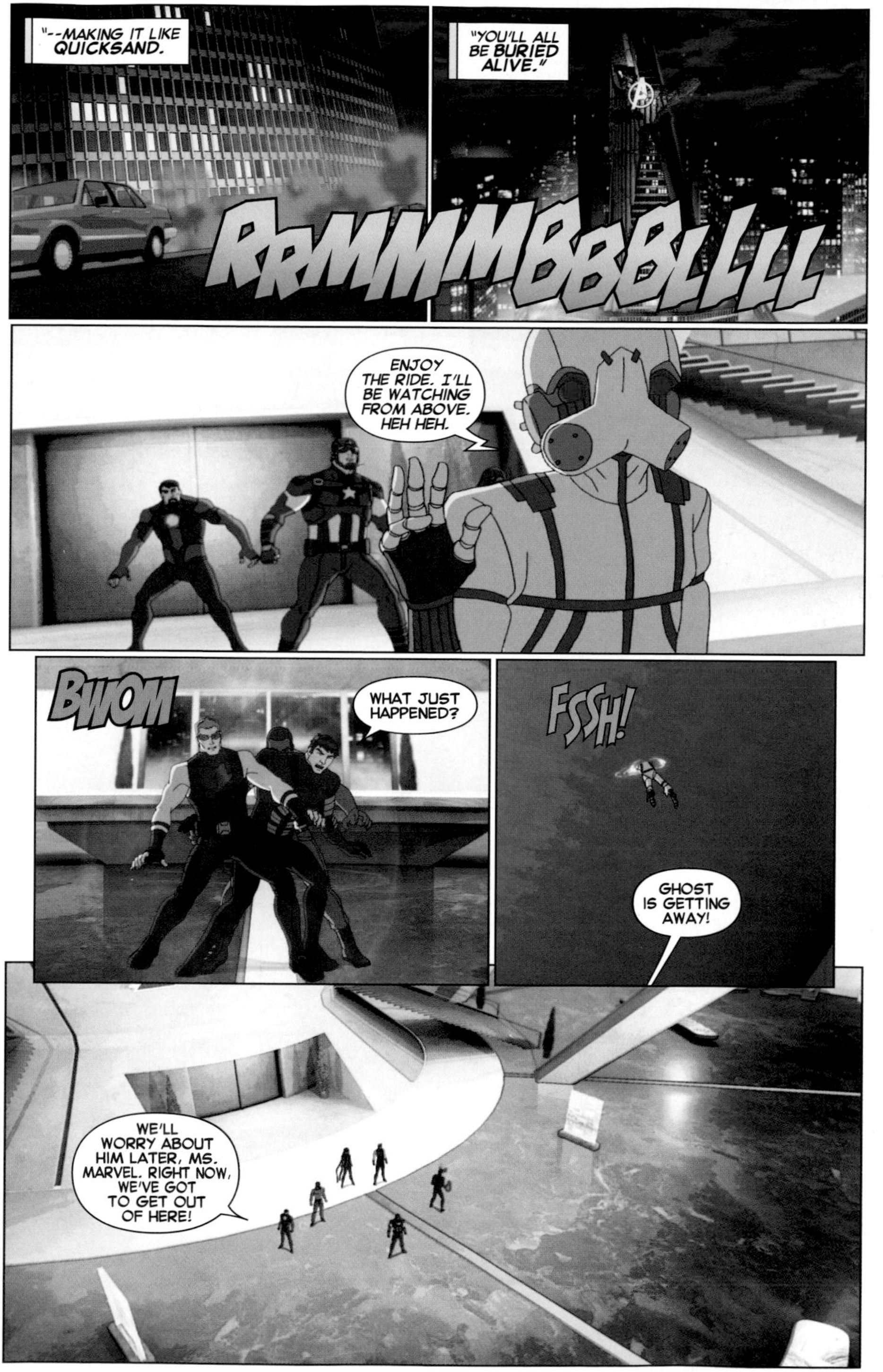
"--MAKING IT LIKE QUICKSAND.
"YOU'LL ALL BE BURIED ALIVE."
RRMMMBBBLLLL
ENJOY THE RIDE. I'LL BE WATCHING FROM ABOVE. HEH HEH.
BWOM
WHAT JUST HAPPENED?
FSSH!
GHOST IS GETTING AWAY!
WE'LL WORRY ABOUT HIM LATER, MS. MARVEL. RIGHT NOW, WE'VE GOT TO GET OUT OF HERE!

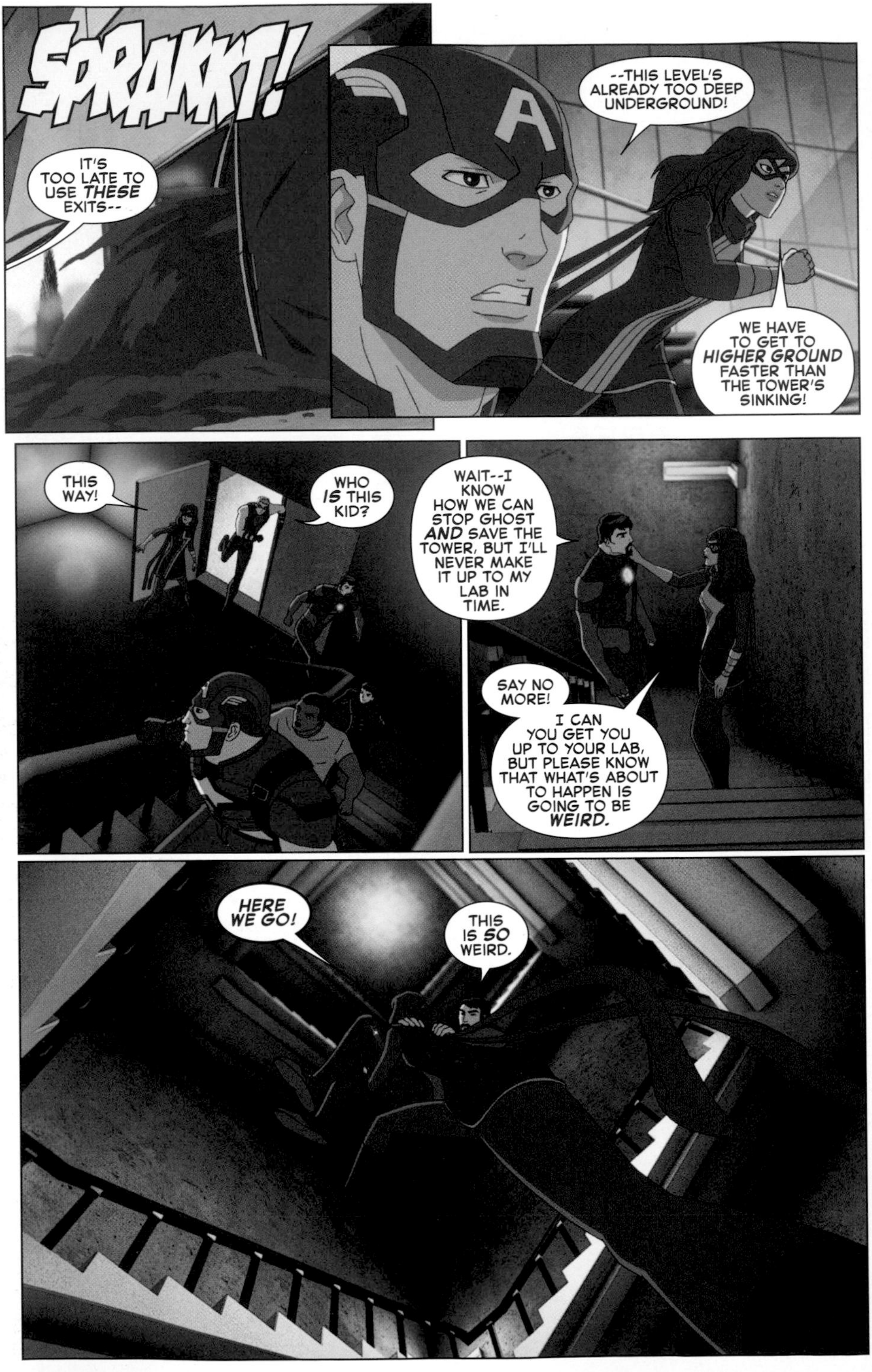
SPRAKKT!
IT'S TOO LATE TO USE THESE EXITS--
--THIS LEVEL'S ALREADY TOO DEEP UNDERGROUND!
WE HAVE TO GET TO HIGHER GROUND FASTER THAN THE TOWER'S SINKING!
THIS WAY!
WHO IS THIS KID?
WAIT--I KNOW HOW WE CAN STOP GHOST AND SAVE THE TOWER, BUT I'LL NEVER MAKE IT UP TO MY LAB IN TIME.
SAY NO MORE!
I CAN YOU GET YOU UP TO YOUR LAB, BUT PLEASE KNOW THAT WHAT'S ABOUT TO HAPPEN IS GOING TO BE WEIRD.
HERE WE GO!
THIS IS SO WEIRD.

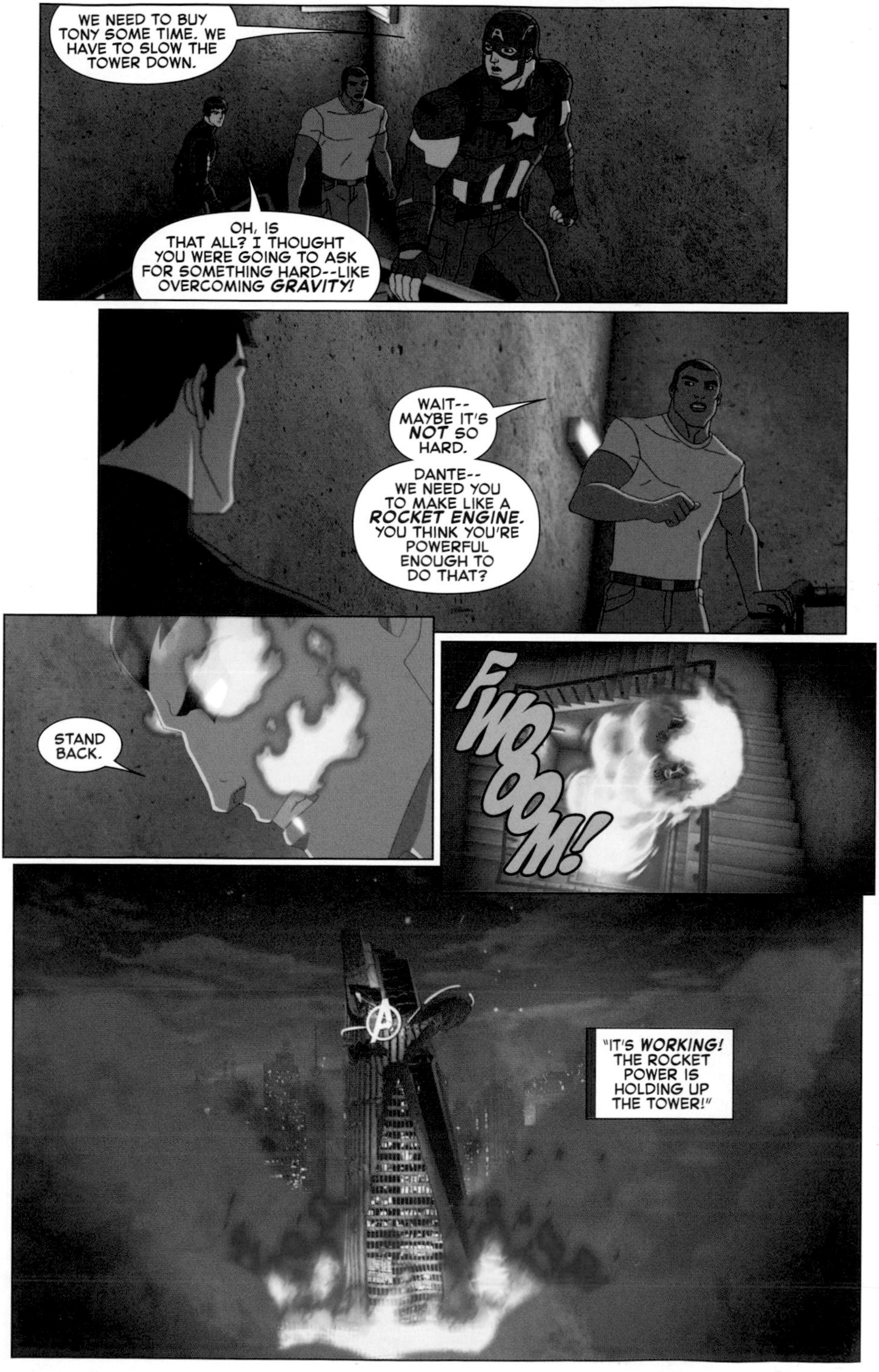
WE NEED TO BUY TONY SOME TIME. WE HAVE TO SLOW THE TOWER DOWN.
OH, IS THAT ALL? I THOUGHT YOU WERE GOING TO ASK FOR SOMETHING HARD--LIKE OVERCOMING GRAVITY!
WAIT-- MAYBE IT'S NOT SO HARD.
DANTE-- WE NEED YOU TO MAKE LIKE A ROCKET ENGINE. YOU THINK YOU'RE POWERFUL ENOUGH TO DO THAT?
STAND BACK.
FWOOOM!
"IT'S WORKING! THE ROCKET POWER IS HOLDING UP THE TOWER!"

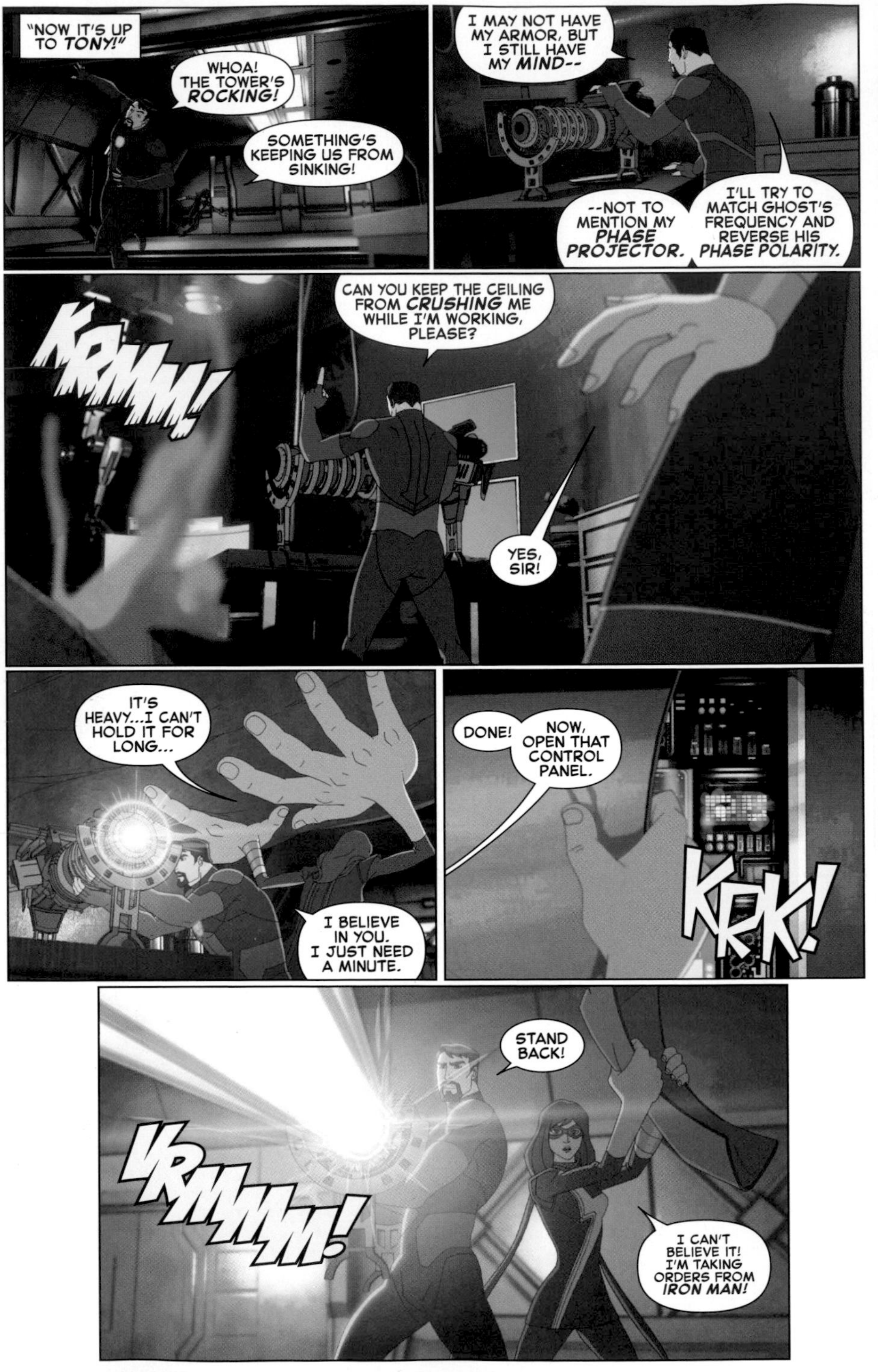
"NOW IT'S UP TO TONY!"
WHOA! THE TOWER'S ROCKING!
SOMETHING'S KEEPING US FROM SINKING!
I MAY NOT HAVE MY ARMOR, BUT I STILL HAVE MY MIND--
--NOT TO MENTION MY PHASE PROJECTOR.
I'LL TRY TO MATCH GHOST'S FREQUENCY AND REVERSE HIS PHASE POLARITY.
KRMMM!
CAN YOU KEEP THE CEILING FROM CRUSHING ME WHILE I'M WORKING, PLEASE?
YES, SIR!
IT'S HEAVY...I CAN'T HOLD IT FOR LONG...
I BELIEVE IN YOU. I JUST NEED A MINUTE.
DONE!
NOW, OPEN THAT CONTROL PANEL.
KRK!
STAND BACK!
VRMMMM!
I CAN'T BELIEVE IT! I'M TAKING ORDERS FROM IRON MAN!

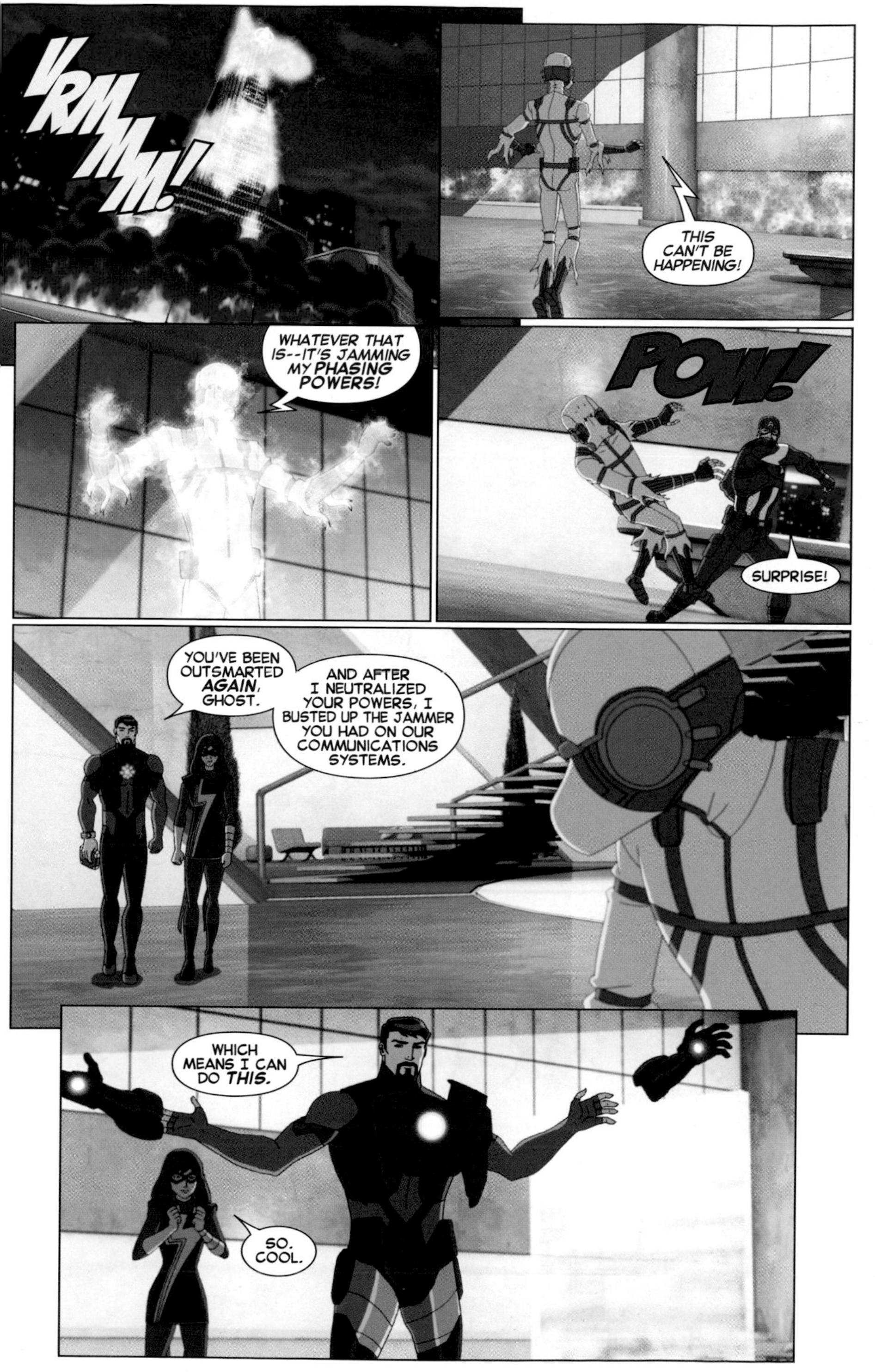
VRMMMM!
THIS CAN'T BE HAPPENING!
WHATEVER THAT IS--IT'S JAMMING MY PHASING POWERS!
POW!
SURPRISE!
YOU'VE BEEN OUTSMARTED AGAIN, GHOST.
AND AFTER I NEUTRALIZED YOUR POWERS, I BUSTED UP THE JAMMER YOU HAD ON OUR COMMUNICATIONS SYSTEMS.
WHICH MEANS I CAN DO THIS.
SO. COOL.

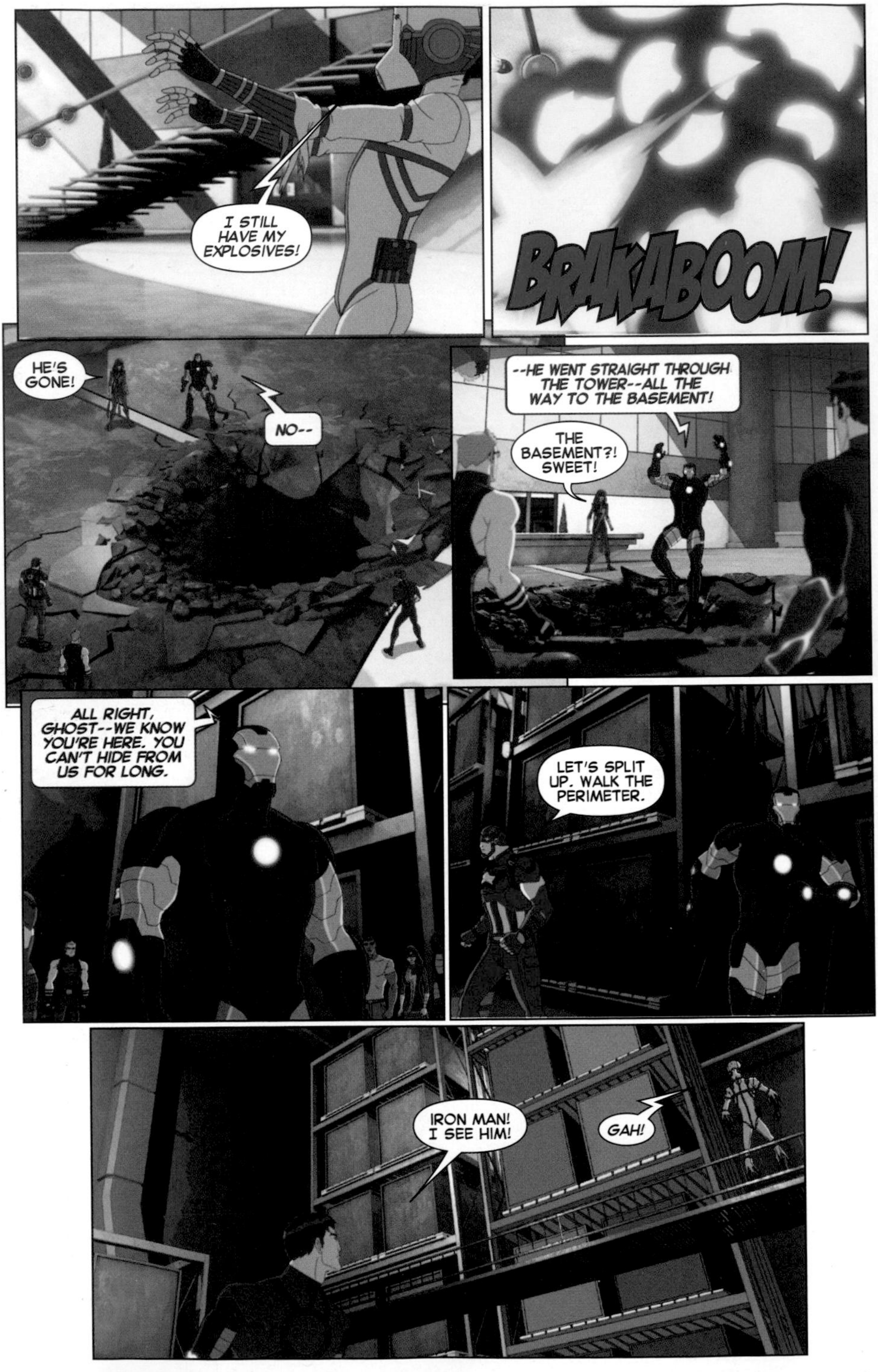
I STILL HAVE MY EXPLOSIVES!
BRAKABOOM!
HE'S GONE!
NO--
--HE WENT STRAIGHT THROUGH THE TOWER--ALL THE WAY TO THE BASEMENT!
THE BASEMENT?! SWEET!
ALL RIGHT, GHOST--WE KNOW YOU'RE HERE. YOU CAN'T HIDE FROM US FOR LONG.
LET'S SPLIT UP. WALK THE PERIMETER.
IRON MAN! I SEE HIM!
GAH!

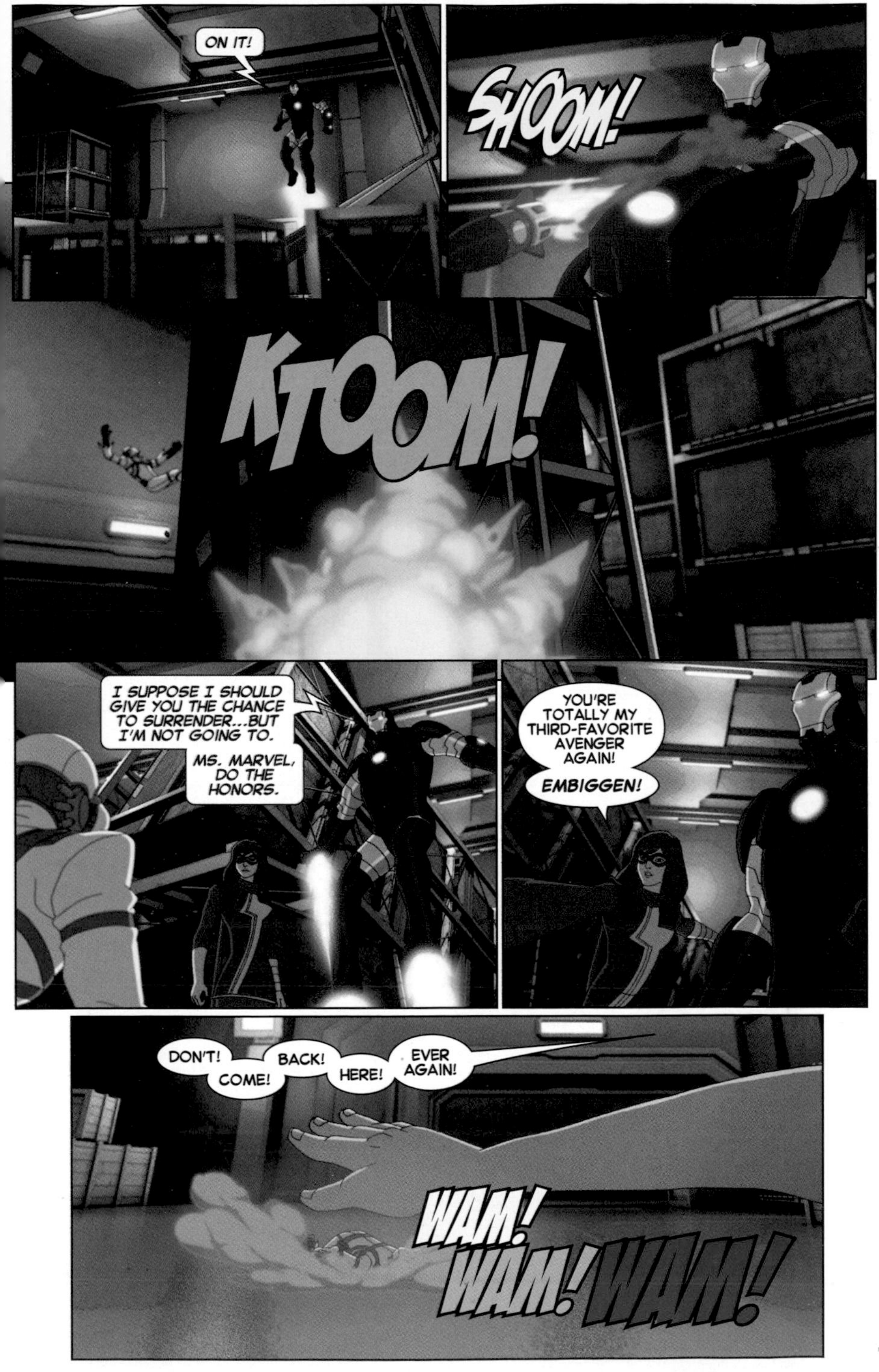
ON IT!
SHOOM!
KTOOM!
I SUPPOSE I SHOULD GIVE YOU THE CHANCE TO SURRENDER...BUT I'M NOT GOING TO.
MS. MARVEL, DO THE HONORS.
YOU'RE TOTALLY MY THIRD-FAVORITE AVENGER AGAIN!
EMBIGGEN!
DON'T!
COME!
BACK!
HERE!
EVER AGAIN!
WAM!
WAM!
WAM!

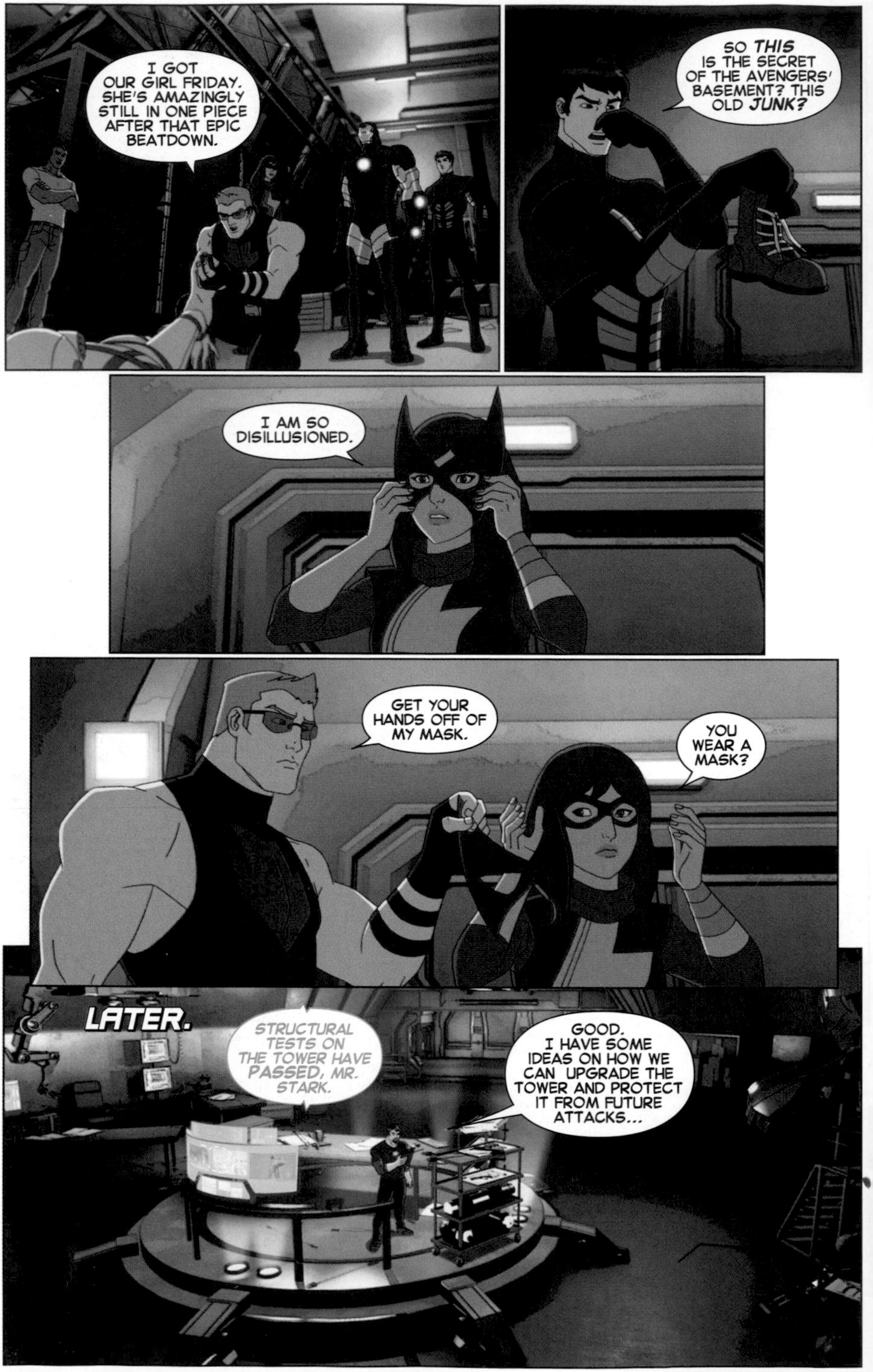
I GOT OUR GIRL FRIDAY. SHE'S AMAZINGLY STILL IN ONE PIECE AFTER THAT EPIC BEATDOWN.
SO THIS IS THE SECRET OF THE AVENGERS' BASEMENT? THIS OLD JUNK?
I AM SO DISILLUSIONED.
GET YOUR HANDS OFF OF MY MASK.
YOU WEAR A MASK?
LATER.
STRUCTURAL TESTS ON THE TOWER HAVE PASSED, MR. STARK.
GOOD. I HAVE SOME IDEAS ON HOW WE CAN UPGRADE THE TOWER AND PROTECT IT FROM FUTURE ATTACKS...

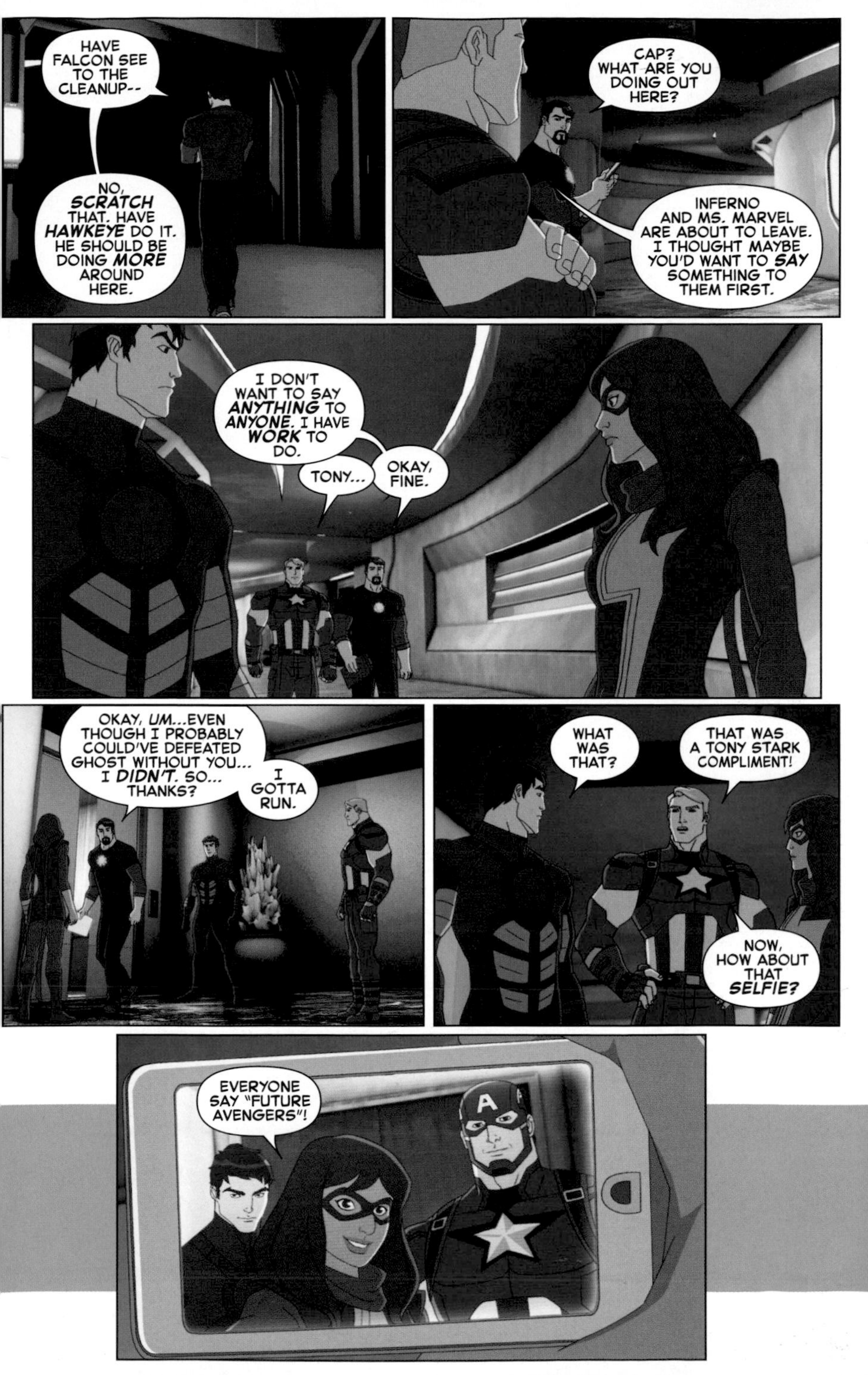
HAVE FALCON SEE TO THE CLEANUP--
NO, SCRATCH THAT. HAVE HAWKEYE DO IT. HE SHOULD BE DOING MORE AROUND HERE.
CAP? WHAT ARE YOU DOING OUT HERE?
INFERNO AND MS. MARVEL ARE ABOUT TO LEAVE. I THOUGHT MAYBE YOU'D WANT TO SAY SOMETHING TO THEM FIRST.
I DON'T WANT TO SAY ANYTHING TO ANYONE. I HAVE WORK TO DO.
TONY...
OKAY, FINE.
OKAY, UM...EVEN THOUGH I PROBABLY COULD'VE DEFEATED GHOST WITHOUT YOU... I DIDN'T. SO... THANKS?
I GOTTA RUN.
WHAT WAS THAT?
THAT WAS A TONY STARK COMPLIMENT!
NOW, HOW ABOUT THAT SELFIE?
EVERYONE SAY "FUTURE AVENGERS"!

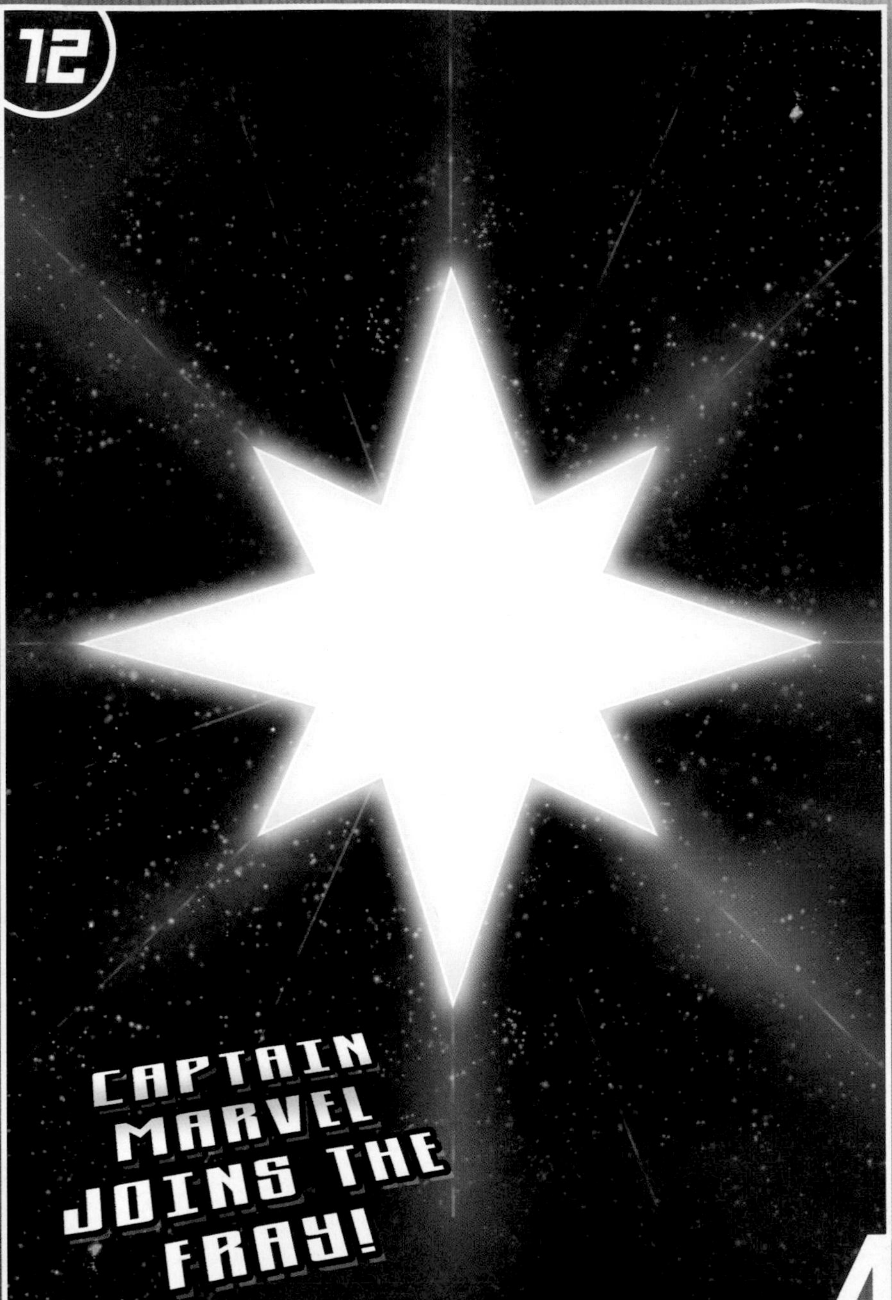
12
CAPTAIN MARVEL JOINS THE FRAY!

CAPTAIN MARVEL

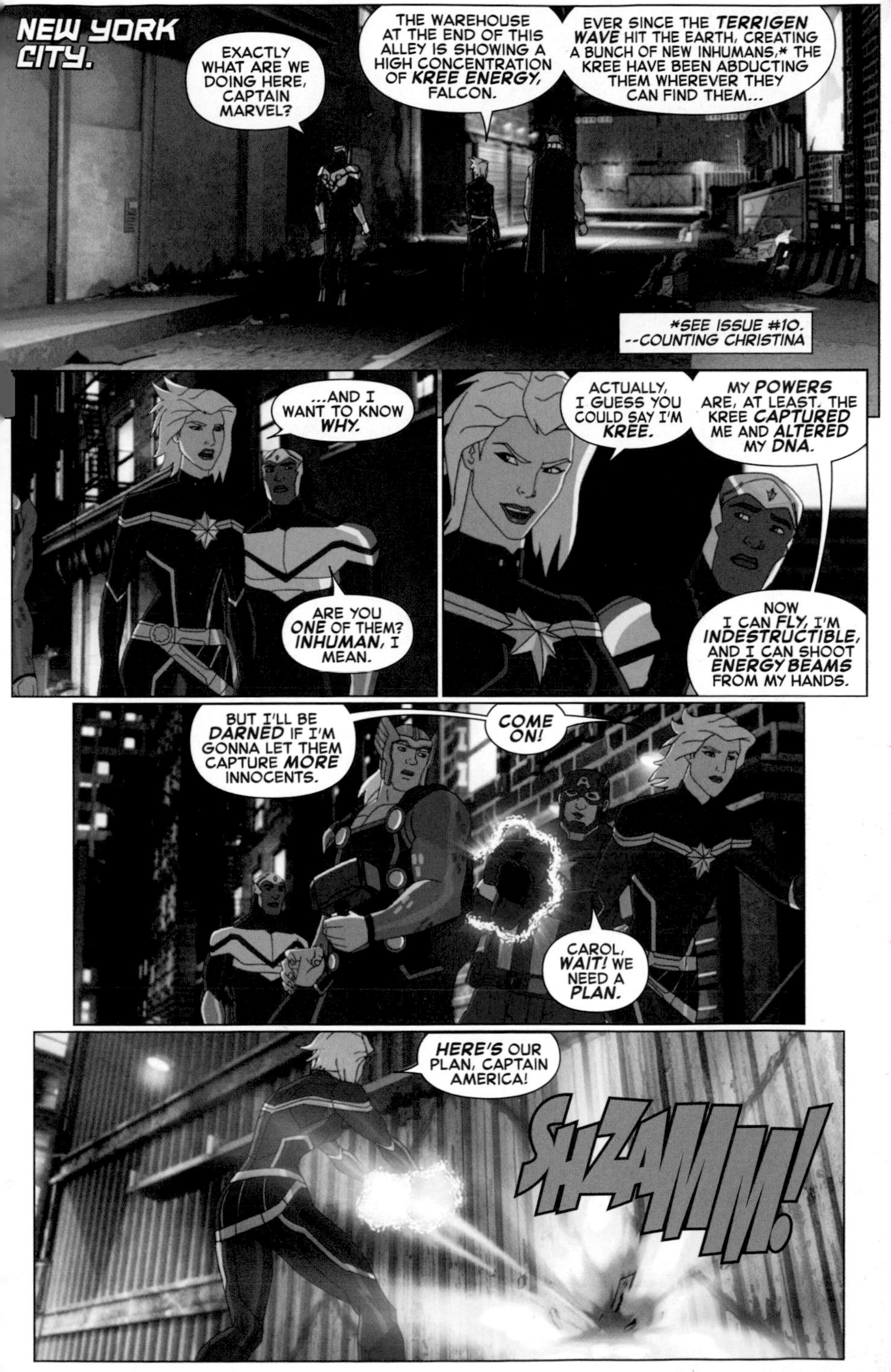
NEW YORK CITY.
EXACTLY WHAT ARE WE DOING HERE, CAPTAIN MARVEL?
THE WAREHOUSE AT THE END OF THIS ALLEY IS SHOWING A HIGH CONCENTRATION OF KREE ENERGY, FALCON.
EVER SINCE THE TERRIGEN WAVE HIT THE EARTH, CREATING A BUNCH OF NEW INHUMANS,* THE KREE HAVE BEEN ABDUCTING THEM WHEREVER THEY CAN FIND THEM...
*SEE ISSUE #10. --COUNTING CHRISTINA
...AND I WANT TO KNOW WHY.
ARE YOU ONE OF THEM? INHUMAN, I MEAN.
ACTUALLY, I GUESS YOU COULD SAY I'M KREE.
MY POWERS ARE, AT LEAST. THE KREE CAPTURED ME AND ALTERED MY DNA.
NOW I CAN FLY, I'M INDESTRUCTIBLE, AND I CAN SHOOT ENERGY BEAMS FROM MY HANDS.
BUT I'LL BE DARNED IF I'M GONNA LET THEM CAPTURE MORE INNOCENTS.
COME ON!
CAROL, WAIT! WE NEED A PLAN.
HERE'S OUR PLAN, CAPTAIN AMERICA!
SHZAMM!

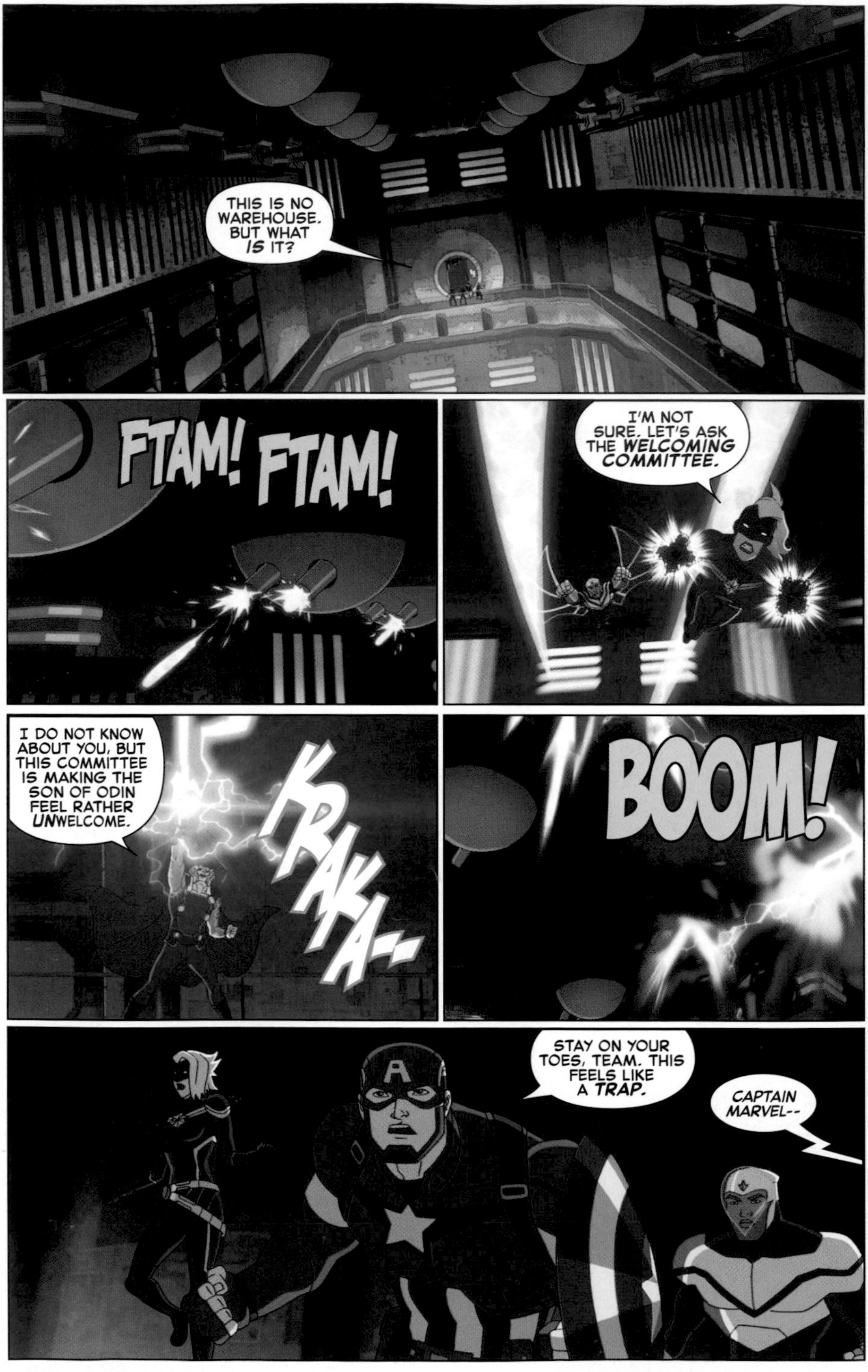
THIS IS NO WAREHOUSE. BUT WHAT *IS* IT?
FTAM! FTAM!
I'M NOT SURE. LET'S ASK THE *WELCOMING COMMITTEE.*
I DO NOT KNOW ABOUT YOU, BUT THIS COMMITTEE IS MAKING THE SON OF ODIN FEEL RATHER *UN*WELCOME.
KRAKA--
BOOM!
STAY ON YOUR TOES, TEAM. THIS FEELS LIKE A *TRAP.*
CAPTAIN MARVEL--

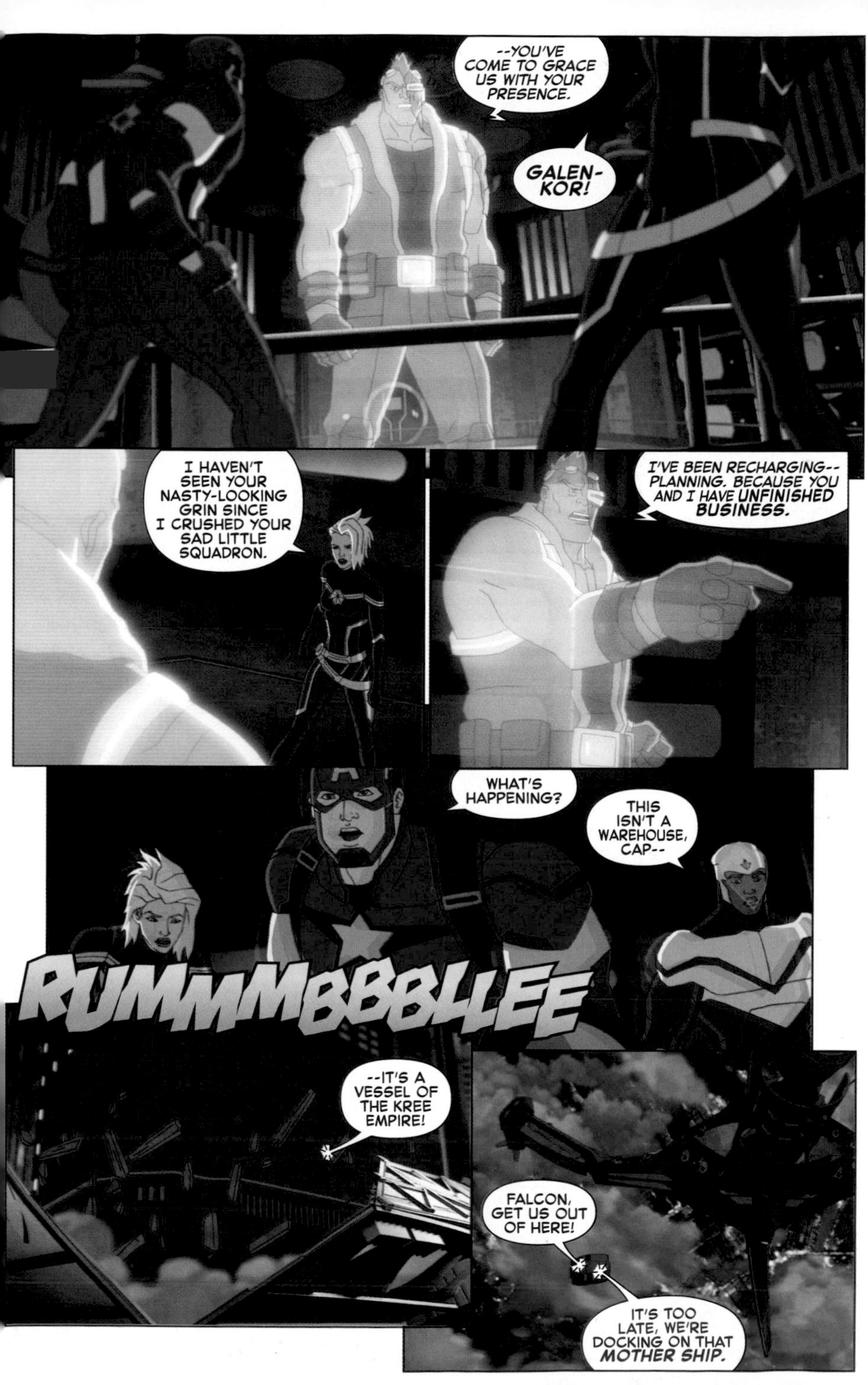
--YOU'VE COME TO GRACE US WITH YOUR PRESENCE.
GALEN-KOR!
I HAVEN'T SEEN YOUR NASTY-LOOKING GRIN SINCE I CRUSHED YOUR SAD LITTLE SQUADRON.
I'VE BEEN RECHARGING-- PLANNING. BECAUSE YOU AND I HAVE UNFINISHED BUSINESS.
WHAT'S HAPPENING?
THIS ISN'T A WAREHOUSE, CAP--
RUMMMBBBLLEE
--IT'S A VESSEL OF THE KREE EMPIRE!
FALCON, GET US OUT OF HERE!
IT'S TOO LATE, WE'RE DOCKING ON THAT MOTHER SHIP.

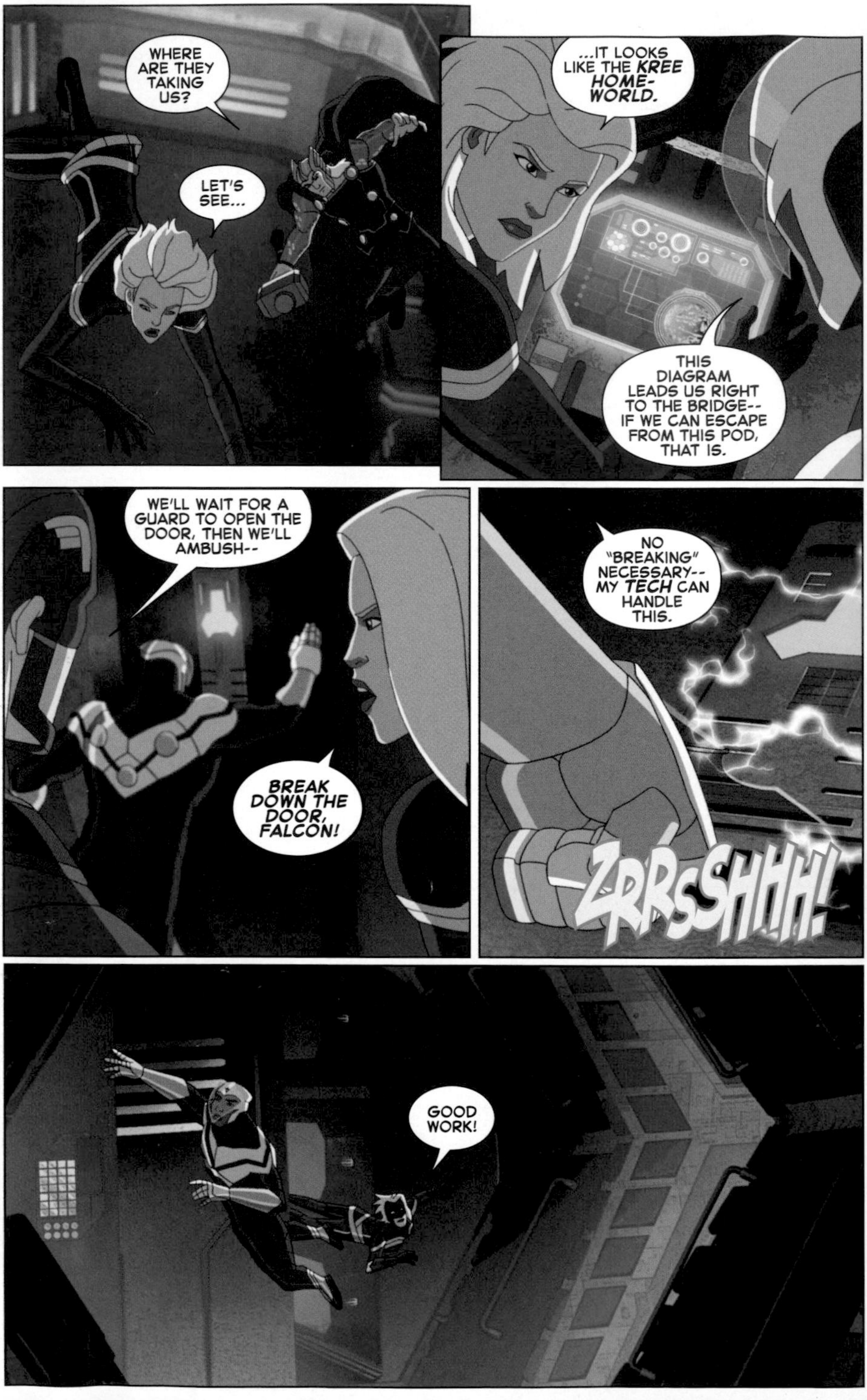
WHERE ARE THEY TAKING US?
LET'S SEE...
...IT LOOKS LIKE THE KREE HOME-WORLD.
THIS DIAGRAM LEADS US RIGHT TO THE BRIDGE-- IF WE CAN ESCAPE FROM THIS POD, THAT IS.
WE'LL WAIT FOR A GUARD TO OPEN THE DOOR, THEN WE'LL AMBUSH--
BREAK DOWN THE DOOR, FALCON!
NO "BREAKING" NECESSARY-- MY TECH CAN HANDLE THIS.
ZRRSSHHH!
GOOD WORK!

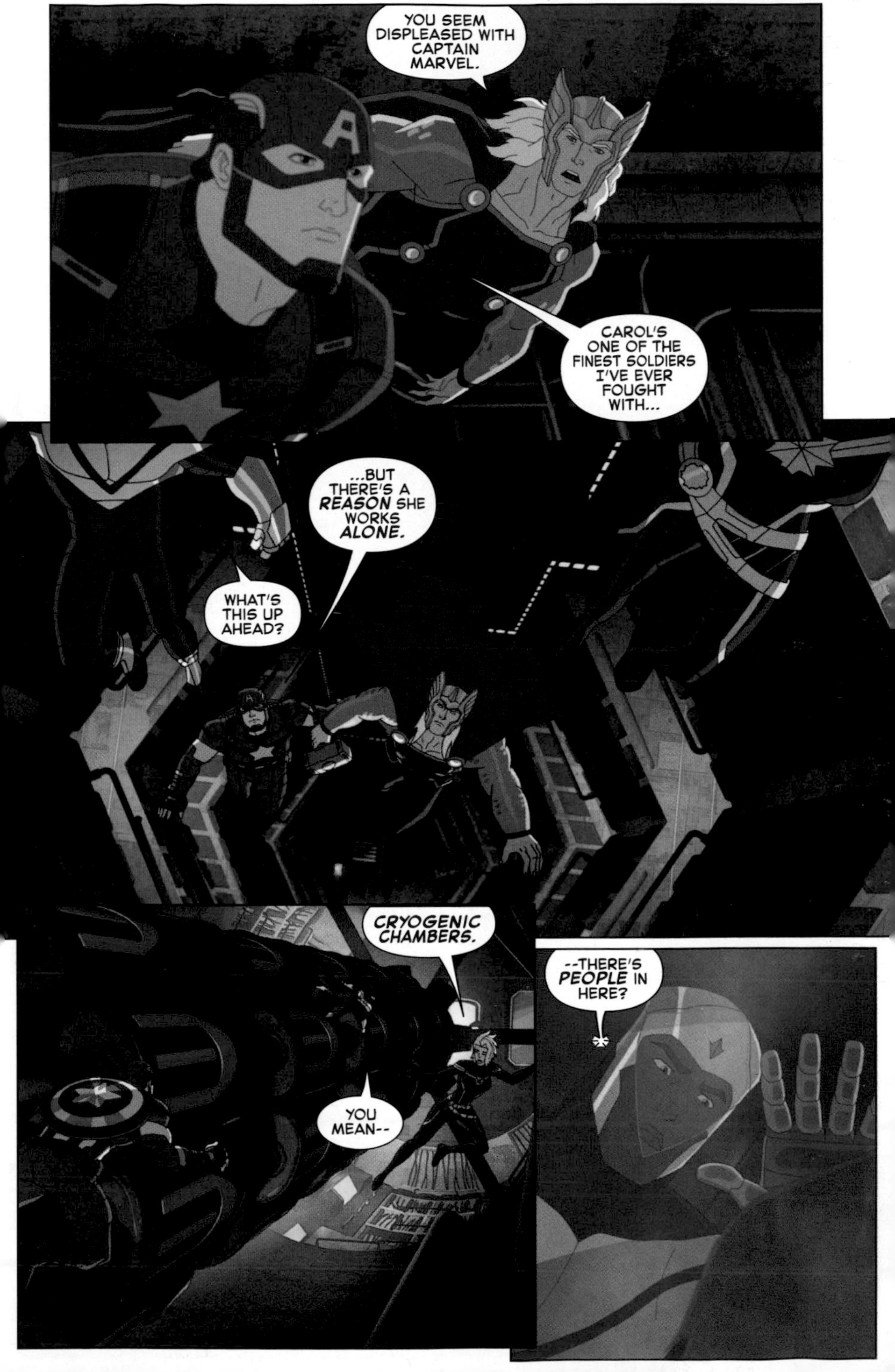
YOU SEEM DISPLEASED WITH CAPTAIN MARVEL.
CAROL'S ONE OF THE FINEST SOLDIERS I'VE EVER FOUGHT WITH...
...BUT THERE'S A REASON SHE WORKS ALONE.
WHAT'S THIS UP AHEAD?
CRYOGENIC CHAMBERS.
YOU MEAN--
--THERE'S PEOPLE IN HERE?

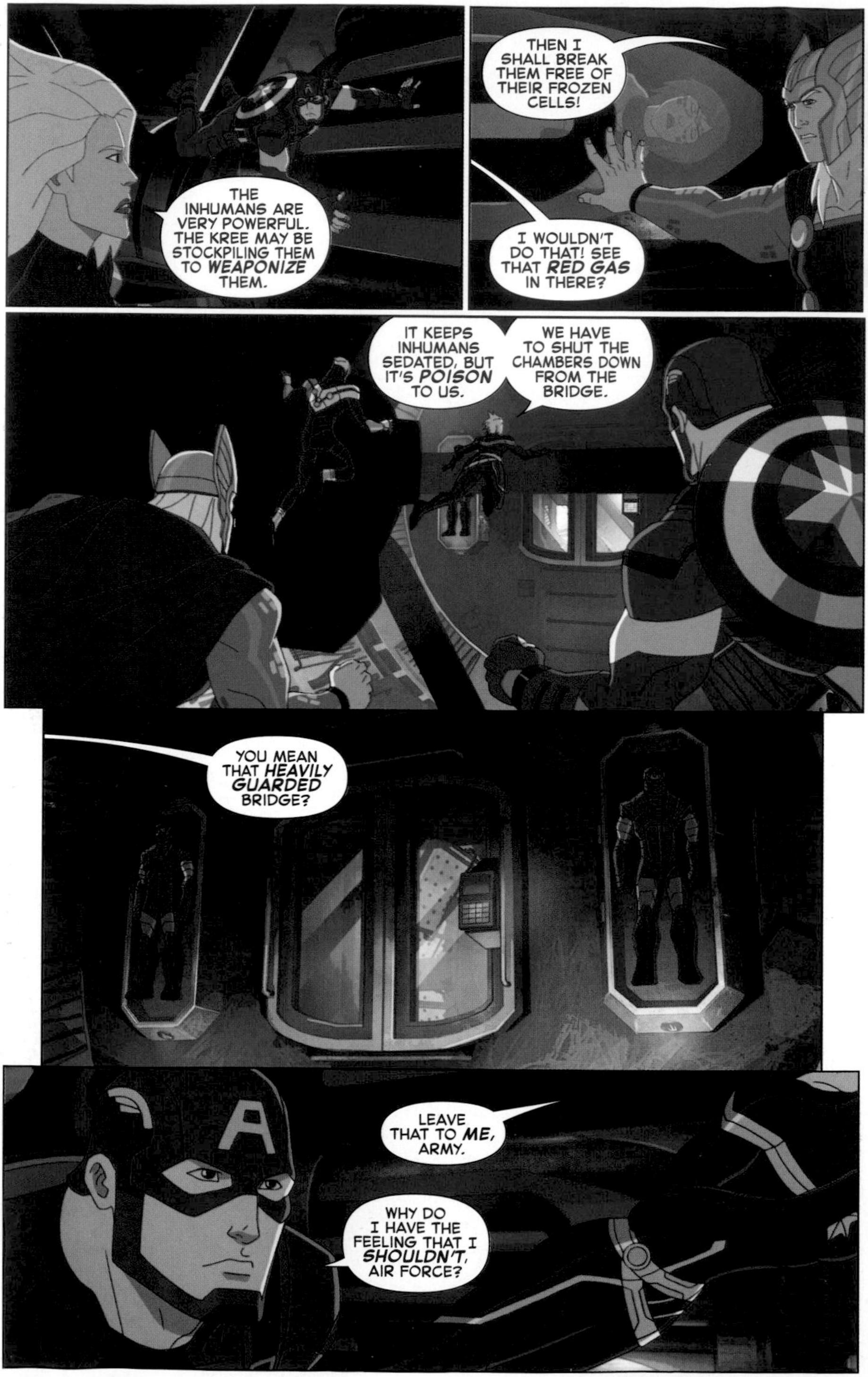
THE INHUMANS ARE VERY POWERFUL. THE KREE MAY BE STOCKPILING THEM TO WEAPONIZE THEM.
THEN I SHALL BREAK THEM FREE OF THEIR FROZEN CELLS!
I WOULDN'T DO THAT! SEE THAT RED GAS IN THERE?
IT KEEPS INHUMANS SEDATED, BUT IT'S POISON TO US.
WE HAVE TO SHUT THE CHAMBERS DOWN FROM THE BRIDGE.
YOU MEAN THAT HEAVILY GUARDED BRIDGE?
LEAVE THAT TO ME, ARMY.
WHY DO I HAVE THE FEELING THAT I SHOULDN'T, AIR FORCE?

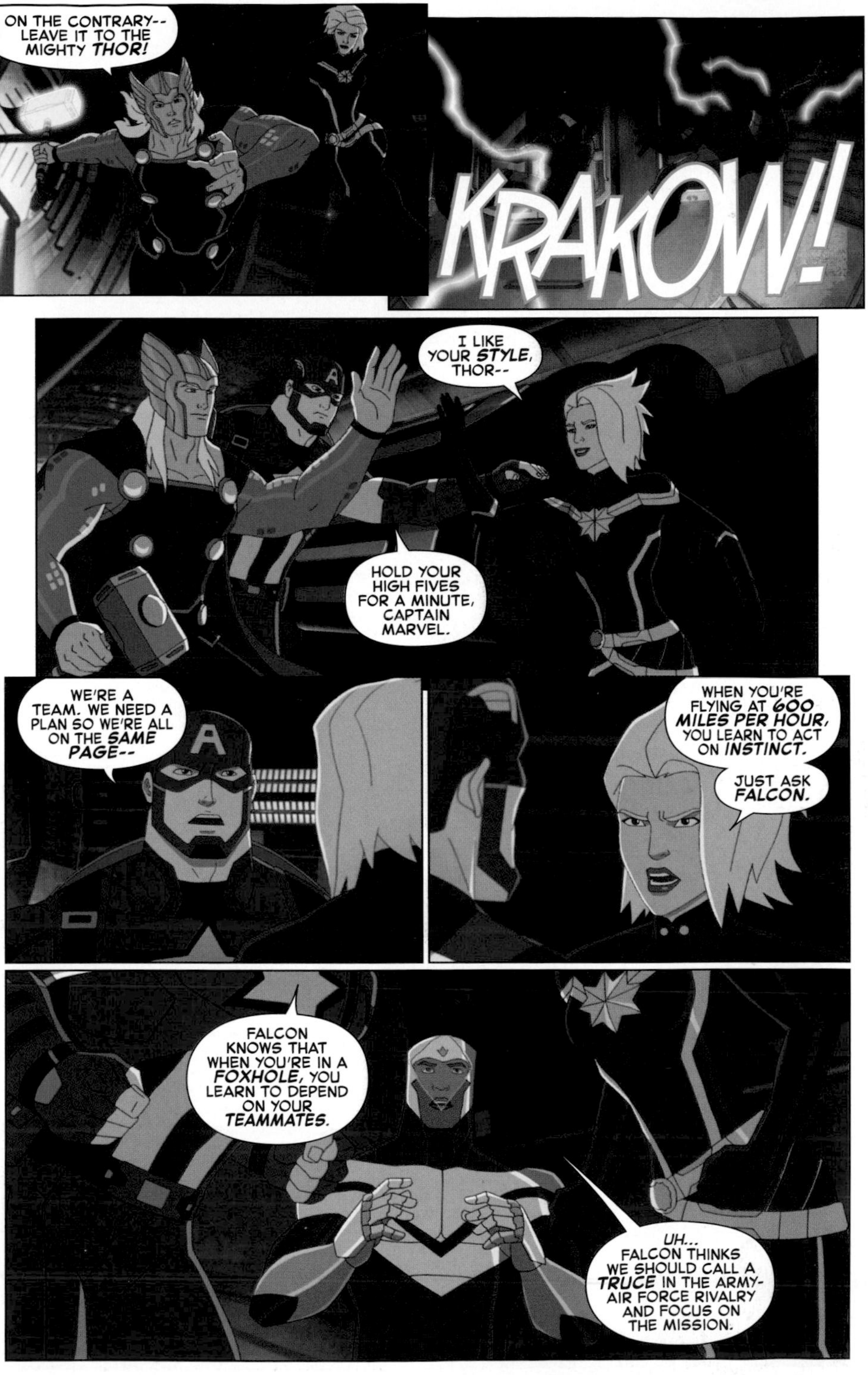
ON THE CONTRARY-- LEAVE IT TO THE MIGHTY THOR!
KRAKOW!
I LIKE YOUR STYLE, THOR--
HOLD YOUR HIGH FIVES FOR A MINUTE, CAPTAIN MARVEL.
WE'RE A TEAM. WE NEED A PLAN SO WE'RE ALL ON THE SAME PAGE--
WHEN YOU'RE FLYING AT 600 MILES PER HOUR, YOU LEARN TO ACT ON INSTINCT.
JUST ASK FALCON.
FALCON KNOWS THAT WHEN YOU'RE IN A FOXHOLE, YOU LEARN TO DEPEND ON YOUR TEAMMATES.
UH... FALCON THINKS WE SHOULD CALL A TRUCE IN THE ARMY-AIR FORCE RIVALRY AND FOCUS ON THE MISSION.

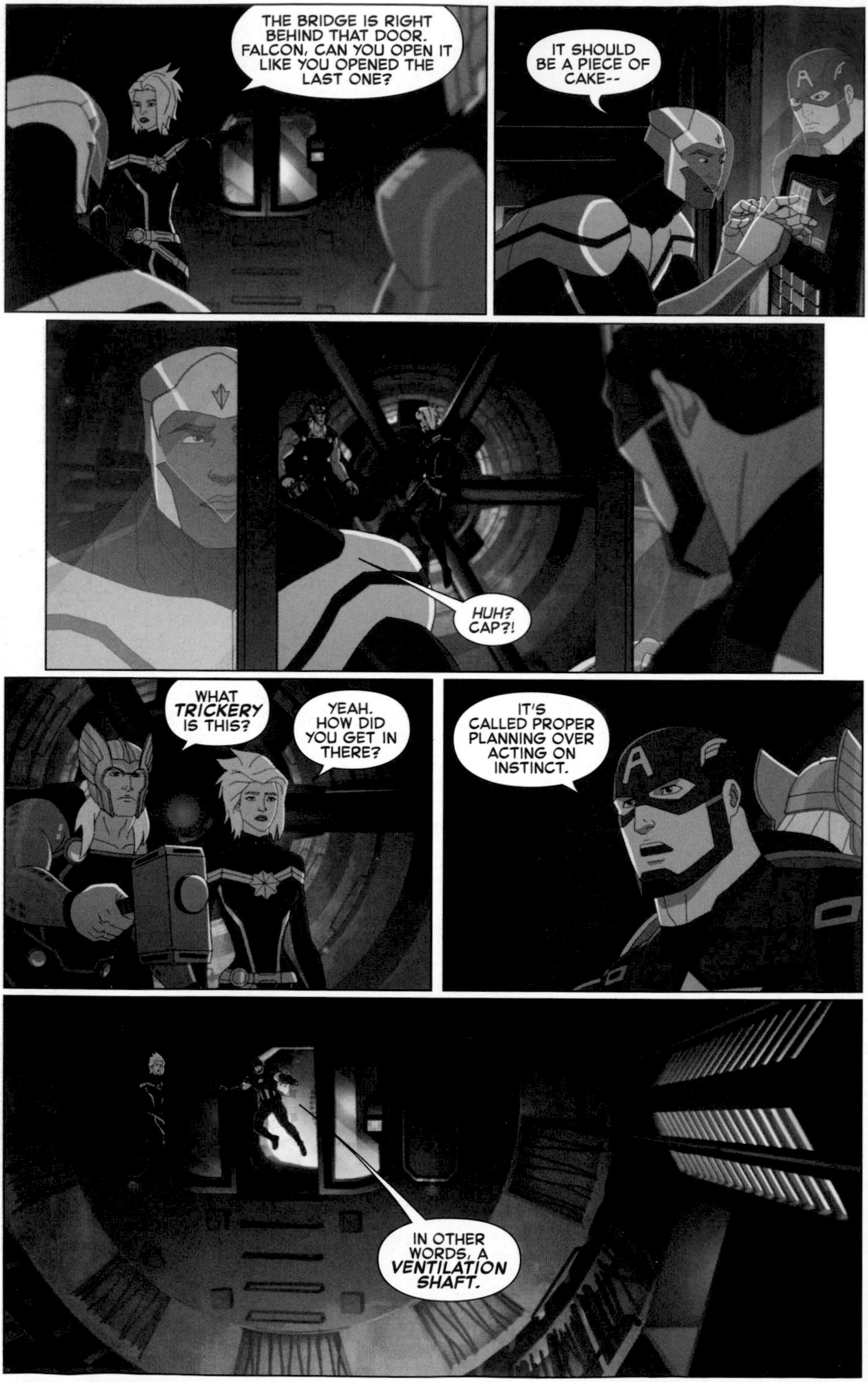
THE BRIDGE IS RIGHT BEHIND THAT DOOR. FALCON, CAN YOU OPEN IT LIKE YOU OPENED THE LAST ONE?
IT SHOULD BE A PIECE OF CAKE--
HUH? CAP?!
WHAT TRICKERY IS THIS?
YEAH. HOW DID YOU GET IN THERE?
IT'S CALLED PROPER PLANNING OVER ACTING ON INSTINCT.
IN OTHER WORDS, A VENTILATION SHAFT.

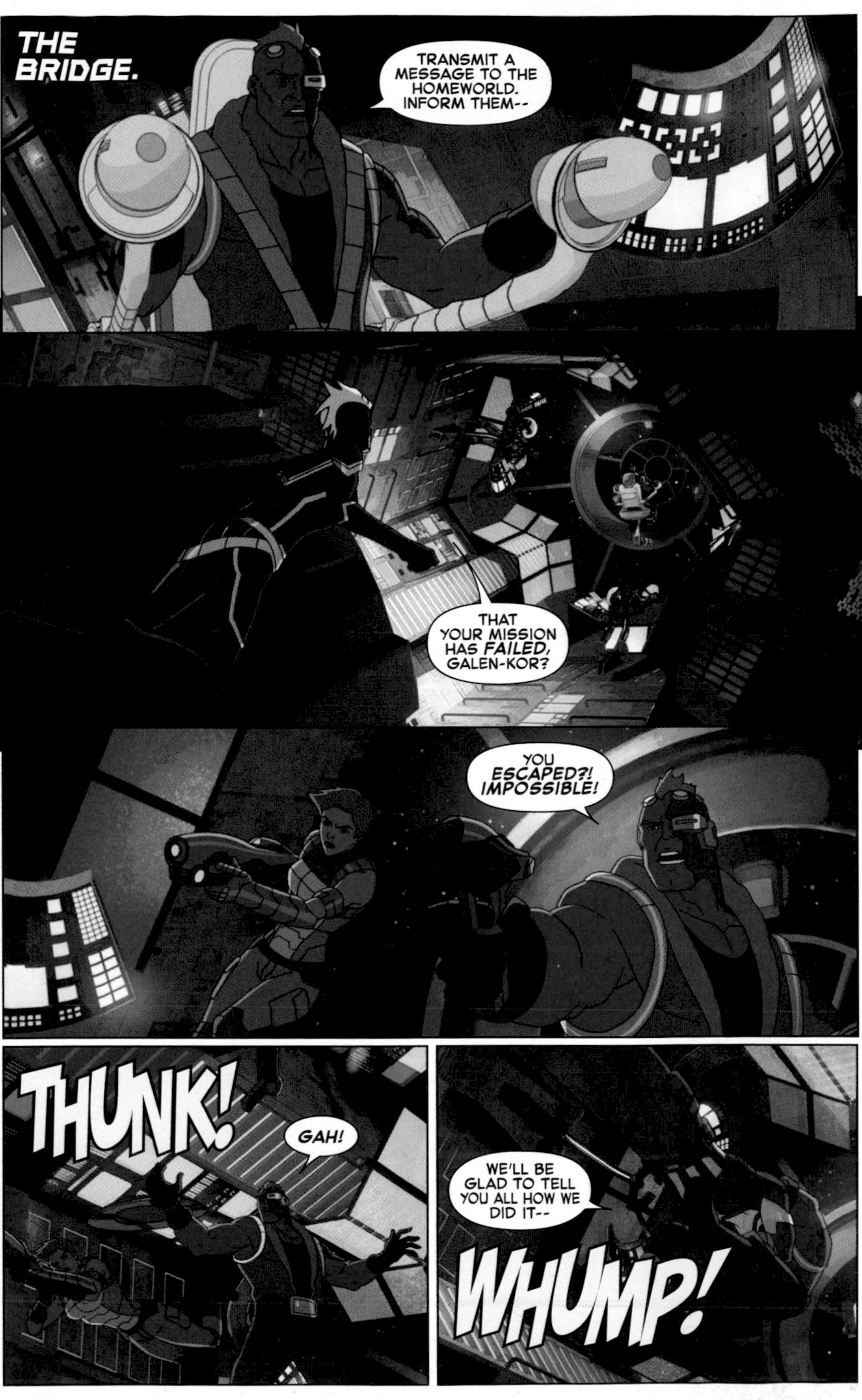
THE BRIDGE.
TRANSMIT A MESSAGE TO THE HOMEWORLD. INFORM THEM--
THAT YOUR MISSION HAS FAILED, GALEN-KOR?
YOU ESCAPED?! IMPOSSIBLE!
THUNK!
GAH!
WE'LL BE GLAD TO TELL YOU ALL HOW WE DID IT--
WHUMP!

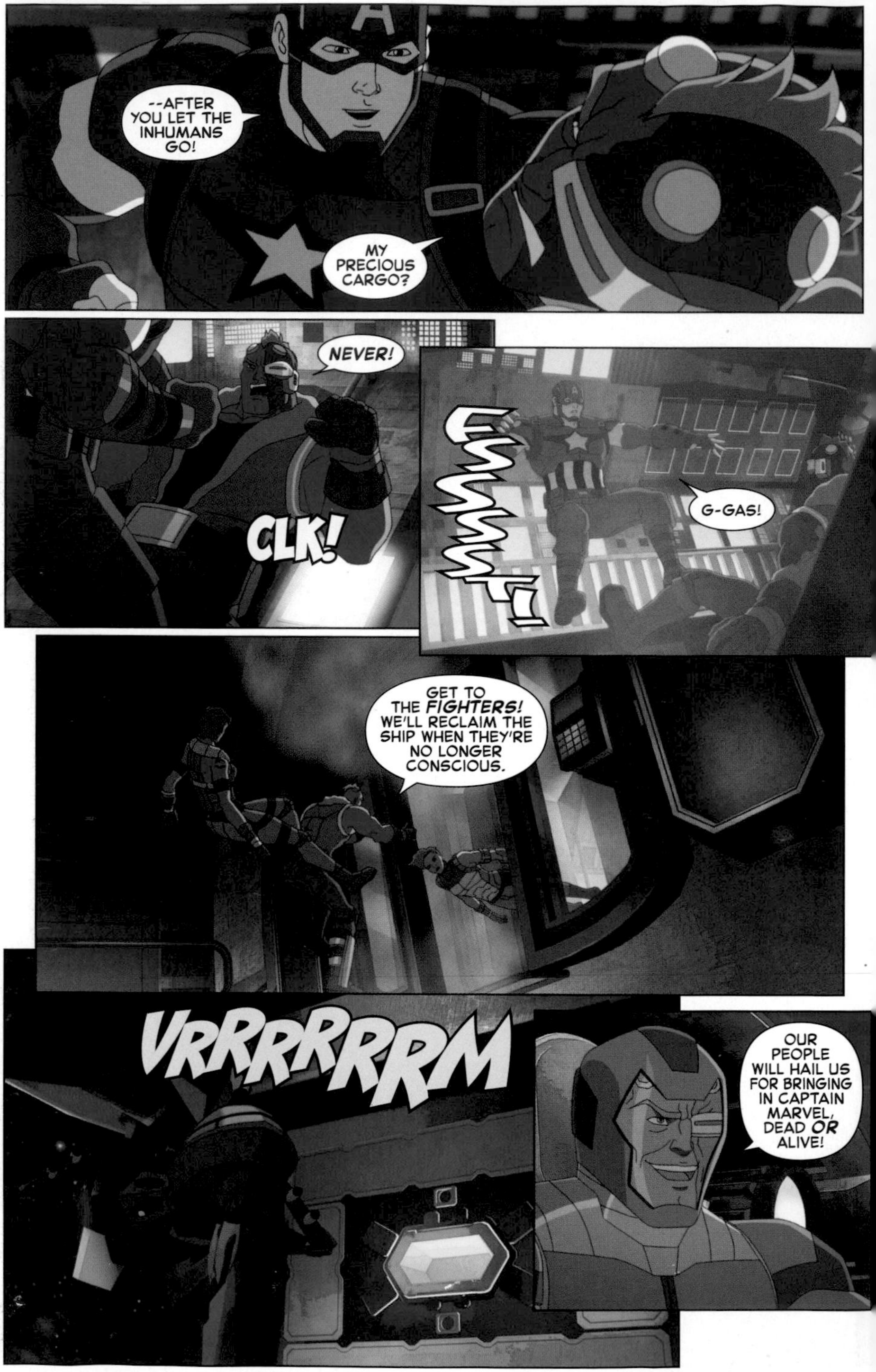
--AFTER YOU LET THE INHUMANS GO!
MY PRECIOUS CARGO?
NEVER!
CLK!
FSSSSST!
G-GAS!
GET TO THE *FIGHTERS!* WE'LL RECLAIM THE SHIP WHEN THEY'RE NO LONGER CONSCIOUS.
VRRRRRRM
OUR PEOPLE WILL HAIL US FOR BRINGING IN CAPTAIN MARVEL, DEAD *OR* ALIVE!

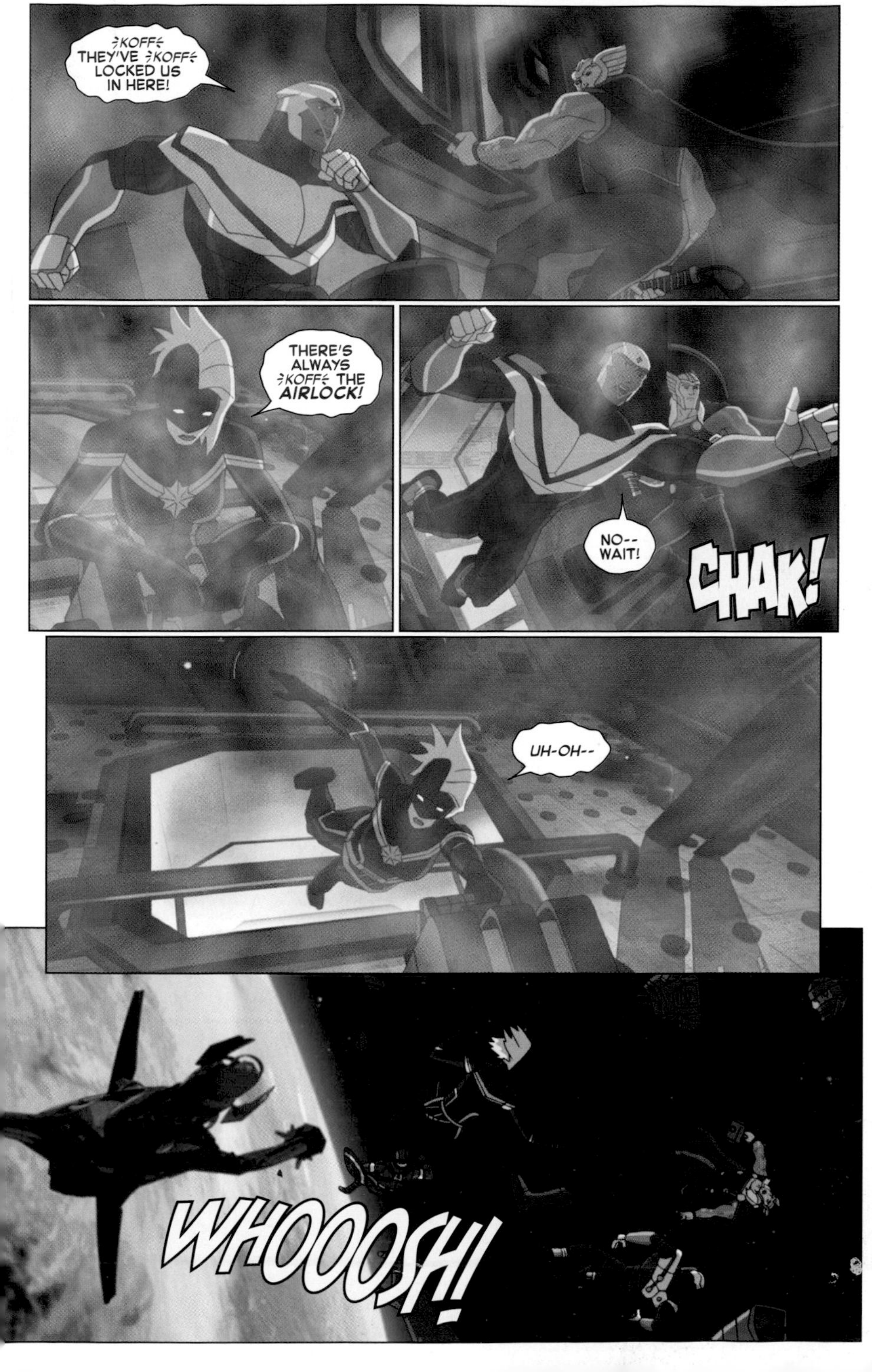

⊰KOFF⊱ THEY'VE ⊰KOFF⊱ LOCKED US IN HERE!
THERE'S ALWAYS ⊰KOFF⊱ THE AIRLOCK!
NO-- WAIT!
CHAK!
UH-OH--
WHOOOSH!

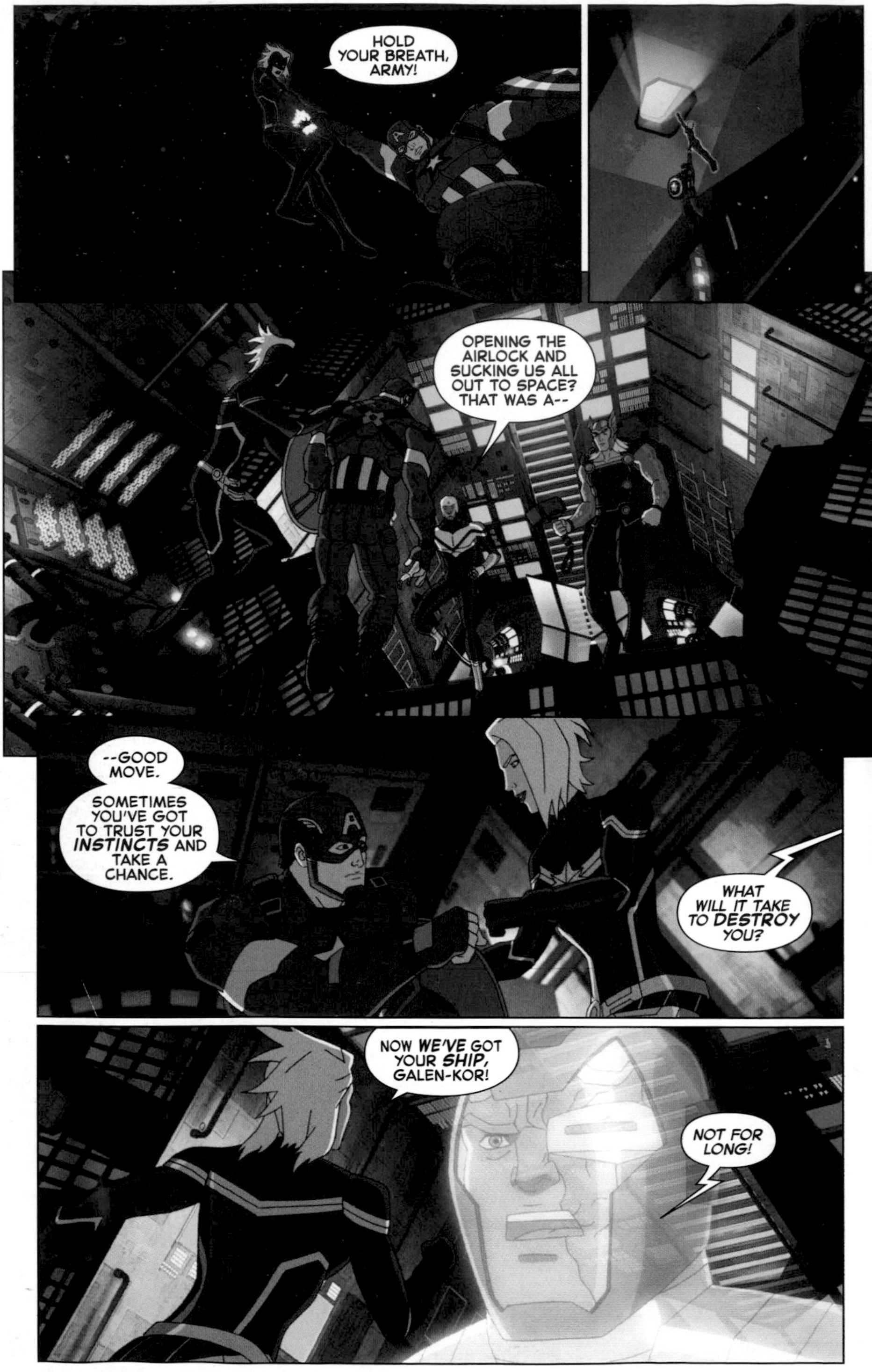
HOLD YOUR BREATH, ARMY!
OPENING THE AIRLOCK AND SUCKING US ALL OUT TO SPACE? THAT WAS A--
--GOOD MOVE.
SOMETIMES YOU'VE GOT TO TRUST YOUR *INSTINCTS* AND TAKE A CHANCE.
WHAT WILL IT TAKE TO *DESTROY* YOU?
NOW *WE'VE* GOT YOUR *SHIP*, GALEN-KOR!
NOT FOR LONG!

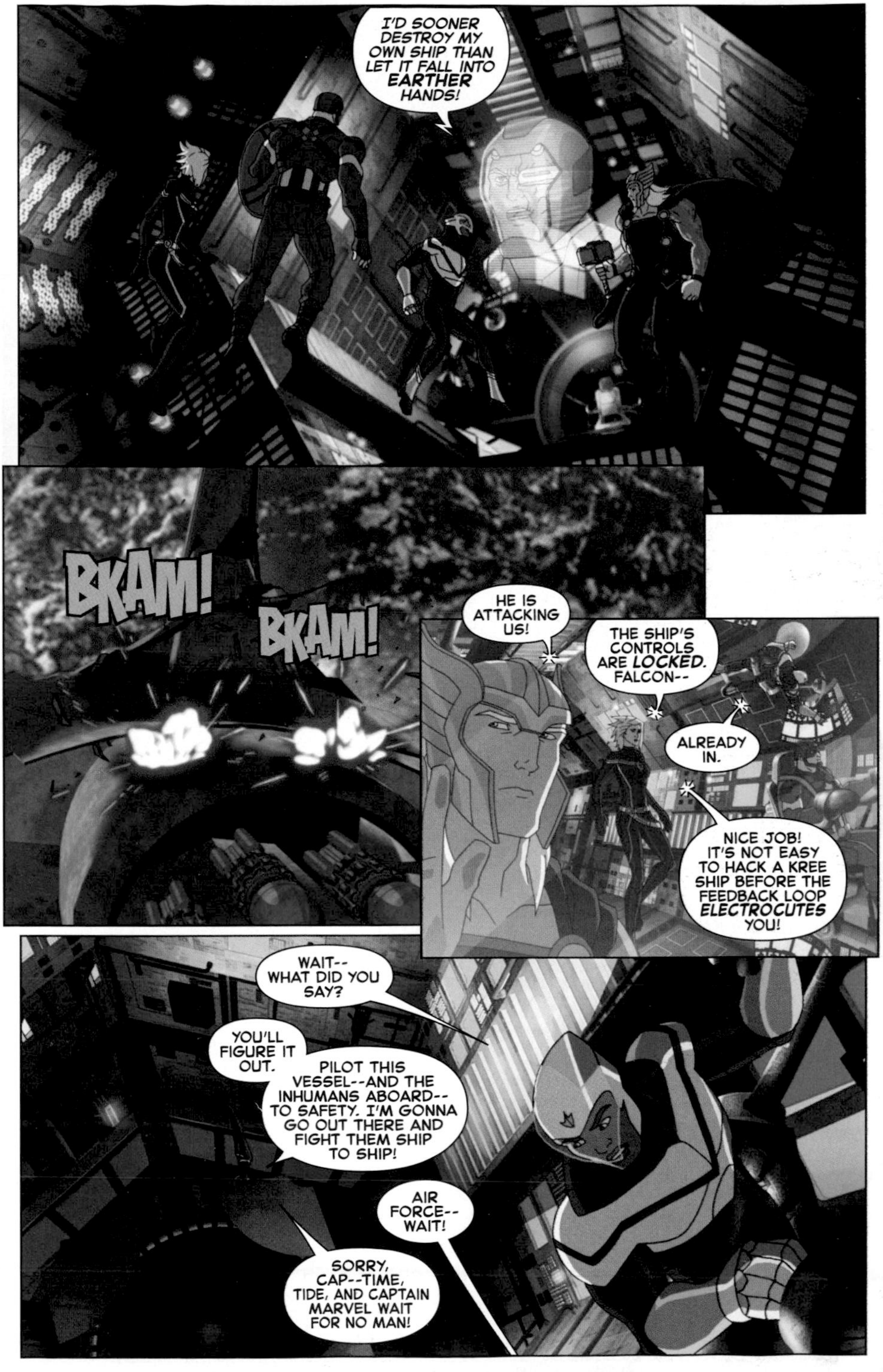

I'D SOONER DESTROY MY OWN SHIP THAN LET IT FALL INTO EARTHER HANDS!
BKAM!
BKAM!
HE IS ATTACKING US!
THE SHIP'S CONTROLS ARE LOCKED. FALCON--
ALREADY IN.
NICE JOB! IT'S NOT EASY TO HACK A KREE SHIP BEFORE THE FEEDBACK LOOP ELECTROCUTES YOU!
WAIT-- WHAT DID YOU SAY?
YOU'LL FIGURE IT OUT.
PILOT THIS VESSEL--AND THE INHUMANS ABOARD-- TO SAFETY. I'M GONNA GO OUT THERE AND FIGHT THEM SHIP TO SHIP!
AIR FORCE-- WAIT!
SORRY, CAP--TIME, TIDE, AND CAPTAIN MARVEL WAIT FOR NO MAN!

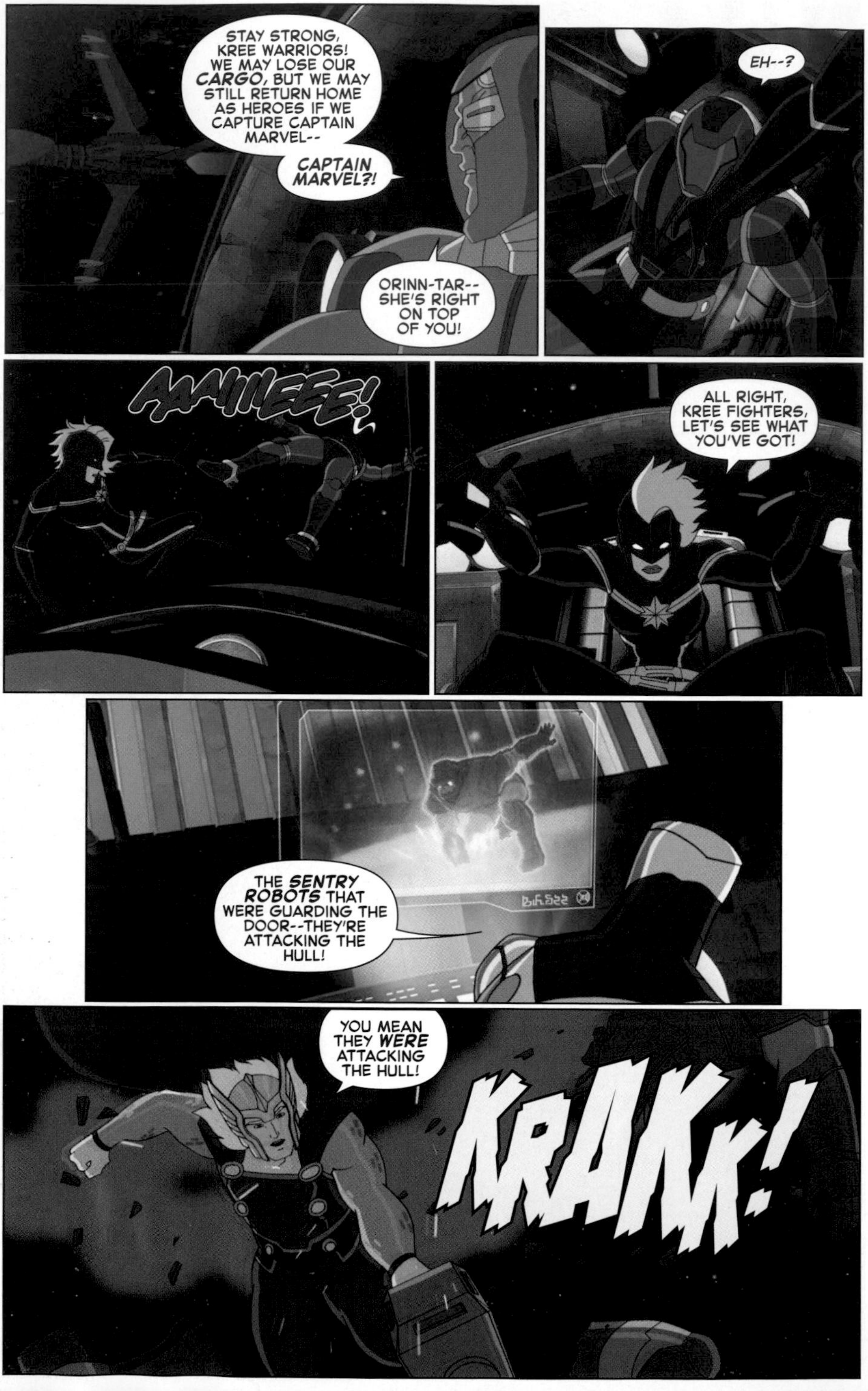
STAY STRONG, KREE WARRIORS! WE MAY LOSE OUR CARGO, BUT WE MAY STILL RETURN HOME AS HEROES IF WE CAPTURE CAPTAIN MARVEL--
CAPTAIN MARVEL?!
ORINN-TAR--SHE'S RIGHT ON TOP OF YOU!
EH--?
AAAIIIEEEE!
ALL RIGHT, KREE FIGHTERS, LET'S SEE WHAT YOU'VE GOT!
THE SENTRY ROBOTS THAT WERE GUARDING THE DOOR--THEY'RE ATTACKING THE HULL!
YOU MEAN THEY WERE ATTACKING THE HULL!
KRAKK!

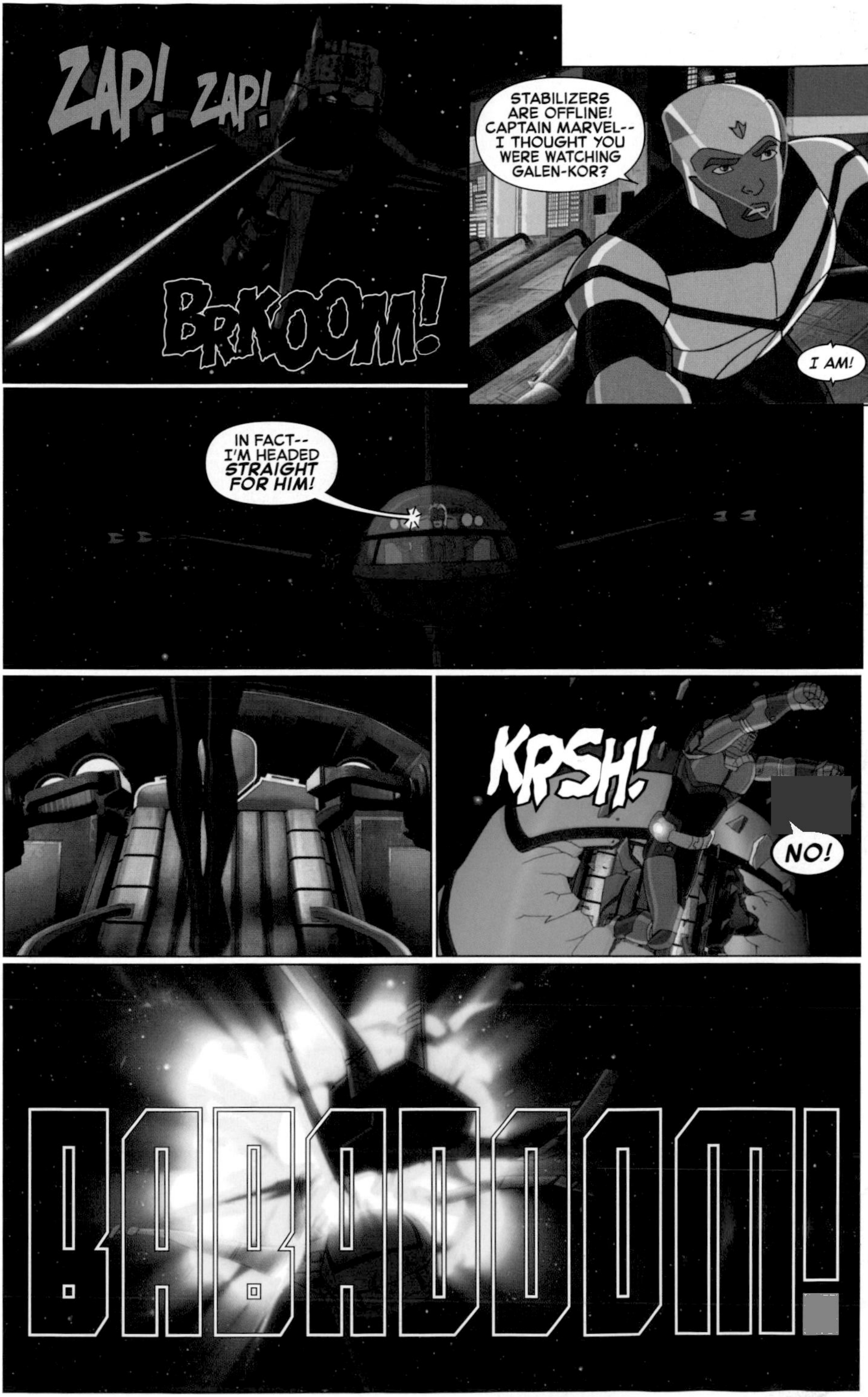

ZAP! ZAP!
BRKOOM!
STABILIZERS ARE OFFLINE! CAPTAIN MARVEL-- I THOUGHT YOU WERE WATCHING GALEN-KOR?
I AM!
IN FACT-- I'M HEADED STRAIGHT FOR HIM!
KRSH!
[redacted]
NO!
BABADOOM!

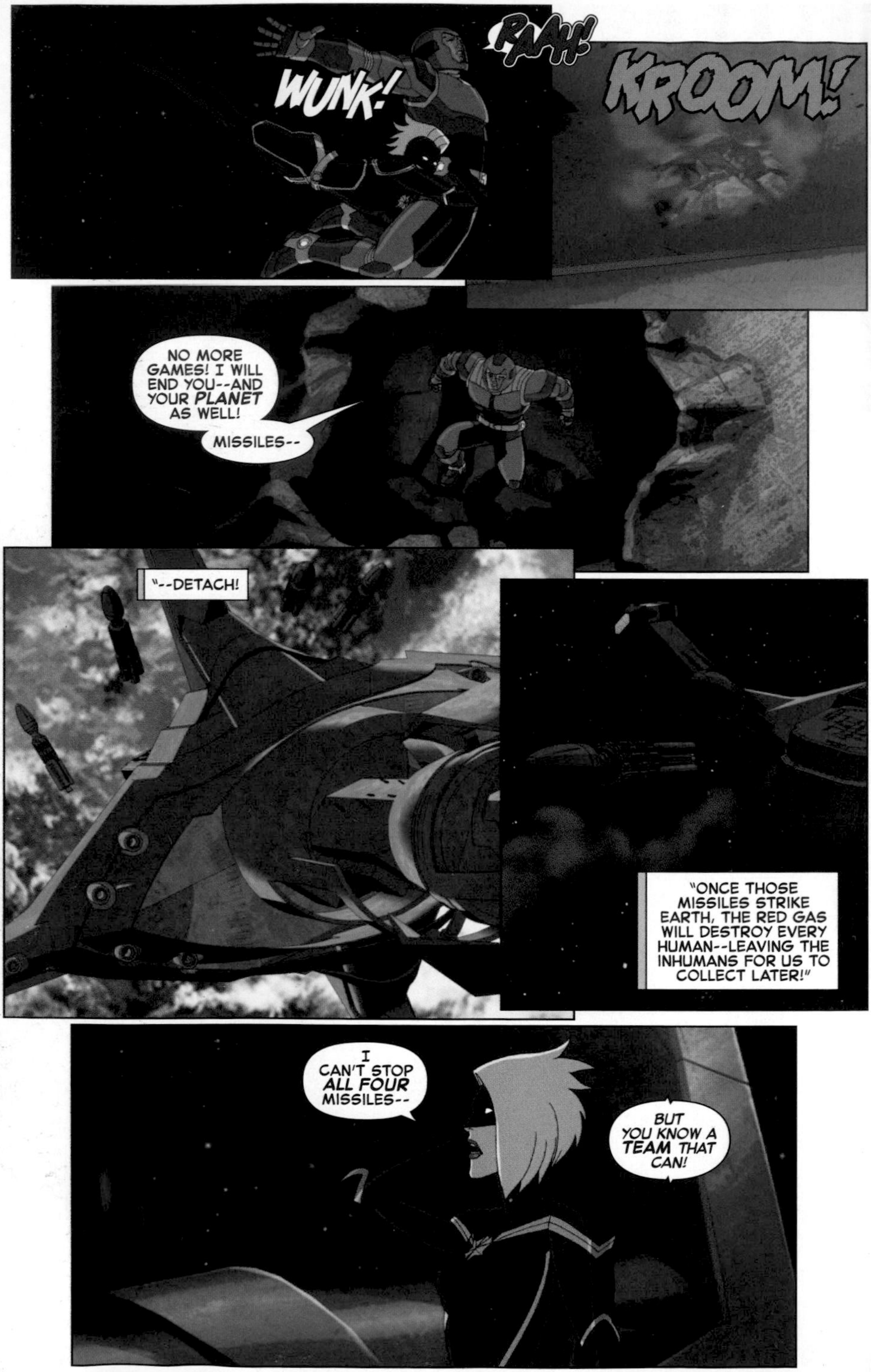
RAAH!
WUNK!
KROOM!
NO MORE GAMES! I WILL END YOU--AND YOUR PLANET AS WELL!
MISSILES--
"--DETACH!
"ONCE THOSE MISSILES STRIKE EARTH, THE RED GAS WILL DESTROY EVERY HUMAN--LEAVING THE INHUMANS FOR US TO COLLECT LATER!"
I CAN'T STOP ALL FOUR MISSILES--
BUT YOU KNOW A TEAM THAT CAN!

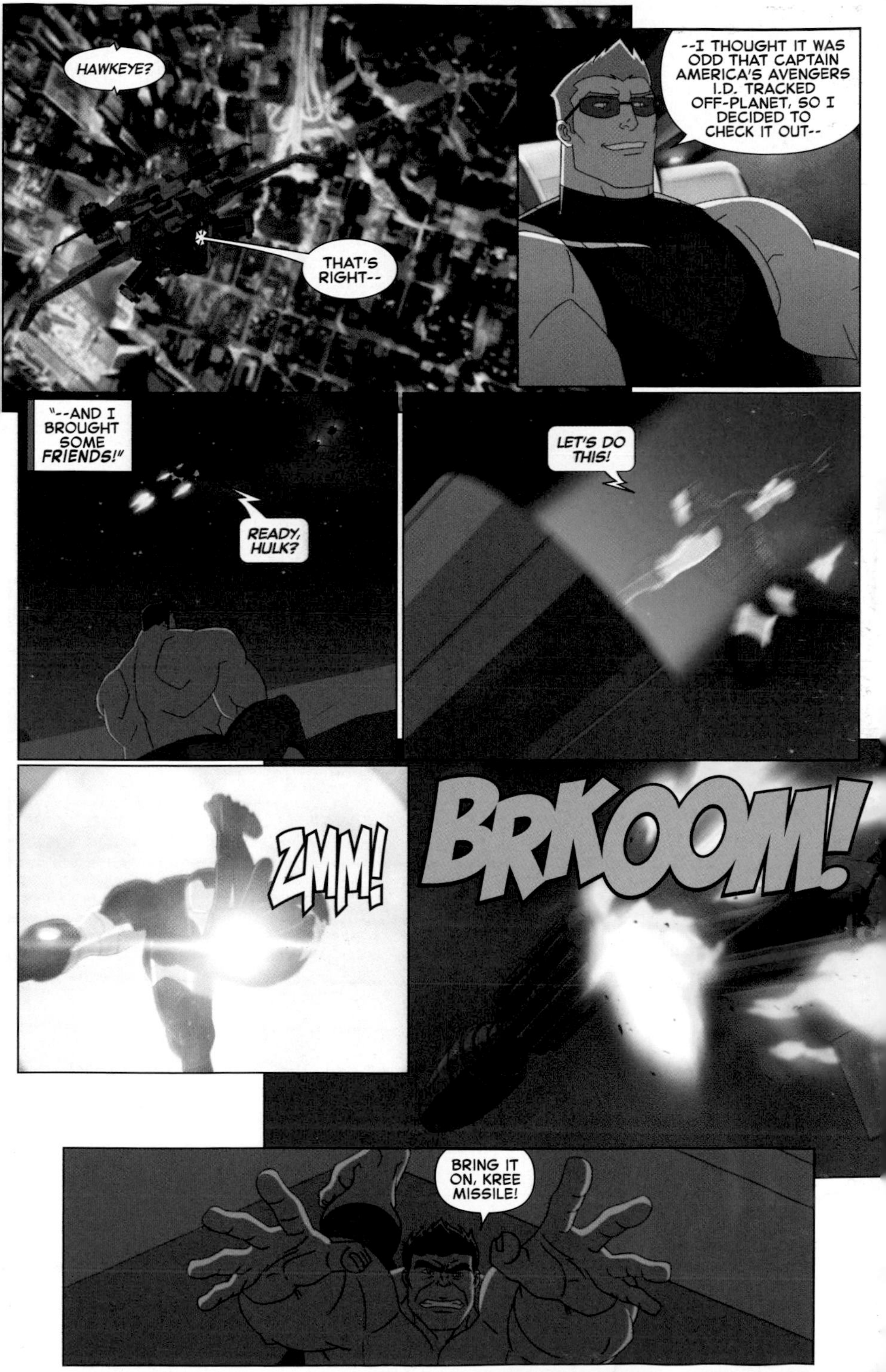
HAWKEYE?
THAT'S RIGHT--
--I THOUGHT IT WAS ODD THAT CAPTAIN AMERICA'S AVENGERS I.D. TRACKED OFF-PLANET, SO I DECIDED TO CHECK IT OUT--
"--AND I BROUGHT SOME FRIENDS!"
READY, HULK?
LET'S DO THIS!
ZMM!
BRKOOM!
BRING IT ON, KREE MISSILE!

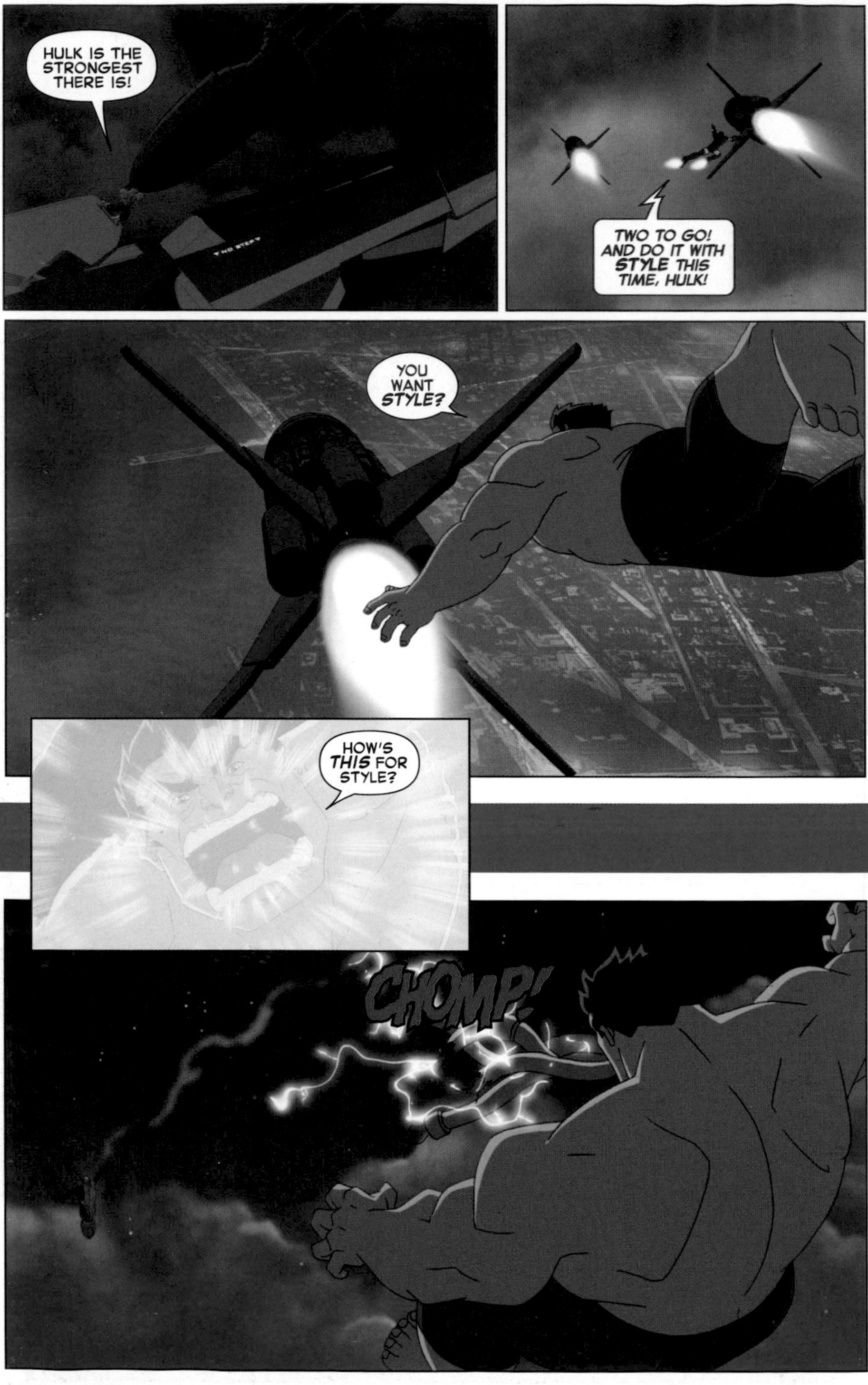
HULK IS THE STRONGEST THERE IS!
TWO TO GO! AND DO IT WITH STYLE THIS TIME, HULK!
YOU WANT STYLE?
HOW'S THIS FOR STYLE?
CHOMP!

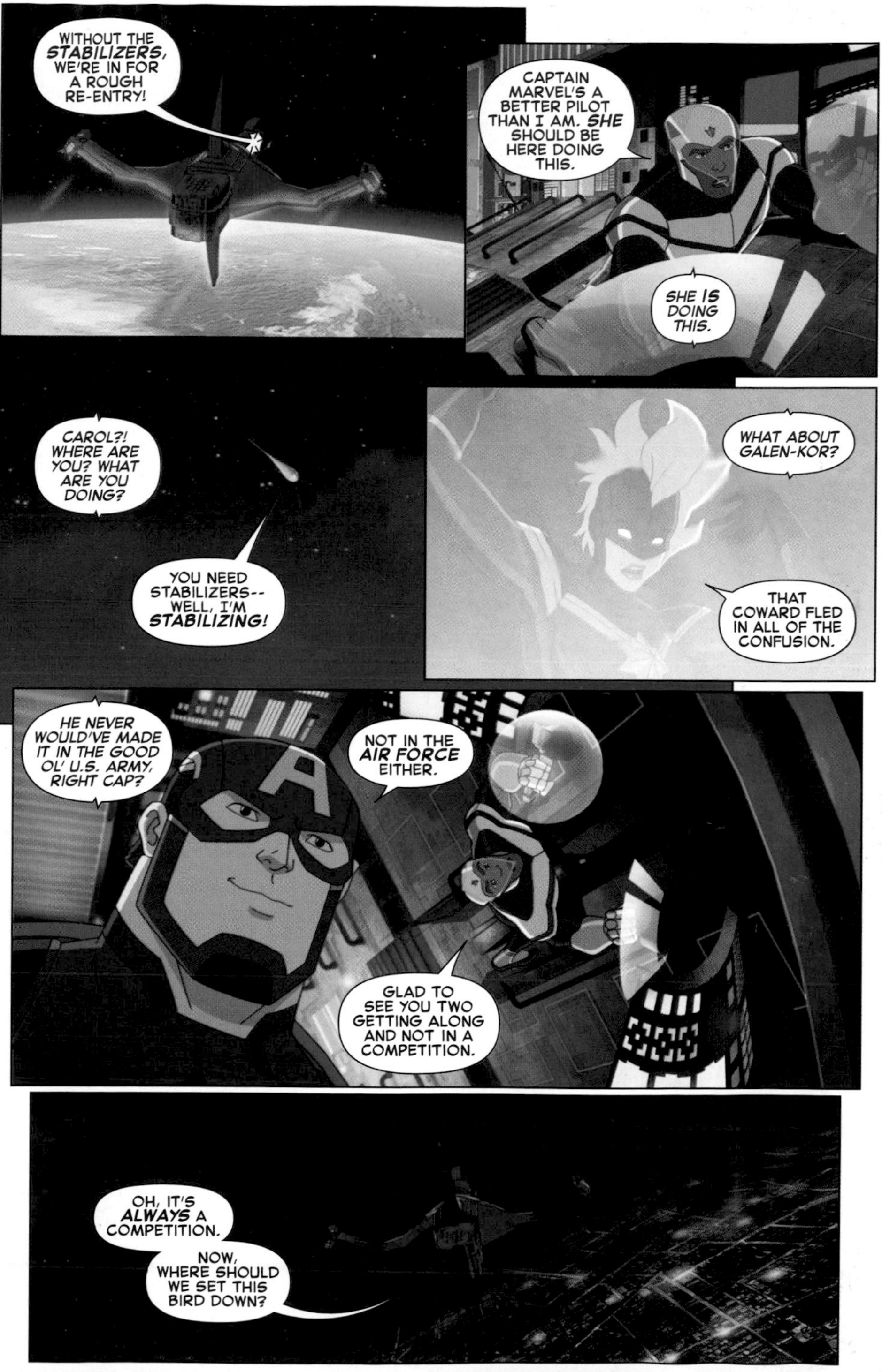

WITHOUT THE STABILIZERS, WE'RE IN FOR A ROUGH RE-ENTRY!
CAPTAIN MARVEL'S A BETTER PILOT THAN I AM. SHE SHOULD BE HERE DOING THIS.
SHE IS DOING THIS.
CAROL?! WHERE ARE YOU? WHAT ARE YOU DOING?
YOU NEED STABILIZERS-- WELL, I'M STABILIZING!
WHAT ABOUT GALEN-KOR?
THAT COWARD FLED IN ALL OF THE CONFUSION.
HE NEVER WOULD'VE MADE IT IN THE GOOD OL' U.S. ARMY, RIGHT CAP?
NOT IN THE AIR FORCE EITHER.
GLAD TO SEE YOU TWO GETTING ALONG AND NOT IN A COMPETITION.
OH, IT'S ALWAYS A COMPETITION.
NOW, WHERE SHOULD WE SET THIS BIRD DOWN?

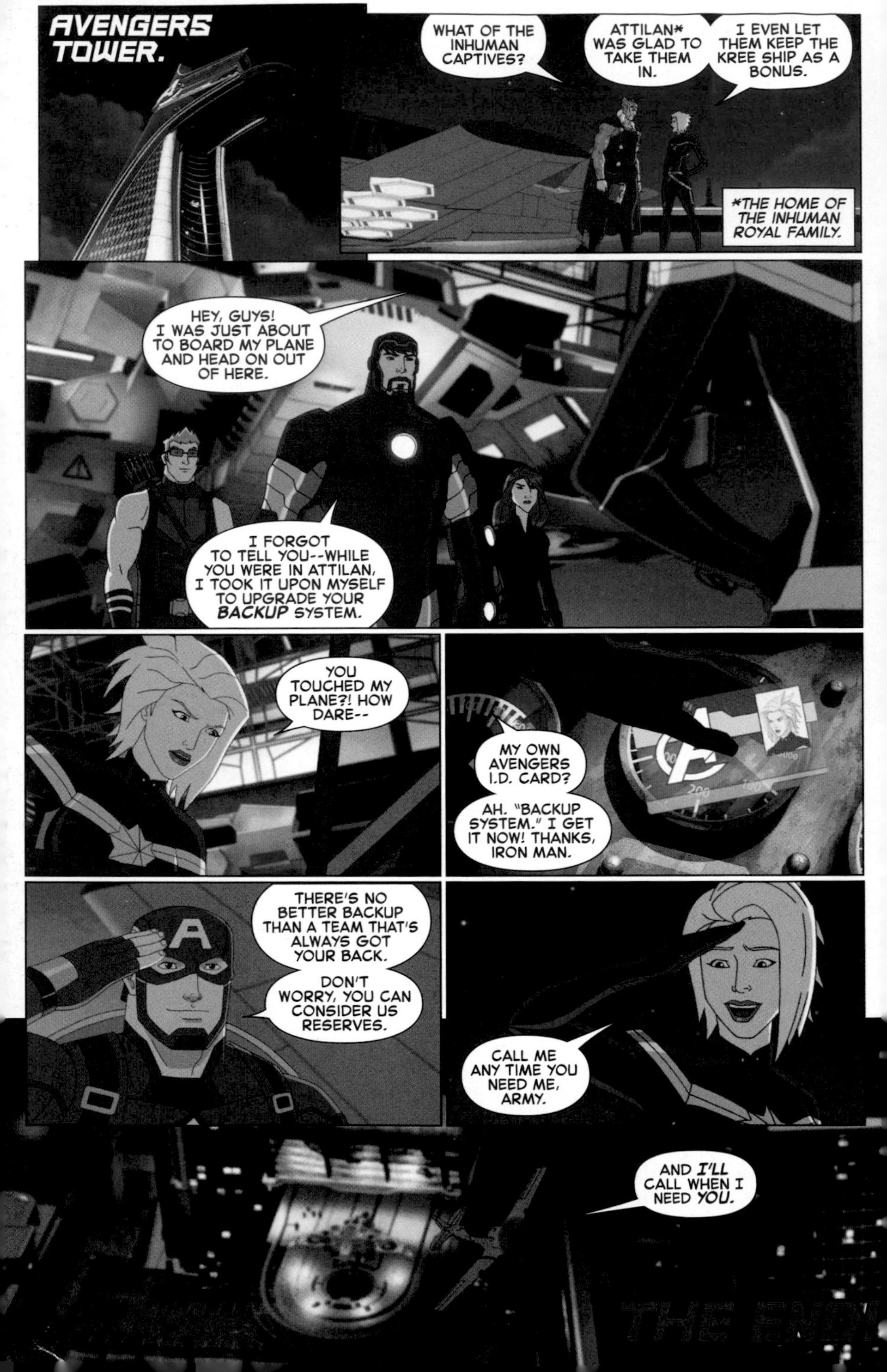
AVENGERS TOWER.
WHAT OF THE INHUMAN CAPTIVES?
ATTILAN* WAS GLAD TO TAKE THEM IN.
I EVEN LET THEM KEEP THE KREE SHIP AS A BONUS.
*THE HOME OF THE INHUMAN ROYAL FAMILY.
HEY, GUYS! I WAS JUST ABOUT TO BOARD MY PLANE AND HEAD ON OUT OF HERE.
I FORGOT TO TELL YOU--WHILE YOU WERE IN ATTILAN, I TOOK IT UPON MYSELF TO UPGRADE YOUR BACKUP SYSTEM.
YOU TOUCHED MY PLANE?! HOW DARE--
MY OWN AVENGERS I.D. CARD?
AH. "BACKUP SYSTEM." I GET IT NOW! THANKS, IRON MAN.
THERE'S NO BETTER BACKUP THAN A TEAM THAT'S ALWAYS GOT YOUR BACK.
DON'T WORRY, YOU CAN CONSIDER US RESERVES.
CALL ME ANY TIME YOU NEED ME, ARMY.
AND I'LL CALL WHEN I NEED YOU.
THE END

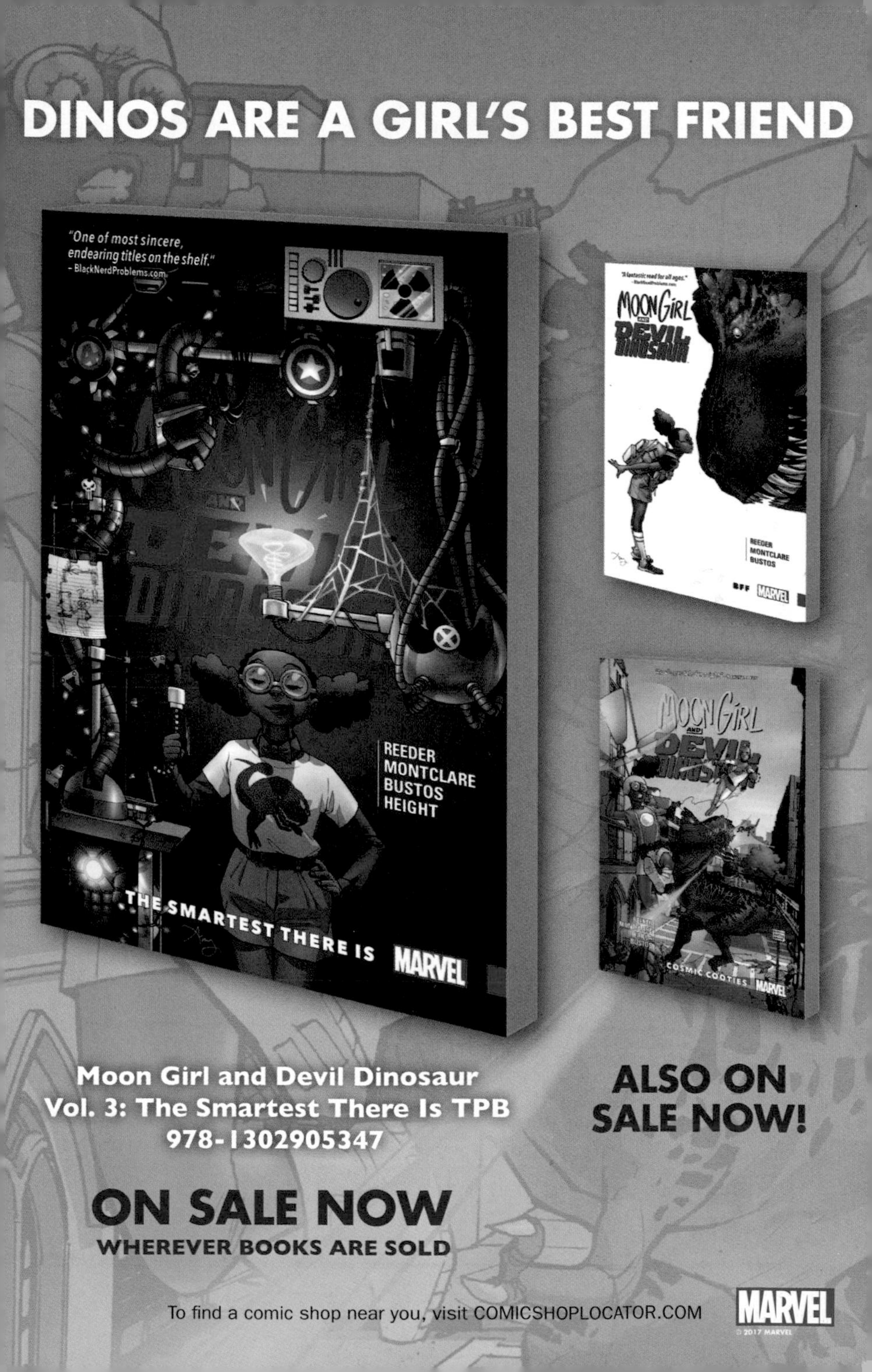
DINOS ARE A GIRL'S BEST FRIEND
"One of most sincere, endearing titles on the shelf." – BlackNerdProblems.com
REEDER
MONTCLARE
BUSTOS
HEIGHT
THE SMARTEST THERE IS
MARVEL
"A fantastic read for all ages."
MOON GIRL AND DEVIL DINOSAUR
REEDER
MONTCLARE
BUSTOS
BFF
MARVEL
MOON GIRL AND DEVIL DINOSAUR
COSMIC COOTIES
MARVEL
Moon Girl and Devil Dinosaur
Vol. 3: The Smartest There Is TPB
978-1302905347
ALSO ON SALE NOW!
ON SALE NOW
WHEREVER BOOKS ARE SOLD
To find a comic shop near you, visit COMICSHOPLOCATOR.COM
MARVEL
© 2017 MARVEL

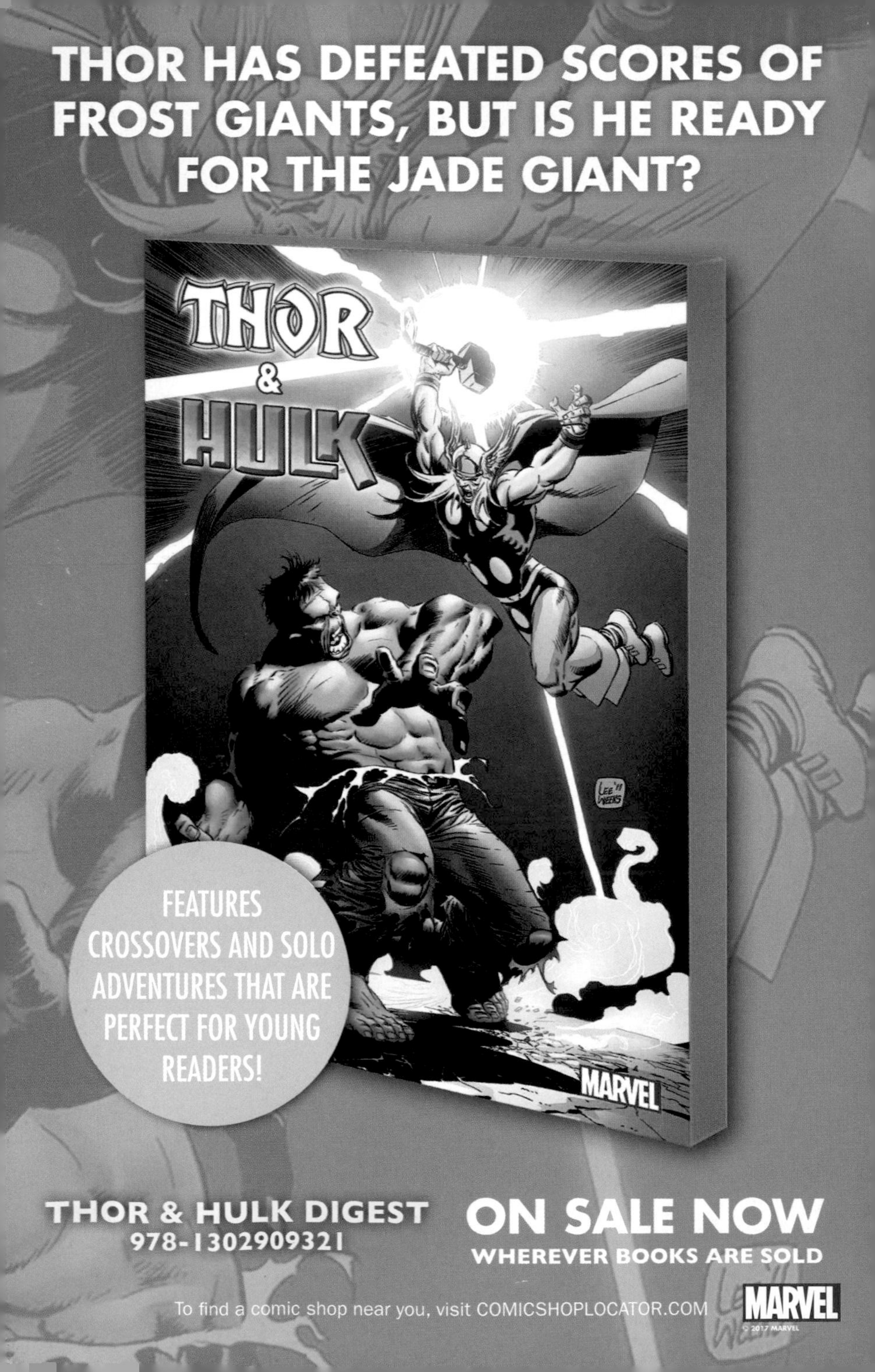
THOR HAS DEFEATED SCORES OF FROST GIANTS, BUT IS HE READY FOR THE JADE GIANT?
THOR & HULK
MARVEL
FEATURES CROSSOVERS AND SOLO ADVENTURES THAT ARE PERFECT FOR YOUNG READERS!
THOR & HULK DIGEST
978-1302909321
ON SALE NOW
WHEREVER BOOKS ARE SOLD
To find a comic shop near you, visit COMICSHOPLOCATOR.COM
MARVEL
© 2017 MARVEL

CREATIVELY COLOR CUDDLY CHARACTERS!

All of your favorite Marvel characters are joined by their Tsum Tsum counterparts in this deluxe coloring book!

**COLOR YOUR OWN
MARVEL TSUM TSUM**
978-1-302-90714-3

ON SALE NOW
WHEREVER BOOKS ARE SOLD

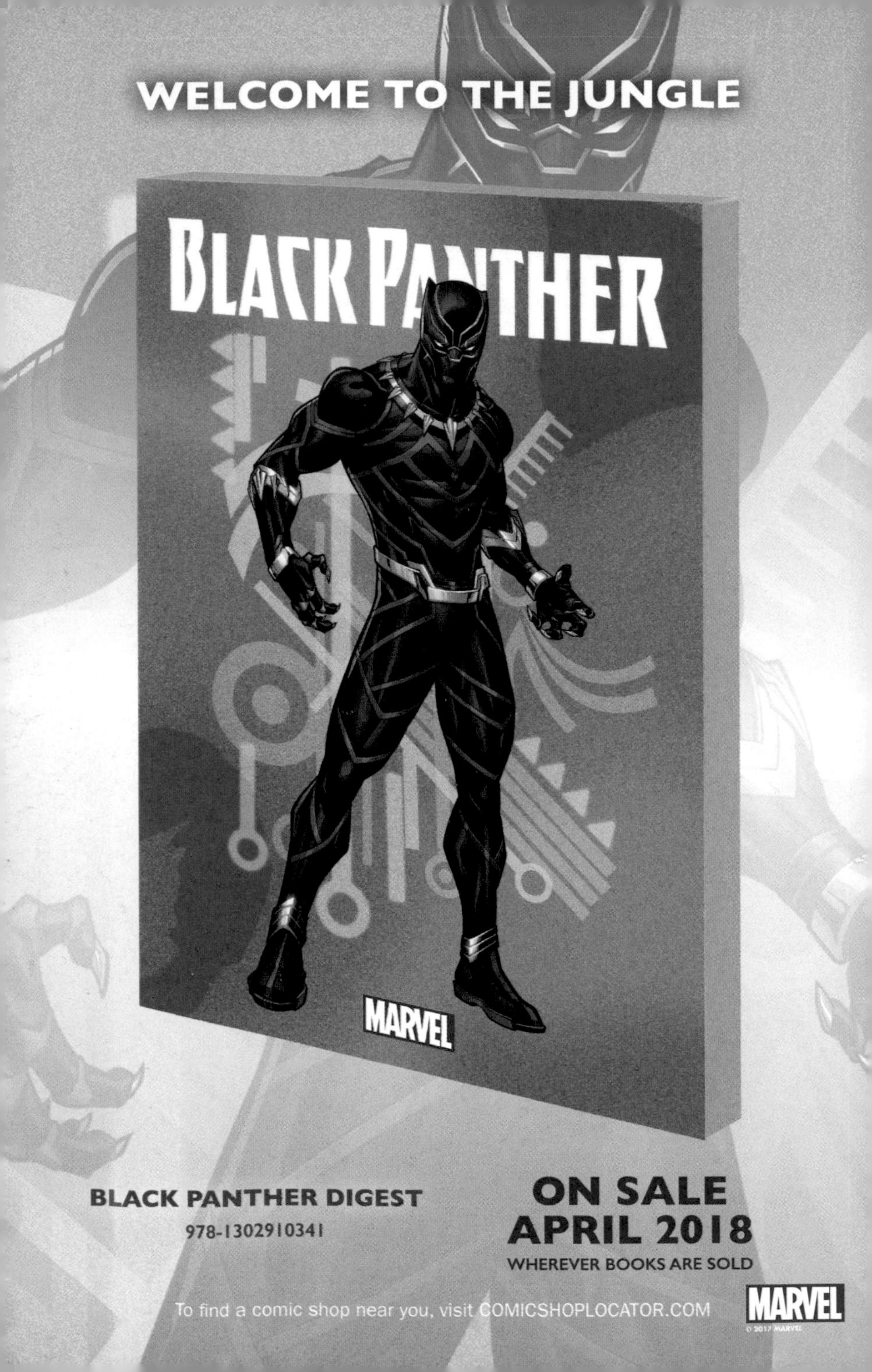
WELCOME TO THE JUNGLE
BLACK PANTHER
MARVEL
BLACK PANTHER DIGEST
978-1302910341
ON SALE
APRIL 2018
WHEREVER BOOKS ARE SOLD
To find a comic shop near you, visit COMICSHOPLOCATOR.COM
MARVEL
© 2017 MARVEL

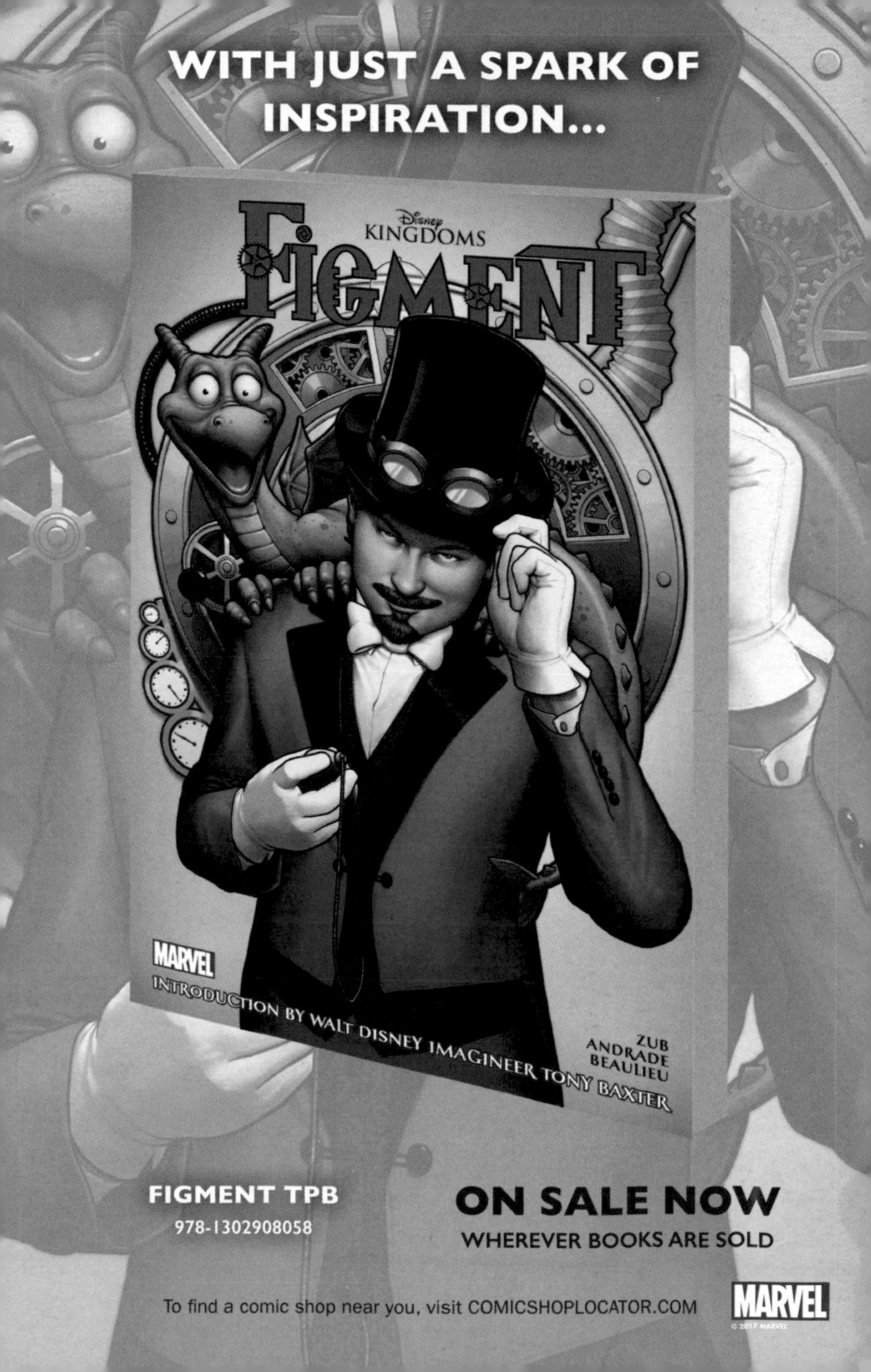
WITH JUST A SPARK OF INSPIRATION...
DISNEY KINGDOMS
FIGMENT
MARVEL
INTRODUCTION BY WALT DISNEY IMAGINEER TONY BAXTER
ZUB
ANDRADE
BEAULIEU
FIGMENT TPB
978-1302908058
ON SALE NOW
WHEREVER BOOKS ARE SOLD
To find a comic shop near you, visit COMICSHOPLOCATOR.COM
MARVEL
© 2017 MARVEL